COUNTRY CHARM
BENNETT SPRINGS SERIES

STEFI HART

Copyright © 2025 by Stefi Hart

All rights reserved.

No part of this book may be reproduced in any form or by any electronic or mechanical means, including information storage and retrieval systems, without written permission from the author, except for the use of brief quotations in a book review.

❦ Created with Vellum

For M & D

CHAPTER 1

Noah

I didn't need to come to a complete stop to read the bold sign nestled at the end of Grandpa Jack's driveway. Even as the last light from the sun faded to black, the glaring red lettering stood out.

I pressed my foot down on the accelerator, keeping the car under control as the back end flicked out and the tires slipped on gravel.

Rational thought escaped me as I sped down the mile-long driveway. What the hell had come over Jack? I'd noticed he hadn't been himself lately, but this…this made no sense.

I didn't wait for the dust to settle before flinging

the door open and storming up the path to the house. I didn't bother knocking—I'd spent more time here than at my own place.

"Jack. Jack, you in here?"

Dark thunderclouds, mirroring my mood, filled the room. I flicked on lights as I moved through the house, not caring if Jack was resting. It wasn't even that late, despite the early darkness. When I entered the lounge, I wasn't surprised to find him sitting in his armchair.

"What the hell is going on? You're selling the farm?" I didn't see the point in beating around the bush. Jack never did.

"Sold, actually."

"Already? What about our plans? The Dexters?" I ran my hands through my hair and turned away, struggling to process Jack's words and the future I'd imagined evaporating before my eyes.

"Why don't you grab us a beer and have a seat before you give yourself a heart attack?"

I wasn't keen to talk about the *for sale* sign anymore, so I took my time heading to the fridge outside under the back veranda. Why Jack didn't keep alcohol inside the house was something I'd never thought to ask. What did it matter now? The farm was gone, and all those little details I'd taken for granted had vanished with it.

The bottles clinked together as I grabbed two. I slammed the fridge door shut too hard, the contents rattling, but I didn't bother to check for damage.

Twisting the cap off both bottles, I dropped them on the kitchen bench as I passed and took a long swig, wishing I'd grabbed a backup. This was going to be more than a one-beer kind of night.

"A local snap it up?" I held the second bottle out to Jack.

"Thanks." Jack lifted his beer and shook his head. "Nah. Bailey Collins. Rolling in dough, from what Alex tells me. Took care of everything over the phone without even looking at the place."

"Typical. City money, no clue about farming."

"Don't be so quick to judge the bloke. You were the one preaching about needing new stock in town."

"I was talking cattle."

"Well, you never know what he might bring."

"It won't be knowledge, and you know it. If he has so much money, he's probably too precious to do the hard work himself and will hire half the town to do it for him. What's the bet he won't last the year?"

"Maybe. But at least it'll give some of our young blokes a job, so we don't lose them to the mines."

"Only until he gets bored and sells the farm. Then what?"

"As I said before, hold off judging until you've met him."

I glared at the walls, not really aiming my frustration at anyone in particular. "Even you have to admit that city blokes don't stick. Country air's too dusty, and they lose all their tack."

Jack shook his head. "We need fresh blood around here. How else do you expect this town to grow? You don't want the rumors about us marrying our cousins to become reality. You never know—this city guy might have a daughter."

I scoffed. "Not one I'd be interested in."

Jack took a long swig, draining his beer. "Any local girls catch your eye?"

"I'm too busy to entertain dating. I've got a future to plan."

~

Bailey

. . .

I was relieved when the three-week settlement suited the previous owner. A tidy deal, signed and settled on my terms, was exactly how I liked to handle business. I needed to see this purchase as a chance to start fresh, to leave my old career behind. It had been a long time since I'd felt excited about doing something for myself. Buying the property based solely on a few photos and a real estate agent's write-up gave me an unprecedented thrill—an act of self-indulgence I didn't regret, despite occasionally wondering if I might.

Driving through the town site of my new neighborhood, I scanned the streets of a place that could only be described as quaint. No other word seemed to fit. It was the polar opposite of my upmarket house in the artsy, ultra-modern inner-city suburb I'd loved but no longer needed.

I turned into the first driveway on the outskirts of town, marked by a green letterbox with numbers long since faded. The large *For Sale* sign with its bold red *SOLD* sticker was the only landmark indicating I had arrived. A pang of dread crept up from my gut, washing over my excitement and settling into a diluted sense of curiosity. I could only hope the transition to my new home would go as smoothly as my dealings so far.

Alex, the real estate agent, had reassured me the house was in perfect order for moving in, requiring little maintenance. But I couldn't shake my apprehension. An aged man living alone—what could I expect? My father, with his obsessive-compulsive tendencies, wasn't a good comparison. He was as far removed from a farmer as one could be.

Red dust spewed like flames around my new black F-Truck, which I'd purchased only two days earlier. My little silver sports car, a gift from my father, had been left parked in my city apartment's garage.

Glancing in the rearview mirror, I watched the dust clouds billow like a flare announcing my arrival —a sight I'd need to get used to, along with the absence of a convenient drive-through car wash. I'd have to resign myself to the bucket-and-sponge method of cleaning. It wouldn't be the easiest transition, but I was up for the challenge.

The driveway stretched long, but it wasn't enough to prepare me for what awaited at the other end. I had expected Alex to greet me, possibly with Jack. After all, I'd offered him the use of the granny flat until he was properly sorted—it was the least I could do, considering how accommodating he'd been.

The welcoming party of six, however, was a surprise. Jack's family, I guessed. Perhaps this was more of a farewell they hadn't yet come to terms with.

Alex had mentioned several times that the sale was due to financial hardship, which explained why I got the property so cheap.

I steered the truck to the edge of the gravel driveway and stopped, giving myself a moment to analyze the situation without appearing judgmental. My father had always drilled into me the importance of being prepared for every situation. Meeting Jack's family so soon hadn't been on my radar.

The dark tint of my windows allowed me a quick glance. My appraisal came to an abrupt halt when my gaze settled on one man who seemed determined to look anywhere but in my direction. "Mmm, not bad," I muttered, taking a deep breath as I opened the door.

Stiff from sitting too long, I stretched my legs and slid down to meet the ground. With a polite smile firmly in place, I turned to greet the group.

"Bailey." The suited man, likely Alex, extended his hand with a welcoming grin.

"Hi, Alex?"

He nodded.

"Nice to finally put a face to the name." Shaking his hand with a firm grip, I turned my attention to the others. "I didn't expect a welcoming party."

"And d'ya think we expected Bailey to be a chick?" The tallest man was the first to speak. His comment didn't crack the stubborn frowns each of them wore, as though my presence—and my gender—were somehow offensive.

I shrugged, unfazed. It wasn't the first time my name had caused confusion, and I was once again grateful for my obviously feminine attributes.

The awkward silence stretched too long. I shrugged again. "Sorry if you're disappointed."

"We were long past disappointed before you stepped out of that fancy truck," the man I'd noticed earlier retorted.

Sexy and feisty. I couldn't help but smile as his eyes raked over me before locking onto my gaze. Many men had underestimated my petite stature, wrongly assuming it gave them the upper hand. I was used to observing their tactics and refusing to be manipulated. Then again, none of them had known my father or the lifetime I'd spent as his protégé. I often suspected he'd given me the name Bailey strategically, to keep people guessing.

When he didn't back down, holding my gaze too

long, I arched an eyebrow and turned to the elderly man. Closing the distance, I extended my hand. "You must be Mr. Kelly. It's a pleasure to meet you."

"Jack, please. Pleasure's mine, Bailey, and welcome to your new home."

"Thanks, Jack." I flashed him a smile. His welcome felt as warm as if I were family, not the stranger who'd bought the home that had been part of his life longer than I'd been alive.

The bargain price I'd celebrated suddenly lost its zing. Judging by the grim expressions on his family's faces, they were all mourning the loss of something I'd been so excited to gain.

Business is business, I tried to convince myself. But somewhere between the city and Bennett Springs, my joy downgraded to guilt. The shiny new truck, far too fancy to call a farm hack, only added to the unease.

Jack introduced me to his family, who, after recovering from the initial shock that I wasn't male, politely welcomed me to town.

Daniel, Jack's older grandson, shook my hand awkwardly. "Ah, sorry about the chick comment." His face flushed a deep red—something I hadn't seen on a grown man before. "Catch ya later. The farm's not going to run itself," he muttered, shoving his hands into his jean pockets and walking off toward a four-wheel drive without a proper goodbye.

"Come on, Noah, we'll give Bailey a hand with those boxes," Mike, Jack's son-in-law, instructed rather than asked his remaining son.

"That's okay," I said quickly. "It won't take me long. But thanks."

"A waif like you shouldn't be lifting boxes." Mike winked before expertly untying the ropes securing them.

My father, Adam, might've seemed like an indoors type, but he'd insisted on survival training that extended to living off the land—and defending myself. With gunshot accuracy of ninety-eight percent, I'd learned to appreciate his rigorous teachings.

"I'm stronger than I look, but if you insist." I gestured toward the boxes, inviting them to help. "Thank you. I'll make coffee when you're done, if you have time."

Noah brushed past me without a word.

"That'd be lovely, thank you," Tracy said, while Mike tipped his head, carrying a large box.

"If the boys need to get back to work, Dad can give me a lift home," Tracy added, glancing at Jack, who smiled warmly. Their brief exchange revealed a sense of family I'd never experienced.

"Of course. Why don't you give Bailey a quick tour?"

"I'll leave you with Jack and Tracy if you don't mind. After all, who knows the property better?" Alex handed me a large wad of keys, extending his other hand for a farewell handshake.

"Great, thanks, Alex. I'm sure I'll see you around town."

"That you will," Alex grinned. "Once you see the size of this place, you'll understand why I'm so certain." With a wave, he called out his goodbyes and left.

I was eager to explore the house I'd bought but hadn't yet seen. I followed Tracy inside, acutely aware of how hard this must be for her. Saying goodbye to a home filled with lifelong memories, couldn't be easy.

The house was large, the décor dated but tolerable. With a fresh coat of paint and the new furniture I'd bought, it would suffice until I decided whether to renovate or rebuild.

The neutral tones of the white bathroom tiles and cream sandstone benchtops were a pleasant surprise. Jack's late wife had clearly been a woman of taste. The home's cleanliness softened my initial guilt. Alex had mentioned she died a few years ago and that Jack hadn't been the same since.

Despite the size of the house, the tour didn't take long.

"I'm sure you'll want a proper look once we leave you to settle in," Tracy said as we walked into the kitchen.

I spotted a large hamper wrapped in cellophane with a big red bow. "Oh wow, is this for me?" I stepped closer to examine the wicker basket.

"Alex likes to introduce newbies to local produce."Tracy laughed, picking up a neatly folded newspaper beside the gift. "He's a nice man. We've known each other since school." Her tone grew wistful. "Some of us don't know when to leave, I guess."

I glanced at her, noting the brief shadow of sadness on her face before her expression brightened as Mike entered, carrying my coffee machine.

"Perfect timing." Mike grinned, setting it on the sandstone benchtop, which, like the white tiles, seemed a feature throughout the house.

"Thanks. You were right—it would've taken me much longer. Can I tempt you all to stay for coffee and cake?"

Mike nodded appreciatively. "I put the cooler

bags from your front seat over there, closest to the kitchen."

"Thanks," I said, unpacking coffee pods, sugar, and teaspoons. "I hope I'm not keeping you from more important things."

"Not at all," Mike replied. "We're due for a break anyway."

"Be honest, Dad—you just want to see how well that tiny machine spits out coffee," Noah quipped.

I grinned, enjoying their banter, though Noah's sharp gaze hinted at lingering resentment.

CHAPTER 2

*B*ailey

I couldn't believe how much land I now owned. It was small compared to the other farms surrounding the town, but it was more than I ever imagined.

Jack and Tracy pointed out landmarks and shared stories about their past. Their memories, built over a lifetime, seemed deliriously happy and cherished. Maggie, Jack's late wife, was at the center of most tales. She came across as someone everyone loved to be around, and the feeling was mutual. I couldn't help but feel a sense of awe at the legacy she had left behind.

I tried to absorb the details Jack offered as he gestured toward dams and a spring-fed creek that flowed year-round. The creek watered the cows and reticulated the gardens. Huge rainwater tanks supplied the house, and Jack mentioned a bore, though I missed the significance of that water source. I figured there was plenty of time to sort out the finer details later. For now, I was content to sit back and enjoy the view.

"The stables aren't as pretty as they could be, but they do the job," Jack said, pointing toward them in the distance.

I had a mare arriving in the next few days, and in the coming months, a stallion. I was pleased the stables would temporarily house them, though I hoped they wouldn't feel cramped. With a bit of luck, my plans for new stables would soon become a reality. For now, I reminded myself to focus on the reason I bought the property. It was far too easy to get caught up in the excitement of owning so much land.

"Do you ride?" I was hoping to find someone who'd join me occasionally.

Jack shook his head. "I prefer to rely on my own two legs. They haven't let me down yet."

I smiled. It was a bit of a schoolgirl fantasy to

assume farmers still depended on horses. I liked the idea of rounding up stock on horseback, turning an otherwise tedious chore into something more enjoyable.

When the American-style wooden barn came into view, my smile widened. It was exactly as I'd hoped—rustic and charming, even more so than the photograph had suggested. The style was my inspiration for replacing the existing stables and house.

"Do you use the barn?"

"Not since—" Jack paused, shaking his head as he shifted in his seat. The emotional toll of the tour was evident. "I've been wanting to hold an old-fashioned barn dance, but that was Maggie's thing. I wouldn't know where to start."

Silence settled between us.

Jack stopped the car a short distance from the barn's double doors, large enough to fit a vehicle through.

I stood back as Jack undid a latch and swung the doors open. I was surprised it hadn't been locked, but if he didn't use the space, vandalism probably wasn't a concern.

The lower story was spacious, more than big enough for worktables and shelves for art supplies. The sturdy staircase, made from jarrah railway sleepers, added to the character. It only needed a balustrade to comply with safety regulations, and it would be perfect. I'd already decided the second floor would make an excellent bedroom.

"I'm afraid it needs a bit of work and a good clean," Jack admitted.

Stepping inside, I ignored the years of dust that settled like a woolen drop sheet over the barn's rustic charm.

"Is there water to this building?"

"There's a tank around the back. The roof is new, and I installed gutters, so it should be full after the winter we've had. Maggie intended to turn this into a quilting retreat but ran out of time. Plans for a kitchen and bathroom have been council-approved if you want them."

I grinned. "I'd appreciate it." I could already picture the barn tidied up, music and laughter echoing across the lush paddocks. I could hardly wait for my dreams to take shape.

"May I ask what your plans are for this space?" Tracy spoke for the first time since we got out of the car.

"I'm not entirely sure, but you might see those barn parties yet, Jack." My intention to establish an art and relaxation retreat felt more certain than ever.

Still, I wasn't ready to discuss it, at least not until my business plan was finalized.

Jack's eyes glistened with unshed tears.

I understood. A man like Jack—a tough farmer—wasn't comfortable putting his emotions on display. Instead, he nodded once, a gesture I'd noticed both Noah and Mike use earlier.

"As sad as I am to see the farm sold, I'm curious to see what you'll do with it," Tracy admitted.

"Well, as I said before, I don't want to see the farm go either. As skeptical as Noah is, I don't have an ulterior motive. I don't know what it feels like to have a connection to anything family-oriented, but I imagine I wouldn't want to lose it if I did. I have a business dream I never thought I'd be able to establish. Now that it's possible, I have no interest in crushing anyone else's."

Tracy's eyes brimmed with tears. "Why would you be so generous to strangers?"

I shrugged, feeling a flicker of unease. Would Tracy still think me generous when she learned I planned to demolish their family home to build a large Cape Cod-style house in its place? That was a worry for another time.

"Maybe those strangers will become my friends." And I genuinely hoped they would.

Tracy held out her arms, but instead of waiting for me to approach, she stepped forward and wrapped me in a warm hug. "I think we'd be friends regardless, but thank you."

I returned the embrace, closing my eyes as a wave of unexpected emotion hit me. The gesture brought back memories of what it felt like to receive motherly affection—something I'd almost forgotten. The realization made me miss my own mother more than ever.

∼

Noah

"Damn," I muttered under my breath. It wasn't the first time I'd fumbled a task since meeting Bailey.

"Come on, Noah, hurry up if we're going to make it to town before dark."

Gathering the wire strainers and spinning jenny, I hoisted them onto the back of the ute. Dan would finish up in his own time. He liked to end the day by riding the perimeter of the paddocks on the quad bike, checking for fences in need of repair. The extra hour of peace and quiet was no doubt part of the ritual.

With two small children, dinnertime at Dan's place was always chaotic. I loved the noise and energy, but Dan was more reserved, content with his own company.

Mike's eagerness to get to town wasn't about the hardware store's closing time but an excuse to meet the boys at the pub for an end-of-day beer. Dan would head home when he was ready. With nothing better to do, I decided to join my father. There was no way I'd grab my usual beer with Jack tonight—not when I felt like an imposter on the land that had been in my family for generations.

I drove, as I had since I was eleven years old. Today, I welcomed the distraction, something to focus on other than Bailey's unnerving arrival.

"So, what do you think?" Mike interrupted my thoughts.

"Of?" I glanced over, catching Mike's eye roll and head shake.

"Bailey, of course. You've been off your game since we got back. Bit of a stunner, isn't she?"

I shrugged, feigning indifference. "If you're into the hardcore corporate type, I guess you could say she's attractive."

Mike laughed. "Get off it. She'd be soft as putty in your hands if you gave her half a chance, and even a blind man could sense that beauty." He chuckled, turning his gaze to the passing landscape.

"I'll take your word for it because I don't plan on venturing anywhere near that one."

Mike dropped the subject, but the conversation played on my mind, tormenting me. Damn my father for being right. The no-nonsense attitude only added to Bailey's appeal—too calculating to be endearing, but alluring and sexy, wrapped up in a tight little body that didn't look shy of a workout.

I cleared my throat. "What do you think Jack will do about her offer?" Steering the conversation toward practicality felt safer.

"He'd be bloody stupid to knock it back. Besides, what choice does he have if he wants to keep farming?" Mike sighed. "Can't believe he never asked us for help. I had no idea he'd racked up the bank loans."

"He knew I was struggling, but he should've given me a chance to help." I slammed my palms against the steering wheel. "Damn, Charlotte." The agitation from the moment I'd seen the *for sale* sign simmered inside, threatening to explode. Losing one farm because of her had been bad enough, but now the land I loved—the land I'd wanted to tend for the rest of my life—was gone.

The pub's car park was packed with work trucks. Knock-off time always brought a flood of farmers unwinding after a hard day. I rarely joined them, preferring to share a beer with Jack at the farm if I wasn't already there working.

Laughter greeted us as Mike pulled open the heavy wooden door. The smell of stale alcohol and cigarette smoke from years past engulfed my senses. Nearby, jeers and taunts accompanied the crack of pool balls.

"Hey, Noah." Whitney, greeted me with a wide smile, her makeup caked on in thick layers.

"Hi, Whitney. Two pints, thanks."

"Is that all I get? It's been ages since you last came to see me, and all you want is two pints?"

Whitney's attempts at flirting were as subtle as a sledgehammer, and I wasn't in the mood. Her reputation preceded her, and in a town as small as Bennett Springs, keeping a distance was the safest bet to avoid gossip.

"Get Mike to bring them over, will ya?" I winked and walked away before she could dig her claws in further.

"Noah, what'd we do to deserve this privilege?

Thought you'd be at Jack's, checking out the talent that rolled into town today. Alex tells me she'd melt the rubber off your tyres."

I shook my head. "She'd eat you alive, Cooper." We'd been friends since primary school, and Cooper hadn't changed—still too eager and always getting himself into trouble.

"So, are you going to take a shot at her?"

"Bailey Collins is not the sort of chick anyone takes a shot at. Add city-born-and-bred to the mix, and I'm running for the hills. You should know that."

"Great." Cooper grinned.

New blood in town, and nobody's cousin. Bailey would have them lining up. I cringed as Mike handed me a glass, just in time to stop me from heading back to the car. Even the ice-cold beer tasted foul to me.

~

Bailey

The furniture delivery guys arrived late in the afternoon after missing my driveway. Too busy talking, they ended up goodness knows where. The mad rush to unload before the light faded left my house in more of a shambles than I'd anticipated.

My biggest concern had been having a place to sleep, but crashing on a mattress in the lounge room for a few days wouldn't kill me. It was the disarray I couldn't handle. Organization was non-negotiable.

Flatpacks had seemed like a good idea at the time—something manageable on my own—but now, surrounded by chaos, all I wanted was for them to assemble themselves. Deciding to start with the lounge area, I began unwrapping the couch and rolling out the rug.

Cushions and knitted throw unpacked and in place meant one box down, a million to go. I sighed, setting aside the empty box and moving on to the next.

The flatpacks weren't difficult, just time-consuming. The instructions were straightforward, but the weight of the assembled pieces posed a challenge.

As much as I hated to admit it, I needed a man.

Skipping Google, I turned to the local paper Alex had left on the kitchen bench alongside the welcome gift.

A carpenter shouldn't be hard to find in a town

like Bennett Springs, where trades were likely nurtured and encouraged. My optimism faded when I saw the only name listed—*Noah Taylor*.

I rolled my eyes, unable to shake the feeling that he'd be around every corner. The town was too small for us to avoid each other.

Flipping the page to H for handyman, I picked up my phone and dialed Cooper.

CHAPTER 3

Bailey

I was pretty pleased with my decision to hire Cooper. He had the furniture assembled and positioned in every room faster than I expected. His rate was more reasonable than I'd imagined, especially since he'd come out after hours and didn't leave until close to midnight. One night in, and I'd already made a connection worth keeping in mind for future work on the farm.

Cooper was good-looking and confident, openly flirting with me while we worked side by side. I didn't mind; it was harmless enough. I wasn't interested in getting involved with anyone, but his sense of humor made it hard to resist. By the time he left, my cheeks hurt from laughing—a feeling I hadn't had since I was a teenager.

He'd given me the rundown on the local gossip—who to avoid, who to cozy up to—but the only person he stayed tight-lipped about was Noah. I got the feeling their friendship ran deep, and I wasn't about to pry.

The next morning, needing a change of scenery, I decided it was time for my first official trip into town. It'd give me a chance to pick up groceries and maybe get a feel for the place.

As I drove in, Alex's words rang true: the town was even smaller than I remembered. No wonder the delivery guys had missed it; anyone who blinked could've driven straight through without noticing.

The shopping center was my first stop. Groceries and beer were all I needed. Inside, the store was surprisingly spacious, which was a relief. Stocking up on supplies I hadn't thought to bring was my top priority—I wasn't planning on heading out again anytime soon.

Jack's kindness stuck with me. I could imagine him dropping by after work to check on me, the way a grandfather might. Coffee or juice didn't feel like enough to offer someone like him after a long day. A cold beer seemed more fitting.

As I wandered through the small strip of stores, I took mental notes of what was available. A beauty salon caught my eye, tucked away in the arcade leading to the supermarket. The sight felt like stumbling across treasure. Even though my unpacking was far from done, the idea of a massage to work out the tension in my back was too tempting to resist.

The scent of sandalwood hit me as I stepped inside, instantly calming my nerves. A blonde woman appeared from behind a sheer curtain, her bright smile lighting up the space.

"Hi, I'm Ali," she said. "Please tell me you're after an emergency appointment that will save us both?"

I laughed, already liking her. "Do I look that desperate?"

"Nah," she said with a grin. "You look beautiful. I'm the one stuck dusting shelves." She pulled a face, exaggerating her disgust.

"How could I say no after that plea?"

She beamed and gestured for me to follow her. "What can I do for you?"

"A massage, please," I said. "Though fair warning, the knots in my back might make that shelf-dusting look appealing."

"Never," Ali said, leading me down a long hallway lined with doors. "I'm guessing you're Bailey. Tourists usually book ahead, and you don't look like a local."

"How do I look different?" I glanced at my jeans and rolled-up shirt.

"That's a compliment," she said, glancing back with a grin. "You look fabulous."

I followed her into a cozy room, the sandalwood scent stronger here, with a hint of lemongrass. She handed me a clipboard and asked, "Any allergies or conditions I should know about?"

"Not that I'm aware of," I said.

"Perfect. Full body massage it is."

Her hands worked magic, easing the tension in my muscles as we chatted like old friends. We talked about my plans for the Cassie farm and the retreat I wanted to open—a space for overworked women to escape and recharge. She seemed as excited about it as I was, throwing out ideas for pamper packages and gift bags.

When she draped a warm towel over my back, signaling the massage was done, she asked gently, "What about your family? Were they disappointed you left for your country dream?"

I hesitated, the words catching in my throat. "My

dad passed last year," I said softly. "And I haven't seen my mum since I was sixteen."

"I'm sorry," Ali said, her tone warm and understanding.

"Thanks," I murmured.

After a quick shower, I felt lighter, ready to tackle the rest of my day.

∼

Bailey

Noah's absence from the farm hadn't gone unnoticed. Jack's afternoon visits were becoming a regular thing, along with the excuses he made for his grandson. I could hear the disappointment in his voice, even though he always tried to brush it off. But his expression gave him away—he was bothered, no matter what he said.

For Jack's sake, I hoped Noah would get over himself and whatever childish tantrum he was throwing. I understood the circumstances weren't ideal, but it was hard to believe Noah couldn't see how much Jack was struggling with the change, too.

COUNTRY CHARM

Still, I didn't regret buying the farm or the arrangements I'd made with Jack—for both his accommodation and the farm's operations. Jack was sweet, always checking in on me, even with his packed schedule. It was obvious he missed Noah, even when he casually mentioned how crazy and demanding farm life could be.

I threw myself into making the house feel like home, doing everything I could to avoid the tension my presence had stirred up. My original plan to bulldoze and rebuild now felt excessive, even ridiculous. Instead, I leaned into a French country style that softened the space and worked beautifully with the neutral tones and existing fittings.

For me, chaos wasn't an option—I couldn't function in disorder. Establishing some kind of harmony in my surroundings was essential. And once I had everything in place, I could finally focus on the part I was most excited about: planning my business.

That afternoon, I was deep in concentration, tangled in a mess of cables as I tried to set up my new home theater system. A sharp knock on the door startled me, and relief washed over me. *Jack will know how to fix this,* I thought.

"Come in, it's open." I called, too engrossed in the cords to get up and answer the door myself.

The door creaked open, then closed.

"I'm in the lounge room," I shouted again, assuming it was Jack.

"Trying to get yourself electrocuted, I'm guessing."

I stood from my crouch and turned, startled to find Noah standing in the doorway. "Oh, hi. Sorry, I thought you were Jack."

"Hey." He stayed where he was, lingering near the entrance. "I came to see Jack, if that's okay."

"Why wouldn't it be?" I frowned. "He's not here, though. If he's not in the flat, I'm sure you'd know better than me where to look."

Noah jammed his hands into the pockets of his jacket. "I didn't like to go barging around on your property without checking it was okay first."

Time away from the place hadn't made him relax any. No amount of white flag sailing was going to win him over in a hurry.

I sighed, trying to suppress my irritation. "Come on, Noah, give me a break. You're free to visit Jack wherever and whenever you want. This situation doesn't have to be as difficult as you're making it."

He nodded once, a quick, sharp motion. I smiled despite myself—he was so much like Jack.

"You look like you could use some help," he said,

stepping farther into the room and picking up the instruction manual from the coffee table.

"Do you mind? Technology's great when it works, but setting it up? Nightmare."

He chuckled, the sound low and a little disarming. "It's the opposite for me. Step back before you fry yourself."

Grinning, I handed him the cables I'd been ready to give up on. "Can I get you a coffee? Or a beer?" I hesitated, unsure if offering alcohol before noon was a faux pas around here.

"Beer sounds great, thanks," he said, already focused on the instructions.

Relieved, I headed to the kitchen and grabbed two bottles from the fridge. When I returned, he'd taken off his jacket and was crouched in front of the TV. I couldn't help but notice the way his shirt clung to his biceps as he worked. Strong, capable hands moved with confidence and precision.

"This setup is impressive," he said, glancing up with a grin as I handed him a beer. "These 3D televisions are supposed to be amazing for football—like you're on the field."

I laughed. "I'll take your word for it. I'm not much of a TV person, but it'll be nice for the quiet nights."

Something in his expression shifted at that, but he took a swig of his beer instead of saying anything.

"I didn't peg you for a beer drinker," he said after a moment. "Figured you'd be more of a fancy wine type."

"What gave you that idea?" I raised an eyebrow, genuinely curious.

"That flash truck you rolled up in. I'm guessing it's yours?"

I nodded my head. Something about his tone made me feel like I was walking into a trap.

"When did you buy it?"

Where was he going with this? What my car had to do with my preference of a drink I was clearly going to find out.

"A week ago."

"Did you leave the red sports car in your garage in the city?"

"What are you, a stalker?"

"I'm right, aren't I?"

He was baiting me. "I've never liked red cars, silver's my color."

Noah shook his head, and his smile faded to a grimace.

"What?"

"Nothing else needs to be said. You summed it up perfectly."

"And you're judgmental. I buy a more appropriate car for my new lifestyle, and it explains why you thought I would like wine better than beer?"

"Forget it, you don't get it." He connected the last cable and hit the power button. The screen blinked to life, vivid and crystal clear.

"Thanks," I said, genuinely grateful.

He shrugged, standing and grabbing his jacket. "Don't mention it. I'll let you get back to…whatever it is you're doing."

"You know, Noah," I said, stopping him before he reached the door. "Just because I have money doesn't mean I have everything."

His jaw tightened, but he didn't respond to my comment. "Have a good day, Bailey." He tipped his head, then pulled open the door and left.

Noah's dismissive attitude grated on me more than I cared to admit. I shoved the discarded polystyrene and plastic bags into the oversized box the television had come in, my movements sharp with frustration. That's when I heard it—the faint creak of the kitchen door swinging open.

"I'm in the lounge room," I called, my voice echoing slightly in the quiet house. Maybe Jack had come by, spotting Noah's car and assuming he was still here.

Silence stretched uncomfortably. No reply.

Frowning, I wiped my hands on my jeans and wandered into the kitchen. It was empty, the door hanging ajar. Cold air slipped through the gap, stirring the curtains faintly.

Noah must've left in such a rush he hadn't bothered to latch it properly. Typical.

Still, unease curled in my stomach as I crossed the room. The cool draft pricked at my skin, and I hesitated at the threshold. My gaze flicked to the verandah, shadows pooling under the railing.

"Hello?" I said softly, sticking my head out the door. The word dissipated into the crisp air, swallowed by the stillness.

The verandah was empty. No lingering figure, no movement. But the quiet felt... heavy, almost oppressive, like the house itself was holding its breath.

Shivering, I closed the door firmly and locked it, the deadbolt clicking into place a little too loudly. I glanced over my shoulder as I stepped back into the house, feeling foolish. Of course, no one was there.

Upstairs, I changed quickly, but the feeling of being watched clung to me like a second skin. With my horse arriving tomorrow, I told myself to focus on the practical—checking the stables, making sure everything was ready.

I moved to the window and peered out toward Freya's new home. From here, it looked fine, but I couldn't shake the sense that something—someone—was just out of sight, watching from the shadows.

∽

Noah

I'd been a jerk—no point sugarcoating it. Ever since the *For Sale* sign went up, I'd been acting like a spoiled brat, letting resentment blind me to the bigger picture. The past few years hadn't been kind to any of us, and the farm had become my emotional battlefield. Moving forward felt like wading through a relentless headwind, but I was trying. God, I was trying.

To break the tension, I started chatting with Jack, filling him in on family updates and the usual small-town gossip.

"How're the wedding plans coming along?" I was hoping to steer the conversation to safer ground.

Jack's face softened. "It's going to be the event of

the year. Ben's struggling with his vows, though. Says it's intimidating since Soph's a writer. Claims it's too much pressure."

That got a chuckle out of me. "He'll figure it out."

Jack nodded and went back to work, his focus shifting to the task at hand. But I could tell he was listening; the small grin on his face gave it away.

"Is Charlotte going to be there?" I asked, trying to keep the conversation alive.

Before Jack could answer, the sound of Bailey's truck interrupted us. The familiar rumble made me glance toward the barn just in time to see her park and climb out. She waved as she approached, her smile warm enough to make the lingering tension melt away.

"Hey," she called. "If I'd known you two were here, I'd have brought some beers."

"You trying to get me drunk?" I teased, unable to help myself. Her smile widened, and I felt the corners of my own mouth tug upward despite myself.

"What are you up to? You look like a kid on Christmas morning," Jack said, stretching his back as he straightened.

"Wait until tomorrow," Bailey replied, practically

buzzing with excitement. "I just checked out the stables. Freya's arriving in the morning."

Freya? Probably a horse. "You ride?" I attempted to keep my tone neutral.

Bailey tilted her head. "I try."

"But you have a horse?"

"Yes, I have a horse."

"What kind?"

Her brow furrowed. "Is this going the same way as the sports car conversation?"

I sighed, realizing how I must've sounded. "No, sorry. You took me by surprise. I like horses."

That seemed to mollify her a little. Her smile returned, albeit faintly. "She's a Friesian."

"Bloody hell," I muttered. "Don't you ever just do simple?"

Her smile disappeared. Damn it. The moment the words left my mouth, I knew I'd overstepped. Again.

Bailey turned to Jack, effectively shutting me out. "Is there a stock feeder in town? Or somewhere you'd recommend for hay?"

"Sure. Kennedy's Stock Feeders is good, but we've got round bales of oaten hay if you're interested," Jack replied.

"Thanks. I'll let you get back to it. I'm going to

clean the barn." She smiled again, but it didn't quite reach her eyes this time.

Jack tried to lighten the mood. "Geez, the things you do for fun. You need to get out more."

Bailey laughed softly, but when her gaze flicked to me, the laughter died. Watching her walk away, her earlier buoyancy dimmed, felt like a gut punch. I hated knowing I was the reason for it.

"Did you have to?" Jack broke the silence.

"What?" I snapped, though I knew exactly what he meant.

"You know what." Jack gave me a pointed look. "She's had a different upbringing than you. Just because she has fancy things and money doesn't mean she has everything."

I scowled. "What, do you two compare notes in the evenings? She already hit me with that speech."

Jack crossed his arms. "Yeah, well, it'd pay to listen sometimes."

∼

Loaded with cleaning products, buckets, a broom, and the bottles of water I'd grabbed last minute from the back of the truck, I got to work. The floor was thick with years of dust and grime, and I knew it would take serious scrubbing to make any progress. My plan was to start at the base and work my way up, even though I'd inevitably end up knocking more dirt down as I went.

Dust filled the air as I swept, rising in lazy swirls that tickled my nose and made me sneeze. I bent to pick up some old hessian sacks, brittle and tattered from time, when something moved in the corner of my eye. My heart stopped. Scales—mottled and coated with dust—slithered into view.

A scream ripped from my throat, loud and panicked, as I dropped the sacks directly onto the snake. It had probably been just as startled as I was, woken abruptly from hibernation. Without thinking, I bolted toward the door, colliding with Noah, who must have rushed in after hearing me scream.

His arms wrapped around me, steadying my frantic movements, holding me in place as I clung to him like my life depended on it.

"Snake," I managed to blurt out, my voice trembling. Noah's arms were the only things keeping me from fleeing entirely.

Jack appeared in the doorway, taking in the scene with an amused grin. "Want me to come back later?" he teased, raising an eyebrow at my grip on Noah.

Heat rushed to my cheeks as I released Noah, feeling like a schoolgirl caught passing notes in class.

"Your first encounter with a snake, I'm guessing?" Noah's grin widening as he crossed his arms.

I nodded, still trying to calm my racing heart.

"Good thing he's sluggish this time of year. Point us in his direction, and we'll take care of him for you."

I gestured toward the hessian sacks in the far corner, where the snake had disappeared.

Noah grabbed a rusty old shovel as he passed me, and I stayed well back, unwilling to be anywhere near where the snake might emerge. He approached the pile cautiously, using the tip of the shovel to lift one of the sacks. As the sack moved, a large, coiled mass was revealed beneath. My hand flew to my mouth to stifle the gasp that escaped me.

The tense silence was broken by Noah's sudden laughter. Startled, I lowered my hand and stared at him, then at the snake.

"Is it dead?" I whispered, unable to see any humor in the situation.

Noah crouched down, far too close to the snake for my comfort.

"Careful," I warned, my voice tight.

He moved closer still, then reached out and

grabbed the snake behind its neck. My stomach turned.

"It's okay," he said, his voice calm as he supported the snake's belly with his free hand. "Just a python. Want to pet it?"

I frowned, torn between skepticism and the lingering adrenaline still coursing through me. "It won't bite me?"

"Nah, it's a constrictor," Noah said, a mischievous glint in his eye. "He'd crush you to death before he'd bite you."

I shot him a glare, refusing to give him the reaction he was fishing for. Summoning my courage, I stepped closer, reaching out with a hesitant hand to stroke the snake's belly. Its scales were smooth and surprisingly soft.

"It's softer than I expected," I admitted, my voice barely above a whisper.

"Yeah, they're like that," Noah said, shifting the snake to one hand as he grabbed the hessian sack with the other. "Best we find him a new home. He won't be thrilled about being woken up early."

With practiced ease, he slipped the snake into the sack, tying the top securely. Turning back to me, he grinned. "I'll leave you to your cleaning. Just scream if you need anything else." He winked before heading outside with the sack in hand.

Jack lingered in the doorway. "You sure you're okay on your own?"

I nodded, mustering a smile. "I'm fine, thanks, Jack."

He nodded back and followed Noah, presumably to relocate the snake far from the barn.

Exhaling a shaky breath, I returned to my work, more determined than ever to get the space ready. If I had to face a few more unexpected surprises, so be it.

CHAPTER 4

Bailey

Eight-thirty-two.

I stood on the front porch, practically vibrating with excitement as Rob from Professional Horse Transport pulled up in front of the house. I'd been up since the first light touched the horizon, eager for this moment. His truck and float were impressive, the kind of setup that could transport a dozen horses in more comfort than a luxury caravan.

Rob climbed out of the cab, a man who looked to be in his mid-fifties but carried himself with the strength and agility of someone younger. Years of handling horses had clearly kept him fit.

"Hello, Bailey." He dipped his head in a polite nod, extending a hand.

"Nice to meet you, Rob." I shook his hand, noting the firm grip of someone used to hard work. It was refreshing compared to the polished manicures and smooth handshakes I was used to in the office world. "How'd my girl travel?" I nodded toward the back of the truck, unable to keep the anticipation out of my voice.

"She's a beauty and a dream to transport." Rob led the way to the float, and I followed closely. "I'll just drop the side down. The door's heavy, so stand clear."

I stepped back as he worked, releasing the latch and lowering the ramp with practiced ease. The horses inside shifted slightly, their hooves scuffing the floor as they adjusted to the change. As Rob moved among them, I couldn't help but notice the affection they showed him—nudging and nuzzling whenever he came within reach. It was clear he had a way with them.

When he finally led Freya out of the float, I had to resist the urge to clap my hands and jump like an excited child. She was breathtaking. Her freshly clipped black coat gleamed, her thick, wavy mane hung elegantly down her neck, and her feathered legs and flowing tail gave her a timeless, almost medieval charm.

"Freya," I breathed, stepping forward to hold out a hand. She nuzzled it gently, and I moved closer, rubbing her sleek neck. "I've missed you, beautiful girl."

She brushed her nose against my arm, her warm breath tickling my skin. It was a small gesture, but it filled me with more contentment than I'd felt in weeks.

Rob handed me the lead rope. "I'll grab the delivery form from the cab for you to sign, and then she's all yours."

"Thanks." I barely glanced up, too absorbed in Freya. "Hey, my warrior goddess," I murmured, planting a kiss on her strong Roman nose. "How do you like your new home, huh?"

Her eyes seemed to take everything in, calm and assessing. It would be a few days before I rode her—she needed time to settle in—but just having her here felt like a victory. Freya had always been my escape, my sanctuary from the stress of being CFO of Collins Mining Group.

"Now that's what I call a horse," a voice said, startling me out of my thoughts.

I turned to see Jack approaching, his expression one of admiration.

"She's something, isn't she?" I stepped back to admire her.

"I've never seen a Friesian in real life. They're pretty rare around here."

"She's been my dream since I was a kid. My father bought her for me after I graduated from university." I smiled, glancing at Jack. "Some might think it's odd, but she's the best friend I've ever had."

Jack chuckled. "Not odd at all. Animals make great companions. Though, humans can be good too —if you find the right ones." He winked, reaching up to rub Freya's neck.

Rob returned with the paperwork and a pen.

"Jack, this is Rob. Rob, Jack." I handed the lead rope to Jack. "Would you mind holding her? Her name's Freya."

Jack took the rope, whispering softly to her as I handled the formalities.

"Well, I'd better be off. Got a full day of driving ahead," Rob said once everything was signed.

"Thanks so much," I replied. "I'll spread the word about the great job you did."

Rob smiled and handed me a stack of business cards. "Take care of yourself—and her."

"Will do." After shaking his hand, I watched him climb back into the cab and drive off.

I turned back to face Jack and grinned as I reached out to rub Freya's neck again.

"I don't know much about horses, but she's magnificent. Noah was the horse-crazy one, but he hasn't ridden in years."

I hesitated, curious. "Why not?"

Jack's expression tightened for a moment before he shrugged. "Bad experience." He rubbed the back of his neck, clearly wanting to change the subject. "Do you have tack for her?"

I nodded. "I'll let her settle in first, though it's hard to resist the temptation to ride her."

Jack walked with me toward the stables. "The horse yards are a bit run-down."

"They're secure, which is the main thing, but I'd love to update them—maybe an American-style barn. Do you know anyone local who could do the work?"

Jack paused, considering. "If you want the best, that'd be Noah. He's meticulous, and I think he'd enjoy the project. Otherwise, you'd have to bring in someone from out of town."

I wasn't sure how I felt about hiring Noah. He didn't seem fond of me—or my money. But Jack's recommendation carried weight.

"Thanks, I'll think about it," I said as we reached the stable.

Freya, calm despite her long journey, followed us easily. Her size was imposing compared to my own, but she'd never given me a reason to doubt her.

"I'm heading into town for feed. Need anything?" I was hoping Jack would tag along.

He grinned. "I'll come with you. Keep you company."

I smiled back, grateful to have him along for the ride though I hated leaving Freya so soon. But she needed feeding, and hay alone wouldn't be enough in the cold nights ahead.

As I stepped into the store, the lady behind the counter called out a hello to Jack, and he grinned.

"Mel, this is Bailey. She bought my place."

Mel's smile faded. "Hello, Bailey. How are you settling in?"

"Great. It would've been so much harder if Jack hadn't been so kind to look out for me." I smiled, but Mel's face remained sullen. "It's a beautiful town, and I love the land." I knew I was babbling, but Mel made it clear she wasn't impressed by me or my purchase of the Kelly farm.

"Is there something I can get for you?" Mel's tone was polite but short, leaving no room for further conversation.

"Ahh, yes, please." I pulled a list from my jean pocket. "Do you have horse blankets?"

Mel glanced at Jack and raised her eyebrows. "What size horse?"

I tried to relax. There was no way I was going to admit the breed. Anyone who knew anything about livestock knew the hefty price of a Friesian mare.

"She's large."

Mel laughed. "Compared to what?"

"A Friesian," Jack blurted.

Mel's eyebrows shot up again, but she said nothing as she reached an array of rugs. "We only have paddock quality stock at the moment," she said, almost apologetically.

"That's fine, thanks." I leaned over and picked a blue rug off the shelf.

"Anything else?"

I rattled off the list of things I needed, and Mel helped me carry them to the counter. Jack was nowhere to be seen. Mel rang up my purchases, and

I handed over my credit card without flinching at the exuberant amount I'd spent.

"If you drive your car around the side, Rick will load up for you. Do you need a hand with all this?" Mel gestured to the load of products spilled all over the counter.

"That's okay. I'll make a few trips if I have to, but thanks for your help." I smiled again, trying for a positive response, with no success. Picking up as much as I could, I turned and almost ran into Tracy.

""Oh, Bailey, here, let me give you a hand." Tracy scooped the contents from my arms before I could object.

"Thanks." There was no point arguing when she'd already taken charge. Instead, I turned, picked up the rest of my items, and followed her outside.

I unlocked the truck, and a woman I hadn't met opened the passenger door for me and Tracy to unload onto the seat.

"Thanks." I smiled in her direction as Tracy offered an introduction.

"Bailey, this is my daughter-in-law, Emily. Dan's wife."

"Hi, lovely to meet you."

"You too. Tracy told me all about you." Dimples creased Emily's cheeks as she smiled. Her honey blonde hair hung in spirals to her shoulders, and her eyes, blue like topaz, were bright, adding to the fresh, cheerful look she radiated.

"Noah mentioned you bought a horse." Tracy tried to sound casual, and I couldn't help but wonder how that conversation actually went.

"My dad bought her for me a few years ago." There was no reason to elaborate on the topic. I had nothing to hide, even if everyone else in town seemed to have an issue with the type of horse I owned.

"So, how are you settling in?" Tracy jumped from one topic to the next like a rabbit in the headlights of an approaching vehicle. It was hard to keep up.

"Your dad's been so wonderful to me. I don't know what I'd do without him."

"Well, when you're settled, Emily and I will have to call in for a visit. It'd be lovely for the two of you to get to know each other. It can be lonely out here if you don't make friends."

Already noticing the isolation, I wasn't at all surprised by her warning. "You're welcome anytime. If I'm not in the house, you'll find me in the barn or the stables."

"Lovely. Well, I must get going, or else Mike will come looking for us. Remember to call if you need anything." Tracy set off, with Emily following along behind.

I spotted Jack at the side of the stock feeders where Mel had told me to park for Rick to load the bags of feed into the back of my truck.

Jack looked up as I climbed from the driver's seat, the grin on his face like that of a young boy.

"Cute pups." I smiled as they jumped over each other, fighting for attention. "Are you buying one, Jack?"

His smile faded, and he shook his head.

"Tracy and Emily are inside. Did you see them?" I thought he might want to, if he hadn't already.

"No, but I'll catch up with them in a moment, if you don't mind. Bailey, meet Rick, Noah's best mate."

I smiled at the young guy who approached us from the stockroom.

"Hey, Bailey, was wondering when you were going to show your face around here. Judging by this lot, I'm guessing we'll be seeing more of you."

"Nice to meet you, Rick." I liked him immediately. He was by far friendlier than the girl behind the counter.

"I'll be back in a few minutes." Jack left as soon as the introduction was over.

"Ali said you were a looker. No wonder Noah spends so much time on the Kelly farm these days."

Clearly, he had no clue what his best mate was up to. His assumption came as a surprise. I arched an eyebrow but didn't react. "Ali's a sweetheart. She made me feel so welcome."

"That's my girl." Rick grinned.

Ali had mentioned her husband during my massage the day before, and I could already see how well-suited they were. Both so warm and friendly—the kind of couple I could picture myself spending time with. Although, being the third wheel wasn't exactly appealing, and if Rick was Noah's close friend, it didn't seem likely for the future anyway.

"Jack likes those pups," I said, changing the subject.

"Yeah, he's in here all the time visiting them. Reckon he wants one but doesn't like to, now that it's not his farm and all."

"Really? That's ridiculous. He can have as many dogs as he wants. He should know that." I was mortified to think Jack would go without because of me. "Has he mentioned wanting one?"

Rick shrugged. "Picked one out after they were born, but came in a few weeks later and said he'd have to leave it because he sold the farm. Came as a bit of a shock, I must say. The sale, not the dog."

I nodded, feeling a pang of guilt. Jack had sacrificed so much already, and I didn't want him missing out on more. "How many do you have left?"

"Can't even give 'em away at the moment," Rick said as he began loading bags into the back of my truck. I felt useless standing there, but I stayed, chatting as he worked. Jack joined us just as Rick was finishing up.

"Rick was telling me no one wants these pups. I think it's strange to have a farm with no dog," I said, glancing at Jack.

Jack frowned but didn't reply.

"I'd like to buy us one each. What d'you say? As a thank you for helping me out all the time," I said quietly, not wanting to embarrass him in front of Rick.

Jack shook his head. "I can't accept it, Bailey. You've been too generous already."

"Think of it as a selfish gift. I want one, and she should have a friend. Don't you think?"

I saw him struggling with the grin that was threatening to appear. The glint in his eyes was all the proof I needed that he was delighted.

"You know them better than me. Will you pick us

two of the best?" I winked at Rick, who grinned back at me. "I'll sort out food and stuff with Mel." Leaving Jack to choose our puppies, I headed back into the store to deal with Mel's inevitable frostiness.

By the time I drove us home, Jack sat in the passenger seat with both pups on his lap. "So, what are we calling them?" I was keen for him to decide. I'd never given any real thought to owning a dog before.

"Well, given Freya has the name of a goddess, who am I to lower the standards? Any other deities appeal to you?"

"I've bought a Friesian stallion, and I plan to call him Erebus. We could go with gods and goddesses all around. Isis is pretty."

"I like Isis." Jack sat in thought for a moment. "And, how about Zeus?"

"Perfect."

We agreed to take shifts with the pups for now, keeping them together during the day. The logic was that they'd entertain each other and not disrupt the work that still needed to be done. Jack insisted on taking them that afternoon, giving me time to spend with Freya. I hadn't thought much about how Freya would handle a puppy snapping at her hooves, but thankfully, that wasn't something I needed to worry about—at least for the moment.

Arranging the tack room took longer than expected, but once it was done, I could finally focus on the endless list of tasks that seemed to grow rather than shrink. I decided to groom Freya, even though she was already spotless.

"Wow, that's some horse," a voice startled me. *Noah.* I jumped, dropping the brush, which spooked Freya. She reared, nearly knocking me over. The calm atmosphere I'd created evaporated in an instant, but I worked to soothe her.

"Sorry," Noah said, stepping closer to stroke Freya from the opposite side. He grasped her halter and whispered softly to her. "I didn't mean to startle either of you." He looked past Freya, catching my eye.

"I was in my own little bubble. She has that effect on me."

"I can see why." Noah's gaze shifted to Freya as he admired her. "I've always loved this breed."

"Jack said you ride. Maybe we could go out sometime."

Noah's eyes flicked back to mine, a frown forming on his face.

"Riding, I mean." Heat rose in my cheeks as I realized how it sounded. "You know what? Forget it."

Noah's expression softened, but he didn't immediately respond. Instead, he picked up the brush I'd dropped and began grooming Freya in long, rhythmic strokes. "My mom asked me to invite you to lunch on Sunday," he said, not looking up as he waited for my answer.

"I'd like that. Thank you."

"I'll let her know." He paused, finally meeting my gaze. "Thanks for buying Jack the pup. I can't tell you what it means to him."

I shook my head, feeling uncomfortable under the weight of his intense stare. "It's nothing, really."

Noah nodded once, handed me the brush, and turned to leave. "See you Sunday," he said over his shoulder as he walked away.

CHAPTER 5

Bailey

Of all nights for me to get the spooks, it had to be the one before the barbecue. The door to the bedroom at the end of the upstairs corridor slammed as the wind howled through a window I didn't remember opening. Of course, my imagination took hold, and the few hours I slept left me feeling worse than if I'd had none.

The morning sun lit up shadowed corners, chasing away my fear of an intruder. Dragging myself down to the kitchen, I went straight to the coffee machine. I was going to need all the caffeine I could get if I wanted to make it through the day without yawning constantly.

Small-town hospitality couldn't differ much from back home—everyone pitching in and making a dish to contribute toward lunch. Noah had insisted the only thing I needed to bring was Jack, if he wanted a lift, but I prepared my signature dish anyway. The creamy pasta salad was always a hit when I'd made it in the past, so it was an obvious choice to repeat. Besides, it was quick and easy.

I put the pasta on to cook before pulling on my boots and heading outside to feed Freya. Isis had spent the night at Jack's, as both pups cried too much to get any sleep—not that I had, anyway. So much for them being working dogs. Jack treated them as if they were his babies. He'd even built a yard for them to stay in during the day when we were busy or had to go out. I hadn't thought much about how restricted I'd be with my latest addition, but I wouldn't change Isis for anything.

Freya called out as soon as she saw me approach. "Hello, goddess," I said, rubbing her neck. "You're hungry, aren't you?" Knowing no one would hear, I chatted to Freya as if she could understand.

With the pasta cooking, I didn't have time for more than a quick rubdown before topping up the water trough and mixing her feed. Not wanting to start the day by burning my lunch contribution, I rushed back to the house.

Although I'd allowed myself plenty of time to get ready, I couldn't help but feel anxious. What was I expected to wear to an event like this? I didn't want to look overdressed but still wanted to blend in as though I'd never known another life. Meeting the neighbors—even though their houses were separated by hundreds of acres—felt like a big deal. Nothing would scream *fish out of water* like the wrong outfit.

As if yet another of Noah's tests, the pressure of trying to fit in was more stressful than any job I'd ever had. I couldn't help but be curious about who would attend—whether it'd be an intimate gathering with a select few, or half the town.

Playing it safe with boots, jeans, and a casual top wasn't an option; the warmth of the sun had already kicked in. Despite being spring, the days could get quite warm, and there was no way I was going to overheat trying to blend.

I rummaged through the dresses I'd bought but never found the right moment to wear. I settled on the short white one with a small flower print. It was cute and sexy, and as close to country-girl style as I owned. Teamed with brown high-heeled cowboy boots I'd bought in Canada and my favorite bag—the one my dad referred to as a saddlebag—it worked. I left my hair to fall loose around my face. It felt strange after having it tied up constantly, but I thought it made me look softer, more feminine. A small amount of makeup—just mascara and gloss on my lips—completed the look. I checked myself in the full-length mirror in my bedroom. Tanned from spending more time outdoors, I was satisfied with the overall result.

I was filling a cooler bag with drinks when Jack walked in the front door. He smiled as soon as he saw me fussing around in the kitchen. "You look lovely," he said. He was always generous with compliments.

"Not too much?" It was unlike me, to be so self-conscious and hesitant. Back in the city, others looked to me for guidance. The thought almost made me laugh, given the responsibility I once had compared to my new lifestyle.

"Perfect," Jack assured me before helping carry my stuff to the car.

As I suspected, the invites extended far beyond Jack and me. It looked like a party, and most of the town had come out to meet me. Mike and Tracy's farm was more beautiful than I'd expected. The house, more like a mansion, sat amidst the most perfect garden I'd ever seen outside of a movie.

I stuck close to Jack, my side pressed against his like a child to its mother's skirt.

"Bailey, this is Whitney. She works at the pub." Jack introduced her to me, and I couldn't help but notice the overdressed woman clinging to Noah's arm, pawing at him at every opportunity.

"So, you're the famous Bailey," Whitney sneered. "Love your boots and bag. Where'd you get them?"

I followed her gaze to the boots I, too, adored. "Alberta," I replied, hoping that was enough.

One word was all it took for Noah to snigger, shaking his head before walking away. I wished I'd lied and pretended they were a gift. Why did it even matter where I got them? I wasn't the only person who'd traveled out of the country. Any points I'd earned for the salad and an outfit that wasn't over the top seemed lost now. I tried to convince myself that I didn't need Noah's approval, but even that defiant thought wasn't convincing.

"Bailey, love, how are you settling in?" Mike's voice pulled me from my thoughts.

"Hi, Mike. The longer I'm in town, the more I love

it," I admitted. "It wouldn't have been the same if Jack hadn't been so kind to me." Especially when your son has been so difficult, I added silently to myself.

"Good to hear. Come over and say hello to Tracy. She'll be delighted to see you." Jack left in search of a beer, and I offered him one from the cooler bag, but he declined.

"Oh, I'm so glad you're here." Tracy wrapped me in a warm embrace, like I was a long-lost friend.

I returned her hug, feeling her warmth seep into me. Tracy was like the Sahara compared to Noah's glacier.

"You don't want to spend the day with us oldies. Come on, I'll introduce you to Dan and Noah's friends."

I didn't object as Tracy linked her arm through mine.

The entertaining area was more than I had imagined, like a picnic scene from a fairytale. The lush green lawn was scattered with large deciduous trees and lined with flowerbeds of plants I didn't recognize but still admired. I wished I knew their names, but I decided to wait until a quiet moment alone to ask. My lack of knowledge was a sure giveaway that I didn't really fit in.

Relieved to see there were only a few faces I didn't recognize, I relaxed.

"There she is," Cooper, the first to notice us, called out, grinning.

I flashed him a smile. I knew I could count on Cooper to make me feel welcome. He drew me into a one-arm hug, too familiar after only a brief encounter, but I didn't want to embarrass him when he was just being friendly.

"Oh, Cooper, for goodness' sake, give me a chance to share her around before you claim her," Tracy swatted his shoulder, and he laughed.

The unfamiliar faces belonged to Sophie and Ben, the couple Ali had spoken about during her massage, and Cassie, Ben's younger sister, the local vet.

Emily and Dan sat on one bench under the canopy of a rather impressive-looking tree. Sophie and Ben were cozy on the other, while Ali, Rick, and Cassie sprawled on the grass.

Cooper dragged over two outdoor chairs, one for me and the other for himself, after Tracy declined, insisting she should get back to the adults. Obviously, she still thought of them as children, a concept I found amusing.

The conversation flowed easily, but I mostly

listened. Occasionally, Cooper would lean over and explain who they were referring to. Even though it wasn't his role, he was quite the attentive host, and I reminded myself I'd have to make it clear my interest was purely platonic.

Noah and Whitney wandered over to join us, and I couldn't help but wonder about their involvement.

"Oh, Whitney, I'm glad you found your puppy," Cassie said, and Ben sniggered.

"What? I don't have a puppy."

Whitney looked confused, and Cassie shook her head. "My mistake. Forget it."

The afternoon passed quickly. The food was better than any restaurant I'd ever been to. Nothing beat home cooking, and I imagined half the dishes were probably made from recipes passed down through generations, meant to continue long after my time.

Cooper made sure I was included in the playful banter and conversation, spending most of the day by my side.

As the sun dipped toward the horizon, the older generation retreated indoors or returned to their farms for chores that couldn't wait. Jack, who hadn't been feeling very well, went for a laydown, even after I insisted I was happy to take him home. He wouldn't hear of it.

Sophie and Ben were the first to leave, as Ben had to fly out in the morning for his job in the mines. The trek to the airport was a long one, and they wanted an early night.

I lingered, not wanting to go home to an empty house so soon. I found myself left with Cooper and Noah after Dan insisted he and Emily head off to get the kids sorted before it got too late. They had school tomorrow, and I suspected Dan still had work to do.

"I'm going to scout up a few more beers," Cooper announced, leaving me alone with Noah.

Not knowing what to talk about, I stood and wandered over to lean against the thick trunk of the tree I'd admired for most of the day. That was when I wasn't distracted by Noah's presence, and the way the denim of his jeans fit snug across his narrow hips, or the fitted black t-shirt that molded to every ripple of his upper body. I didn't want to be attracted to him, especially when he reminded me over again that I was an imposter, but some things were out of my control, and Noah's attractive factor was one of them.

Noah wandered over and stood in front of me.

"He's one of my best mates."

I waited for him to continue, but he didn't. "Is he off-limits for me to be friends with too?"

"No, so long as you're just friends."

"Oh, so you're going to dictate what relationships I can have, are you?"

"I don't want him to get hurt, and I've seen it happen before."

More like you've experienced it, I thought, curiosity almost getting the better of me. But I stopped myself before I could ask who'd damaged him so badly to taint his opinion of me enough to not give me a chance.

I wanted to be annoyed at him for judging me again, but I couldn't. Instead, I reached up and traced the line of his face from temple to chin. "I'm not like that, Noah. I've been hurt too."

He wouldn't look me in the eye, but he didn't move away either. He was difficult to read. I let my hand drop to his shoulder and, leaning forward, brushed my lips across his cheek toward his ear. "I don't plan on hurting anyone." I took a deep breath, knowing the effect of too much alcohol in the afternoon sun was making me bold. Running my hands over his shoulder and following the curve to the base of his neck, I moved my lips to meet his. Soft and warm, I could taste beer on his mouth as he responded to my touch, parting his lips slightly as I traced his bottom lip with the tip of my tongue.

Running his hand up my arm, I shuddered. He gripped my wrist, jerking my hand from behind his neck. "This will never happen. You should go." Noah glared at me. "I'll bring Jack home in the morning," he added, before stalking away.

CHAPTER 6

Bailey

Work was the only thing that kept me from replaying the humiliation over and over again in my mind. After Noah dismissed me as he did, I buried myself in tasks, pouring every ounce of energy into being productive. Keeping busy was the only thing stopping me from climbing into my truck and driving until I hit home turf.

No one liked rejection, but experiencing it repeatedly didn't soften the blow.

Noah was off-limits. I knew that from the

moment his critical gaze sized me up on day one. Now I'd overstepped, and I had no idea how to come back from it. If anyone had witnessed the rejection, Noah wouldn't be the only one I'd want to avoid.

If he'd visited Jack in the past few days, I wouldn't know. I'd been holed up in the room I'd turned into my study, designing a website, business cards, and flyers. That was the fun part of building a business. The barn's construction and maintenance? Not so much.

Knowing I couldn't put it off any longer, I picked up my phone and called Cooper.

"Hey-hey, beautiful girl," he answered on the second ring.

"Oh, hi, Cooper. It's Bailey."

"So caller ID revealed. What's up?"

"I have a barn in need of an overhaul. You interested?" I held my breath, hoping his schedule wasn't too packed. The last thing I wanted was to hire someone from out of town—or worse, ask Noah for help.

"I'm finishing up at the Kennedy place this afternoon. I can come by first thing tomorrow to check it out."

"Perfect. Thanks." A grin spread across my face as I hung up.

My whole business was built around the barn so, until Cooper gave the go ahead, my plans were in limbo. However, that didn't stop me from penciling in possible dates for the first few retreats. Manifestation was a powerful tool. I'd have to run them past Jack before announcing them online, but it was progress.

The crop paddock near the barn offered a picturesque view, but the sound of machinery would shatter the tranquility I'd be promising my guests. Farm work wasn't something I factored into my business plan, but hoped it would be easy enough for me to work around.

"You've been busy. I haven't seen you since you left me at the party," Jack said as he pulled open the sliding door I knocked on.

I looked up to see Jack standing in the doorway.

I opened my mouth to explain, but he waved me off with a laugh. "Noah told me he sent you home. Said he didn't want to disturb me."

"Yeah, something like that," I mumbled, wondering what else Noah had told him.

"You've been busy."

I guessed he was referring to my absence. It was unusual for us to go days without seeing each other, but I couldn't face seeing anyone, not even Jack, until I knew how far my humiliation spread.

"I know I'm getting ahead of myself, but I'm contemplating dates for the retreats, and I wanted to run them by you first." I held out the paper I'd written them on for his appraisal.

He scanned the page. "They look fine to me, but I'd better run them past Noah. My head isn't as sharp as it used to be. Maggie used to think for both of us." Jack's eyes glistened, and that faraway look he got when he spoke of her was back.

"It'd be an understatement to say you miss her, huh?"

"Yep. We were a team. She kept me on my toes, never let me slack off." He laughed, a sound filled with love, longing, and sadness.

I'd never known love like that. My parents' relationship was no model, and my own experiences were disasters. My one serious relationship had been built on lies, not love. He'd used me as a ladder to climb his career. When I found out he was cheating with my father's assistant, I wasn't heartbroken—just angry. Love was blind, but I'd add *foolish* to the saying.

"Can I ask how she died?"

Jack let out a deep breath. "Stubbornness."

I smiled, expecting nothing less from him.

"Really, it was. She refused to admit she wasn't well. Worked herself into the ground, riding trails with Noah or helping me on the farm. When she came off her horse one day, I found her hours later, sunburned and dehydrated. That's what it took to get her to a doctor."

He shook his head, the memory still raw. "Tests showed breast cancer. By the time they caught it, it had spread. I gave the barn a makeover, hoping she'd see it and fight harder to recover. But it had her before the surgery."

"I'm so sorry, Jack," I whispered, guilt clawing at me. "And then I come along—"

"Nonsense. You've given me more than anyone else would've. I'm grateful you came along."

Jack stood, squeezing my shoulder as he passed into the kitchen. "Coffee or beer?"

I wanted something stronger but settled on beer.

"Good choice." He grabbed three from the fridge and walked back. My eyebrow shot up at the extra bottle. Then the sliding door opened, and my other brow followed.

"Perfect timing." Jack smiled, his usual self again.

Noah stepped inside. "Hello, Bailey."

His bright green eyes locked on mine, and I realized I'd never noticed their shade before. Maybe it was because they weren't hidden behind his usual furrowed brow.

"Hi, Noah." I shifted in my chair, suddenly conscious of my tiny denim shorts and fitted tank.

I fidgeted, taking a long swig of beer, as if finishing it quickly would allow me to escape faster.

"Go easy on the beer, Bailey. We both know what happens when you drink too much," Noah teased.

"Don't kid yourself, Noah. You've never seen me drink too much." My words came out sharper than intended, but I didn't care.

Noah smirked.

Jack looked between us. "Okay, children. If you want to fight, take it outside."

I wished I could. Anywhere but here, with Noah grating on my nerves.

"Bailey, why don't you run those dates by Noah?"

"That's okay, Jack. I trust you. Besides, it's too soon to set in stone, so if anything changes, I'll work around it." I stood, pulling at my tank top to cover the bare skin above my shorts.

"Thanks for the chat and the beer. Bye, Noah."

I spun to leave, but my diary slid off the pile of books in my arms, hitting the floor. Flustered, I bent to grab it, no longer caring about the skin I exposed, then hurried out the door.

As if things weren't already bad enough with Noah, now his smugness was unbearable.

∼

Noah

Bailey obviously hadn't noticed the photograph slip from between the pages of her diary. Jack bent to pick it up, staring at the two smiling faces in the picture.

"What happened to her parents?" Thinking out loud, his tone casual but curious.

"How should I know? We've barely shared a civilized conversation," I replied, shrugging off the question.

"Yeah, and no points for guessing who's responsible for that," Jack shot back, holding out the photo. I took it, glanced down briefly, and then held it back toward him.

"You can drop it off when you leave. Save me the trip," he said, passing the responsibility to me.

Jack gave me one of those looks, and I knew better than to argue.

Knocking on her door was the last thing I wanted to do, but there I was, standing on her porch. Best-case scenario, she wouldn't hear the light tap of my knuckles against the wood. It would've been easier if Jack had just handed it to her the next time he saw her and no doubt an arrangement we'd both be more comfortable with.

A sharp yap sounded from the other side of the door, warning me to stay put. Not that I had any intention of entering uninvited.

When she finally opened the door, the reason for her delay became obvious. Her skimpy denim shorts had been swapped for a scrap of silk city girls insisted on calling sleepwear. Her wet hair stuck to her skin, dripping water down to the tip of her breast. The fabric clung, soaked through, and left little to the imagination. I couldn't help noticing the dark outline of her nipple beneath the translucent material. Desire hit me hard, and I shifted uncomfortably as it pressed against my zipper.

The faint scent of her bath products wafted toward me, sweet and feminine, and I had to fight the urge to step forward, pull her close, and feel her against me.

Clearing my throat, I held out the photograph. "Ahh, you dropped this."

Her hand brushed mine as she reached for it. That small touch sent a jolt through me, but the moment was over as quickly as it started. Thinking she had it, I let go. The photo slipped from her fingers, floating to the floor before either of us could catch it.

Isis darted forward, snatching it up in her mouth before we could move.

"Drop it, Isis," Bailey commanded, her voice firm.

The little dog had other plans. With a playful growl, she bolted through the house, her tiny legs moving at an impressive speed, Bailey hot on her heels.

If the photo hadn't been important, I might've laughed at the scene. Feeling partially responsible for not delivering it safely, I followed after them.

Bailey stood in the center of the room, her hands on her hips, while Isis darted back and forth on the couch, staying just out of reach. The puppy's movements matched Bailey's, shifting from one end of the couch to the other as if she were playing a game.

I moved carefully, sneaking up from behind. When the moment felt right, I lunged for the dog, but Isis was faster. She jumped off the couch and disappeared under an armchair, the photo still clutched in her mouth.

My momentum carried me forward, and I slid over the furniture, landing with a thud on the floor at Bailey's feet. Before I could recover, she stepped forward, her foot catching my thigh and throwing her off balance. She tumbled down, landing in a heap on top of me.

I looked up at her, trying to ignore the way her silk nightie clung to her body as she sprawled across me. Before I could say a word, Isis bounded over, dropping the photo beside us and wagging her tail like she'd won some kind of prize.

∽

Bailey

I wanted to curl up and disappear under the nearest object big enough to hide me. What a sight I must've been, wearing next to nothing and landing in a tangled mess of arms and legs with the very man who'd rejected me less than a week ago.

Noah rolled to his back, shifting our position and leaving me straddling him. Awkward and twisted, I tried to untangle myself, all while adjusting my skimpy attire. Isis, over enthusiastic for a tumble, sat on his chest, trying her hardest to lick his face despite his protests and attempts to push her away.

Leaning forward, I picked her up and heaved her onto the couch, freeing Noah, who quickly sat up to escape her affection.

With the dog out of the way, the distance between us was minimal. Too minimal. I fought the longing to lean forward. Being rejected twice in one week would do nothing for an ego that was already battered and bruised.

"Sorry," I muttered, putting my hand on the couch to steady myself before easing off him.

He gripped me around the waist to help, but instead of letting go, he groaned softly, changed his mind, and pulled me down against him. His hand tangled in my wet hair, guiding my head down toward his.

His mouth met mine, claiming me with a passion I hadn't expected but desperately wanted. My confusion faded as I gave in, wrapping my arms around him and pressing my body against his. The sensations overwhelmed me—the way his lips moved on mine, parting them, his tongue stroking mine in a rhythm that made my pulse race.

One of his hands pressed to the middle of my back, pulling me closer until my chest was flush against his. The warmth of him seeped through the thin fabric of my nightie. He trailed kisses down my neck, and a moan escaped my lips as my head fell back. He slid the strap of my nightie off my shoulder with his mouth, dipping his head to capture my nipple between his lips.

I gasped as his teeth grazed the hardened bud, sending a jolt of heat straight to my core. His hands slid to my hips, then lower, gripping my ass firmly as he rocked his hips, making me move with him.

Before I realized what he was doing, he slipped his hands beneath the silk of my nightie and pushed it up. He lifted his mouth from my breast long enough to rid me of the only thing I was wearing. I gasped, but his mouth swallowed the sound as he kissed me again, his lips hot and demanding.

His hands trailed down my arms, over my back, and stopped at my hips. He pulled back slightly, his eyes meeting mine before dipping to take in all of me.

"That's all you were wearing, I guess," he said, a lopsided smile tugging at his lips.

I rolled my eyes. "I'd say you know for certain now."

"Shit. Sorry, I didn't realize." His grin widened as his hands roamed lower, brushing the inside of my thighs. "Were you expecting me?"

"You interrupted my shower," I shot back, squirming as I tried to free myself from his hold. His hands were far too close to where I wanted them, and his cocky comment didn't help. "And no, I wasn't waiting for you or expecting you or anything."

I leaned forward to grab my crumpled-up nightie from beside him. Turning it this way and that, I struggled to fix the mess I'd made of the partially wet fabric. "Screw this," I muttered, tossing it to the floor and standing. I turned my back to him and snatched the mink throw from the couch, flicking it out before draping it around my shoulders.

Noah let out a low whistle. "You're beautiful, but I guess I'm not telling you anything you don't already know."

I spun around to glare at him. "What? Just because I'm a city chick, who loves herself and waits around for you to show up? Get your head out of your ass and act like an adult, Noah."

As I spoke, my gaze fell to the photo on the floor—the one that had started this whole mess. I bent down to pick it up, clutching it tightly as my chest ached. "My mother didn't want me," I said softly, looking up to meet his eyes. So what make you think I'd believe you do when you turned on me the moment I arrived?"

Pity flashed in his expression, and I hated it.

"I don't need you to feel sorry for me," I snapped. "But know that I wasn't expecting you, nor did I expect this." I gestured between us. "Now, if you don't mind, I'd like to go to bed."

Noah nodded once, standing as he adjusted his clothes. He reached out to pat Isis on the head. She opened one eye, then closed it again, clearly too exhausted to care what we'd been doing.

I followed him as far as the kitchen but stopped short of the door. I needed some distance. Noah was far too easy to get caught up in, and my judgment was clearly off when it came to men. Best to stick to being friends and nothing more. We had to deal with each other too often to risk creating a rift—especially when lust between us seemed to take over far too easily.

After he left, I went to bed, physically and emotionally worn out. Getting my business off the ground was going to take more time and effort than I'd expected—especially since I'd gotten distracted along the way by adopting a puppy when I already had a horse to look after.

Tomorrow, Cooper would come by to quote the work on the barn. I couldn't wait to see some progress. With my vision and his skills, the end result was going to be something special.

CHAPTER 7

Bailey

I was up before the alarm, though I didn't feel remotely well-rested. All night, I'd tossed and turned, finally falling asleep just as the bitter chill of early morning set in. The few warm spring days hadn't been enough to banish the cold nights, and I couldn't seem to shake the shards that penetrated too deep to shake off the warmth of the sun didn't come close.

Cooper showed up just after seven. Even though we hadn't discussed a particular time, I was surprised. More than once he'd reminded me that he wasn't a morning person.

I'd always loved the early hours when most people were still asleep and the world felt like it belonged to me. Normally, the rising sun sparked new ideas and inspired my day, but that morning? Nothing. I didn't feel inspired. I didn't feel much of anything.

Freya nuzzled my neck, brushing against the faint mark Noah had left. It was as if she wanted to remind me where he'd been before he started hurling his ridiculous accusations—not that I'd easily forget. The memory of his bunch burned into my flesh. I didn't linger at the stable. Horses were sensitive, and I didn't want Freya to pick up on my mood. It wasn't her fault I felt so off-kilter.

Cooper, even first thing in the morning and half-asleep, was good company.

"Hey, do you want coffee before we head off?" It had been hours since my first cup, and I could use another.

"I'd love one," he said, staggering up the steps as I held the kitchen door open for him. "Thought I'd never get here this morning, so I skipped breakfast."

"Chicken and cheese croissants work for you?"

He grinned. "Will you marry me?"

I wrinkled my nose. "You're too good for me. You need a nice girl. I'm damaged goods."

"Sure, I bet that's the excuse you dish up to all the boys," he teased.

I laughed, thinking back to my awkward encounter with Noah the night before and wishing it were true.

Men weren't exactly lining up to knock on my door. I wasn't sure if it was my fault or my dad's. Probably both. It didn't help that I earned more money than most of them and didn't need anyone to take care of me. Men seemed to hate that. As if their manhood was measured by what they could do for me.

A knock at the door pulled me out of my thoughts. Not that I was expecting anyone, but Cooper beat me to answer.

"Hey, Noah, you here for breakfast too?" Cooper leaned casually against the doorframe.

"Nah, I wanted to speak with Bailey, but it's not urgent. I'll come back later," Noah said, his tone clipped.

"I can step outside if you want some privacy." Cooper smirked at me over his shoulder.

I could already hear this minimal exchange making the rounds among our friends.

Noah shook his head, his frown deepening. "It can wait. Enjoy your breakfast." He gave me a brief glance before turning and walking away.

Cooper closed the door, seemingly unfazed by Noah's departure, and leaned back against the kitchen bench. "Anything I can do to help?"

"Not unless you want some orange juice while you wait. I'll make coffee as soon as I get these in the oven."

"Sounds good. Want a glass?"

"Thanks. Glasses are in the top drawer under the microwave." I gestured toward it as I finished assembling the croissants.

"What work do you have lined up for me today?" Cooper poured two glasses of juice.

"Finishing the reno Jack started on the old wooden barn. You know the one?"

"Of course. So many memories of that place. When we were teenagers, we'd hang out there and drink all Jack's homebrew. Noah used to nick it from the cellar."

"What cellar?" This was the first I'd heard of a cellar, and I loved the idea of uncovering hidden parts of the farm.

"Noah never told us where it was. Probably for the best."

I laughed, imagining a teenage Noah, all charm and trouble. "How did he explain the missing bottles?"

"He didn't have to. Jack always blamed Dan since he was older. Everyone knew Noah was the favorite."

"You spent a lot of time here as a kid?"

"Yeah. Maggie used to cook these huge weekend spreads. We never said no. Best cook ever—don't tell my mum." He winked.

I handed him his coffee, adding milk and sugar as he'd requested. As I sipped my own, I asked, "So what's up between you and Noah?"

He ran a hand through his hair, his cheeks coloring slightly. "I didn't want to step on his toes if you two were…you know, seeing each other. He doesn't need that happening to him again."

"Need *what* happening to him again?" I kept my tone even, trying not to sound too eager.

"You haven't heard about Charlotte?"

I shook my head. The name was vaguely familiar, but I hadn't paid much attention to it.

"Charlotte was Noah's wife," Cooper said, taking a bite of his croissant.

"He's married?" My voice pitched higher than I'd intended.

"Was. Don't worry, you're not the homewrecker in this story."

I raised an eyebrow but stayed quiet, not wanting to feed into his teasing.

"Long story short, she cheated on him with Rick's younger brother, Matt. When Noah found out, she was already pregnant—with Matt's kid. She took everything he worked for in the divorce, forcing him to sell the small farm he'd bought. The day Maggie came off the horse, Noah was supposed to meet her after work, but he came home early and found Charlotte in bed with Matt."

I sipped my coffee, letting his words sink in. It wasn't what I'd expected to hear. Talking about Noah's past felt invasive, but I couldn't help being curious.

"Look, he's one of my best mates, and I wouldn't be telling you this if I didn't think it was important," Cooper added. "I think Noah's into you. But you're a city girl, and that's kind of a libido crusher for him." Plating up the croissants and passing them over to Cooper, the silence gave me time to process Noah's what he'd said. It wasn't any wonder I was off side from the moment I showed up.

"Well, thanks for the insight," I said, setting my empty mug down. "When we're done eating, let's head out to the barn and see what the damage is."

"Thanks for breakfast. It was delicious," he said, rinsing his dishes and stacking them in the dishwasher beside mine.

Scooping up Isis, I followed Cooper outside, ready to get to work.

"Roughly how long do you think it will take?" I glanced at Cooper, hoping he didn't think I was impatient.

"Hard to give a definite time frame. Supplies can take weeks to be delivered, but with all the council approvals done, there won't be any hold-ups there." Cooper flicked through the pages of notes he'd scribbled while I bounced ideas off him. "The repairs are reasonably minor, so it's mostly fit-out," he added, more to himself than to me. "At the most, maybe two months."

I couldn't help but grin. His answer was exactly what I'd hoped for. That gave me enough time to complete the timetable, source art supplies, and come up with projects for the ladies to work on. Then there were menus, meditation and pamper sessions to consider, plus marketing and, if all went well, a barn party to kickoff. The next two months were going to be busy, and I couldn't wait.

"So, what do I have to do first?" Overeager and unwilling to waste a moment.

"Now that I have the measurements and an idea of what you want, I'll write up a quote, and then you can start choosing tiles and all the fittings."

"That's the fun part." As minimal as it was, this was progress, and it thrilled me.

Heading back to the house, Cooper continued to share stories of his delinquent times on the farm. Pulling up outside the front of the house, he kept the engine running. "I'll get started on the quote and be in touch."

"Thanks, Cooper." Picking Isis up off my lap, I swung out of the car. "See you soon."

Too lovely a day to spend indoors, I decided to take Isis to the stables and spend a few hours with Freya. I'd restrained myself from riding for too long, and I couldn't hold back anymore. With the next few months set to be hectic, I wanted to make the most of my free time.

As I reached the stables, Jack and Noah drove past. Jack called out from the open window. "Hey, Bailey, want me to take Isis out for a while and give you a chance to ride that beauty?"

"Would you mind?" I held my hand up to shield my eyes from the sun.

"Not at all. Besides, Zeus is missing her."

Walking over to the truck, I scooped Isis up and put her in the back with her brother. "Hey, Noah," I said casually as he got out of the cab and fastened the spare chain attached to the crossbars on the ute to Isis's collar.

"Hey," he replied, his clipped tone doing little to mask his irritation. "Have fun with Cooper this morning?"

I smirked. Jealous, was he? I hadn't seen that one coming. "Cooper's going to be working on the barn for me, so it was pretty exciting."

"You know, I would've done it."

"You've got enough to do. Besides, I thought you might've seen it as me having an ulterior motive."

Noah rolled his eyes but didn't respond, likely because Jack was within earshot. "Cooper's a good worker. You won't be disappointed."

With a quick pat to both pups, I stepped back. "If she gives you any trouble, I won't be far from the stable. Is there anywhere I'm not allowed to ride?"

Noah scoffed. "What, on your farm?"

I glared at him and redirected my question. "Jack, is there anywhere you'd prefer I didn't go?"

"It'd probably be best if you didn't attempt the paddocks with the cattle or the crop paddock. Maggie used to ride the track separating the fenced-off areas—you could start with those," Jack said, pointing to the wide paths used for vehicles.

"Great. I won't get in your way?"

"Nah, once we're parked up, we won't be driving along these paths for a few hours." Jack waved as Noah shifted the truck into gear, leaving me standing in a cloud of dust.

∽

Noah

"Did you have to do that?" Jack snarled.

"What?"

"She's considerate and generous with her land, and you have to fling it back in her face every time."

I kept my gaze forward. Yeah, I was on her case constantly, but I couldn't seem to help myself. Jack wasn't any better lately, always backing Bailey and taking his foul mood out on me. Even if I provoked him, I liked to think blood should be thicker than water.

She certainly had Jack whipped. He couldn't see past anything she did as out of the ordinary. Her extravagant life had me on edge. Normal people didn't live the way she did, and abnormal strangers weren't usually so generous.

I knew her type, manipulative and conniving, just like Charlotte. Jack couldn't see it, but I wasn't fooled. I was waiting for the sugar-coated Bailey to shed her sweetener and cause us further grief.

"So why'd you tell her to ride Maggie's route?" I glanced at Jack quickly and then back to the road. "You want to see how good she is on the back of that beast of hers, don't you?"

Jack grinned. "Ah huh, and I can't wait to see that beauty under rein. Magnificent creature, and she'll look like a doll on top of it."

I nodded once. Couldn't argue there. Bailey, tiny with hair as black and wavy as that of Freya, atop such a strong, powerful animal? It'd be something to see, no doubt about it.

I hadn't ridden since Maggie died. It'd been our shared passion. Seeing the Friesian, a horse I'd only ever dreamed of owning, ignited something in me. The want to feel the freedom and speed of the animal as we moved as one, like a well-choreographed tango. Maggie had been a passionate horsewoman, giving in to the horses' will to go. I expected Bailey to be a pony-club trained rider, edging on the side of caution, not the wild display Jack was hoping for.

Coming to a stop at the next gate, Jack got out to open it so I could drive through, and waited on the other side to close it. I liked the way the farm was set up, with paddocks coming off a large driveway. Especially appealing in winter when getting out to open and close half a dozen gates meant getting saturated.

Jack climbed back in the cab, and we were on our way again. With Bailey paying for fencing supplies and Jack having spare cash since the sale, the cattle yards were finally getting the attention they were overdue for.

"How rich is she?" I wondered aloud, glancing at Jack, waiting for him to scold me for being nosy.

"I'd say *loaded* would put it mildly." Jack shrugged. "She's generous with it, and money doesn't seem of great importance to her."

I pulled the truck up alongside the fence line we'd be working on that afternoon.

"I don't know. Have you checked out that horse?

It'd be worth more than my car and yours put together."

Jack chuckled. "Yeah, and it'll probably travel faster than them too."

"Wait and see if she can handle it. An English-style trot isn't going to be enough to get you excited." I began hauling fencing gear off the back of the truck. Unclipping the chain from each pup's collar, I lifted them down one at a time.

"Stay close," I told them. Not that they listened as they frolicked in the open.

We got to work immediately. I didn't like to dilly-dally, but then again, neither did Jack. Probably from him I'd picked up the straight-to-action trait. No one was going to do the work for us, so we didn't have time to waste.

The sound of hooves thundering up behind us was enough to make us both stop and turn. The power and speed of such a large horse was something worth witnessing. Spectacular, with a more graceful gait than I'd expected given its size. Atop sat Bailey, delicate yet seemingly skilled. Her wavy black hair streamed out behind both rider and horse. Jack was right—a sight worth stopping work for.

Bailey pulled the horse up and circled back. As she approached, I couldn't help but smile. The grin on her face proved the ride had been as good as the sight. I'd never seen her look so happy. Her cheeks were pink from exposure to the cold wind, her eyes lit up as bright as the blue sky behind her. She looked more a part of this life than I'd ever seen her. Maybe I'd been too quick to dish out labels.

Her transition wasn't the normal one of hard labor and financial hardships so many other farmers suffered. Cashed up and living a life of luxury, Bailey made the move from city to country look easy. And they say money can't buy happiness. Seeing her at that moment, I'd be willing to argue with whoever came up with that.

"She's got some go in her," Jack called, holding up a hand to flag Bailey for her attention. "Is she as nice to ride as she is to watch?"

Bailey nodded, enthusiastic. "Light on her feet, but her power is mind-blowing." She looked at me, waiting for my comment, but I had nothing to add. She didn't need me to tell her how wonderful the horse was. She already knew that. No doubt she was confident enough to know how good she looked in a saddle. It surprised me to see her riding in jeans and a shirt. I'd expected jodhpurs and fancy gear to go with the custom saddle she sat in. Though, I was pleased she didn't insist on the tacky diamante bridle

Charlotte always had. Even though my horse had been a quarter horse and a gelding, Charlotte insisted on dressing him up like a little girl's pony-club horse. Money couldn't buy class, and Bailey had plenty of it. No frills necessary.

"Well, I'll let you get back to work. Are you sure you're still okay to look after Isis?"

"Of course, honey. Zeus would be devastated if you took her away now."

"Thanks. Hey, I was planning to cook a roast tonight if you'd both like to join me? It's not much fun cooking for one."

"Sounds great, doesn't it, Noah?"

"Um, yeah. Thanks." I wanted to talk with her about the night before, apologize really. It was unfair of me to act like I knew anything about her, or that she was full of herself just because she had a seemingly simple life. She appeared alone all the time. That couldn't be easy on her.

Bailey grinned. "Any requests for dessert?"

"Whatever you make will be lovely. No need to go to any trouble, though."

I couldn't help but feel like the third wheel. Jack was closer and more comfortable around her than I was. As much as I tried to relax and let my guard down, it didn't feel natural to me.

The slightest frown creased her otherwise flawless face, but she was too polite to say what she was thinking. "Well, I'll see you later, then."

I nodded once, and Jack held up his hand in a wave. "Enjoy your ride, love."

CHAPTER 8

Bailey

Not wanting to leave Jack and Noah in a dust cloud, I nudged Freya into a trot, easing her away from them. Once I'd put enough distance between us, I gathered the reins, gave a gentle squeeze of my heels, and urged her into a canter. The rhythm of her hooves on the dirt felt steady, hypnotic, and thrilling all at once.

Finally, I let her go, urging her into a gallop. Freya responded instantly, muscles bunching and stretching beneath me as she surged forward. With every powerful stride, my heart pounded in sync with her hooves, a thrilling duet of exhilaration and freedom. The rush of adrenaline, mingled with the sheer joy of riding, was intoxicating—like lightning in my veins.

The wind tugged at my hair, whipping it into a wild tangle behind me, but I didn't care. In that moment, the world fell away. There was no endless to-do list waiting for me at the house, no doubts about the retreat or the choices I'd made. No confusion about why Noah despised breathing the same air as me. Just me, Freya, and the open path.

This life—this choice I'd made—still felt like a dream at times, like I was living on borrowed time before reality came crashing back. But would it? Could it? Maybe this was my reality now.

Eventually, I slowed Freya to a walk, letting her cool off. Her breaths came in steady snorts, the rise and fall of her shoulders matching her pace. As much as I wanted to stay in the saddle, the practical side of me whispered reminders. There were errands to run, dinner to make, and a dozen small tasks clamoring for attention.

After dismounting, I led Freya back to the stable, my fingers trailing along her sleek neck. Once inside, I grabbed a soft brush and ran it over her coat, taking my time. The repetitive motion was soothing, a small ritual that always felt grounding. I draped her blanket over her back, adjusted it snugly, and carried her tack to the shed, placing everything in its rightful spot.

Before leaving, I snagged two carrots from the feed bin. Freya's ears perked up when she saw them. "You've earned it, girl," I murmured, holding one out. She took it delicately, crunching with enthusiasm, and I couldn't help but smile.

The walk back to the house was filled with the lingering peace that came after a good ride, but as I stepped inside, the familiar weight of responsibility settled back onto my shoulders. I set the oven to low and grabbed my laptop and diary, settling at the dining table. The roast was already filling the kitchen with its rich aroma, and the thought of Jack and Noah returning to a hearty meal made me smile.

Flipping open my diary, I ran my fingers over the neat columns of handwritten notes. My father used to tease me endlessly about it. *Bailey,* he'd say, *you've got all the tech in the world. Why scribble in that thing like it's 1985?*

I'd roll my eyes every time. He couldn't grasp it, but I needed this backup, this tactile proof that my plans existed beyond fragile screens and fickle networks. Maybe it was my trust issues or just my way of staying grounded. Either way, it worked for me.

As the afternoon light shifted, I thought about the barn dance Jack had mentioned. The idea had stuck with me, and now it seemed like the perfect way to launch the retreats. Guests could arrive early, enjoy the celebration, and dive into the experience.

The thought made me smile, but it also brought a pang of loneliness. The quiet life here was beautiful, but the isolation was real. And then there was Noah. My chest tightened at the thought of him, that maddening, impossible man who seemed determined to keep me at arm's length.

Every time I thought we'd connected, he'd retreat, his walls growing thicker. I couldn't decide if it was stubbornness or self-preservation, but either way, it stung.

Shaking off the thought, I reached for my phone and dialed Ali. Her warm voice greeted me almost instantly. "Hey, Bailey. I was just thinking about you."

"Oh?"

"In a non-creepy way," she added with a laugh. "I've been working on ideas for those retreat packages, if the offer still stands."

"Of course, it does." Relief washed over me. Ali's

enthusiasm was infectious, and her involvement would add so much value to the retreats.

We set up an appointment for tomorrow morning, and by the time I hung up, my spirits had lifted. It wasn't just about the business; it was about connection, about carving out a place for myself in this town.

Returning to my laptop, I started researching art supplies. The possibilities were endless, and my excitement bubbled over. But I had to be practical. Storage was limited, at least until the renovations were done, and I didn't want to risk anything spoiling or going unused.

The timer beeped, pulling me from my thoughts. I added the vegetables to the roast and got to work on dessert. The rhythm of peeling, slicing, and mixing was almost meditative, a comforting routine that reminded me of simpler times.

When the pie was ready to go into the oven, I grabbed a beer from the fridge and headed back to my laptop. There was still furniture to order, and the upstairs dormitory was proving to be a puzzle. Bunk beds felt too juvenile, but single beds could crowd the space. I'd find the right balance eventually.

I always did.

Jack had mentioned Maggie's love for patchwork

quilts and her dream of turning the barn into a quilting retreat. In her honor, I bought bed covers that reminded me of her style. I wished I could've made them myself, but sewing wasn't exactly in my wheelhouse. Dad wouldn't have permitted such a menial task, and back when Mom was around, I was too consumed with school and horses to care about learning.

The thought of Mom left a hollow, aching void inside me. It threatened to crack open like a geyser, spilling over everything I tried so hard to keep together. I figured the photo incident with Noah had dredged it all back to the surface—memories I usually kept buried deeper than I cared to admit.

I could never understand why Mom had turned her back on me when I was sixteen. I told myself—and anyone who asked—that I'd moved on, that it didn't bother me anymore. But lately, that lie was unraveling, little by little.

Their divorce had been the obvious choice. I didn't point fingers or lay blame. Separately, they were good people, even wonderful in their own ways. But together? They were combustible. Dad wasn't cut out for marriage, but Mom—Mom had always been patient, nurturing, and everything a kid could hope for in a parent.

So why had she changed after the split? Why had she left me behind?

I'd sent countless letters over the years. Not one got a reply. Nothing I said or did could make her want me in her life. She'd have to want that herself—and she didn't. Not once in all this time.

Still, I didn't want her back out of obligation. I wanted the warm, understanding woman who used to know what I was feeling before I even said a word. But now I couldn't help wondering if that version of her was something I'd dreamed up. A fabrication to keep me sane.

I pulled a photograph from the back of my diary. It was too easy to think about sending her my new address, just in case she decided to get in touch. But I knew better. Sighing, I slipped the picture back into the pages, toward the back where I always tucked it.

Every year, I transferred it to my new diary, always promising myself that if I stumbled upon it on some random day, I'd reach out to her again. Of course, I never did. It was a hollow ritual—a false hope I clung to despite knowing better.

The thought haunted me. This year, maybe, she'd reach out before I had to break the vow I'd never had the courage to keep.

But why would she? Years of silence had made it clear where she stood.

The memories were murky, painful, and a waste of time. I forced them aside, locking them away where they belonged. Dwelling on the past wouldn't change anything. It only served as a reminder of how few people really cared.

I had too much to do to get lost in that spiral, anyway. The first retreat was fast approaching, and I needed it ready before spring ended. Summer heat would scare off bookings, though sometimes I wondered if a beachside location might've been a smarter choice. Not that it mattered now. If this went well, maybe I could open another retreat for the summer months—or finally launch that school holiday art program for kids.

A knock at the kitchen door startled me, pulling me out of my daydream.

I crossed the room, opened the door, and found Noah standing there, hands shoved deep into his pockets. He looked uncomfortable, glancing up at me with a furrowed brow.

"Hey, you're done early," I said, surprised.

"Yeah. Sorry—if it's a bad time, I can come back later," he said, hesitating. "Jack sent me over. He's in the shower."

I stepped aside, holding the door open wider. "Come on in. Sorry about the mess. I feel so cramped working in the study." I caught myself babbling and clamped my mouth shut. "Want a drink? Beer? Juice? Coffee?"

"A beer would be great, thanks."

I grabbed two from the fridge, set them on the counter, and plucked the bottle opener out of the drawer. When I turned back, I caught Noah watching me.

"What?" I raised an eyebrow.

"Nothing," he said quickly, taking the beer I handed him. "Thanks." He took a long swig. "So, how's the business coming along?"

"Slow," I admitted. "There's not much I can do until the barn's finished."

He nodded, his gaze shifting to the table littered with my notes. After a beat, he said, "About the other night—I'm sorry for what I said. Things got out of hand. I didn't mean for it to end that way."

I shrugged, even though his words hit harder than I wanted them to. "It probably would've ended badly no matter what."

He looked like he wanted to argue but stopped himself. "I'm not in the market for a relationship," he said finally, his voice low. "And I don't want to feel like I'm using you."

I turned away, pretending to check on the roast. Hearing it out loud didn't make it hurt any less, though I wished he hadn't said anything at all. Some things were better left unspoken.

Jack arrived soon after, his presence breaking the tension. He filled the room with his usual warmth, recounting childhood stories with the ease of someone who loved his memories.

"I could talk about this ratbag all night if someone doesn't stop me," Jack said with a grin, clapping Noah on the back. "What about you, Bailey? Got any funny childhood stories?"

I hesitated. Funny stories? My life hadn't been miserable, but laughter hadn't exactly been a cornerstone. "Not really," I said finally. "Mom loved nature's treasures. Dad loved the treasures he got from nature. They were just…busy, I guess."

Jack nodded.

"What did your dad do?" Noah asked casually, but I knew the question wasn't as simple as it sounded.

"He owned CMG," I said, bracing for the reaction.

Noah let out a low whistle. "I didn't make the connection. That's…obscene."

I looked down, picking at my nails. His words made me feel small, ashamed of something I'd never been ashamed of before. A tear slipped down my cheek, and I wiped it away quickly, angry at myself for letting him get to me.

When they finally left, I exhaled a breath I didn't realize I'd been holding. Noah was too much hard work. He made me feel lonelier than I already was.

That night, as I drifted to sleep, the faint sound of a child crying lingered in the distance. It haunted me, but I pushed it aside, chalking it up to exhaustion and my own restless thoughts.

CHAPTER 9

Bailey

Just because I lived in a remote setting didn't mean I needed to neglect my appearance. I looked forward to my appointment with Ali for more than just the female company. After we finalized the pamper sessions to include in the retreat fee, I could finally publish the website.

Excitement bubbled inside me. The hours I'd spent on the site the day before were going to pay off in the long run. I couldn't wait for Cooper to get back to me with a quote so he could start the renovations. Nothing thrilled me quite like progress, especially when it involved a project I cared so much about.

"Hey, Bailey, you're early." Ali greeted me with a bright smile as soon as I stepped through the door.

"Sorry, should I come back in a little while?"

"Not at all. Come through." Ali led me down the dimly lit corridor, the soothing scent of sandalwood and hot wax wrapping around me like a warm blanket. I instantly felt myself relax.

"I'll start with the body massage," I said as we reached the treatment room.

Ali nodded and left me to undress.

"Honestly, Ali, if you could bottle what you're doing, you'd make a fortune," I said as her hands worked their magic. I hadn't even realized how much tension I'd been carrying until she started kneading it away.

Ali chuckled. "So, have you finished unpacking all those boxes yet?"

"Yeah, finally. It's such a relief to have that done. Now I can actually focus on why I came here."

"Good. Does that include socializing?"

"Of course. What do you have in mind?"

"Tonight at the pub. Friday night usually brings in a good crowd, and I'm hoping some of the crew from the Taylor's barbecue will be interested in getting together."

"That sounds great." The idea of finally checking out the local bar and getting to know people better had me eager for the evening.

"Perfect." Ali continued the massage in silence, leaving me to my thoughts.

As much as I wanted to discuss the retreat packages, my mind wandered to what I had in my wardrobe that might help me blend in with the locals. The more events I attended, the easier these decisions would get—or so I hoped.

Ali moved on to the facial, and I tried to relax, letting the cool products soothe my skin.

"Does your mind ever go quiet?" Ali teased, laughter in her voice.

I opened my eyes, frowning. "What do you mean?"

She laughed outright. "I know you're trying to relax, but the tension in your face gives you away."

"Sorry, I can't help myself."

"We'll chat during the pedicure and manicure. I've got some ideas for the retreat I want to run past you anyway."

"That'd be good. Once we finalize everything, the website can go live."

Ali smiled and continued the treatment in silence, but my brain refused to settle. The harder I tried to relax, the more impossible it became, so I gave up. Hydrating my skin was the priority, and I'd had plenty of downtime since moving here anyway.

"Okay, so I've drawn up some package ideas for you to look at," Ali said once we moved to the pedicure chair. She handed me a manila folder, and I burst out laughing.

"You've been itching to talk about this too, haven't you?"

"Just a bit." Ali grinned. "It's not often something new happens in this town—at least, not something good enough for me to sink my teeth into." She pointed at the file I was flipping through. "That's your copy. I put together treatment options at the same price, plus a few discounted extras if guests want more. But if it's not what you had in mind, I can adjust it."

I skimmed through the pages. Ali had thought of everything.

"Well, that was a short discussion. This is exactly what I was hoping for." I looked up to see Ali beaming. Her excitement was infectious, and I smiled back. "Now we just need to figure out what furniture you need for the room so we can start ordering."

"Oh, I have a portable massage table I can bring. You don't need to go to any expense," she said, looking a little embarrassed.

"No way. I'm not letting you haul something back and forth for every retreat. Honestly, I planned for this."

Ali nodded but didn't look entirely convinced.

I didn't want Ali to back out, so I changed the subject. "Tell me, what sort of thing should I wear to the pub?"

Ali grinned and launched into a full description of what she was planning to wear, along with the usual attire of others.

Even though I didn't have to be at the pub until seven, I stayed inside to work on my website. I would've liked to take Freya out for a ride, but I didn't want to mess up the manicure Ali had spent so much time on—especially after she warned me she expected my nails to look the same when I left the salon, at least for one night. She'd even convinced me there'd be plenty of time to ride Freya on the weekend.

Ali was right, of course, but guilt crept up on me. I hadn't been spending anywhere near enough time with her since I arrived. Once the barn was underway and the business sorted, I'd be able to schedule my time better.

Baking was a great distraction, and with my laptop at the table, I could flip between the two with ease.

Deep in concentration, trying to get the wording for my website just right, the slamming of a door upstairs startled me. I frowned and glanced toward the staircase. I couldn't remember there being a window open, so I wondered where a wind strong enough to create such force had come from.

Pushing away from my computer, I climbed the stairs to check it out. As I walked into each room, my heart raced. The feeling of someone watching me made the skin of my arms prick with goosebumps, and the hairs on the back of my neck stand on end.

"Hello?" Even if someone was there, I doubted they'd answer, but the word slipped out before I could stop it.

All the windows were closed.

The door to the bedroom at the end of the corridor was shut, and that was obviously the one that had slammed. I hesitated as I reached for the handle. It was ridiculous getting worked up over a closed door. Pushing it open, I saw not only was the room completely empty, but the window was closed too.

I had to admit it was odd. Doors don't just slam, even if this one had. Perhaps there was a draft coming from somewhere. It was an old house, after all.

Leaving the room, I pulled the door closed behind me to prevent a repeat of the incident. I didn't need to give myself any more reason to freak out. I still wasn't entirely comfortable with the isolation the large property provided.

Heading back to the kitchen, a knock at the door made me jump. Clapping my hand over my mouth to stifle a cry, I took a deep breath and tried to calm myself before answering it.

I hesitated a moment. Peering through the crack, I was relieved to see Noah standing on the other side.

"Hey, come in." I didn't care if my invitation was out of the ordinary. Having company, even if it was Noah, helped me reach a sense of calm.

Noah frowned. "What's up? You don't look so good."

"Now there's a line to win every girl's heart," I tried for sarcasm.

"You know what I mean. You look—I don't

know." Noah wedged his hands into his jean pockets and looked down.

"Just spooked myself, is all."

Noah glanced up and frowned.

"Forget it. Did you want something?"

"Oh yeah, Ali called about tonight and suggested I ask if you need a lift. I think she's worried you'll back out." Noah attempted a smile but looked more uncomfortable than before.

"It's been months since I went anywhere, so trust me, I won't back out." I grinned, feeling the tension dissolve. "I can drive. I don't intend on drinking much, anyway."

Noah shrugged. "No problem, I'll see you there then."

"Great." There was no way I was going to rock up to the pub on a Friday night with Noah as my escort. If what Ali had said earlier about the pub drawing a crowd was true, I had no interest in becoming the next town headline.

Dressed in dark skinny jeans and a fitted cream top, I pulled on the brown boots I'd worn to the barbecue. At least I wouldn't risk Noah's disapproval if I were questioned about where I bought some of my other shoes.

I was past caring if my clothes were dressier than

others. I didn't have anything more casual. Besides, the city girl in me needed an excuse to dress up for a night on the town.

After taking Isis over to Jack, who insisted she have a sleepover at his place, I grabbed my brown leather jacket and saddlebag before heading out. It was just past seven, but I had no intention of being the first to arrive, only to sit alone in the corner like a loner.

I needn't have worried. The car park was nearly full. I spotted Cooper's truck as soon as I pulled in, and with a bit of luck, he'd have my quote ready and could give me a starting date.

I pushed the thought aside, sliding out of my truck and pulling on my jacket. The nights were cool after the sun went down, and the breeze had picked up.

Heads turned when I pulled open the heavy door to the main bar. The attention stolen from Whitney, who stood behind it, earned me a look of death, which only darkened when Noah approached. A flick of his head was enough to make her change direction toward the area reserved as a restaurant.

What was Whitney's problem? Were she and Noah an item? No one had ever indicated that was the case. Maybe they were a thing of the past, or perhaps Whitney was hoping for a future with him. I pushed the thought aside. I wanted to enjoy the night, not spend it trying to piece together Noah's personal life like a jigsaw puzzle with no edges.

Ali, Rick, and Cooper were already seated at a table for ten. I was curious who else would be showing up. Ali had mentioned inviting those from the barbecue, and I figured she was talking about the younger crowd. I wasn't disappointed to see Whitney was working and wouldn't be joining us for dinner. There was something about her that rubbed me the wrong way. I didn't want to admit it was a hint of jealousy, but I feared that might be the case.

"Hi, Bailey." Ali waved.

"Hey, you weren't kidding when you said the place draws a crowd. I got a shock when I saw the car park so full."

Ali laughed. "It's practically the only place in town that stays open on a Friday night, but the food's good, and the guys can play pool."

"You forgot the most crucial ingredient, Ali." Rick raised his beer in a toast that didn't need any further explanation.

"You ready for another round?" I reached into my bag for my purse.

"Just about." Rick gulped half the contents of his glass in one mouthful.

I had a feeling we were in for a messy night.

"I'll come with you. The others should be here soon." Ali linked her arm through mine.

"Any specific orders?" I called over my shoulder as Ali guided me toward the bar.

"Don't worry, I know what they have." Ali didn't wait for a response. "You look amazing, by the way. Anyone would think you spent the entire day at the salon."

I laughed.

"Like you need it." Ali rolled her eyes. "So how's the website coming along?"

"It's live, and hopefully getting heaps of hits as we speak." Even without dates, I wanted to spark some interest. I'd add the dates as soon as Cooper confirmed how long the renovations would take.

"You'll have to give me the link so I can check it out."

I nodded, then turned my attention to the bar. Whitney was standing in front of us, waiting for our order.

"Hey, Ali, what can I get for you?"

"Hi Whitney, you remember Bailey, don't you?"

"Yeah, we met at Noah's on the weekend. So what

can I get you?" Whitney continued to ignore me, repeating her previous question.

"Another round for me and the boys. What about you, Bailey?"

"Same, thanks."

Whitney raised her eyebrows and smirked, but said nothing. Pouring the five glasses, she placed them on the bar.

When Ali reached for her purse, I insisted I was paying and handed the cash to Whitney. It was going to be a real test getting all five glasses back to the table without spilling them, but we managed.

Cassie showed up with Sophie and Ben. Emily and Dan arrived not five minutes after them.

The conversation was rowdy, the boys already a few beers in, having met earlier to make arrangements for the buck's night. Cooper, as best man, was organizing it, but since he lived at his parents' house, the party was being held at Rick and Ali's.

"Oh, before I forget." Sophie reached into her purse and pulled out a large pearly envelope, passing it to me.

"What's this for?" I took the envelope and hesitated before opening it. I glanced up.

Sophie smiled. "Open it and you'll see."

I lifted the flap and removed an ivory and peach

card. Without even reading it, I knew exactly what it was: an invitation to Sophie and Ben's wedding. "Oh, it's beautiful. Thank you." I paused, my heart a little heavy. I hoped they weren't inviting me out of obligation. "I wasn't expecting this."

"But you'll come, won't you?" Sophie's voice was full of hope.

Not normally the hugging type, I surprised myself when I leaned over and hugged Sophie. "I'd love to come." My voice was softer than usual, and for a moment, I almost felt the sting of tears welling up in my eyes. The gesture, so kind and unexpected, caught me off guard. I wasn't ready for it, but I wasn't about to push it away either.

"Good." Sophie returned the hug warmly, her smile making me feel like everything was just a little bit better.

Where Ali was bubbly and welcoming, Sophie had always been more reserved but equally warm in her own way. If the business and farm didn't work out, the friends she'd made here would be worth the move.

"Hi, kids." Mike wandered over to join us, his easy smile immediately making the atmosphere feel even more relaxed. "Tracy's been meaning to call in, but doesn't want to be a pest." He directed his comment toward me.

"She's not a pest. Please tell her to come over anytime," I reassured him with a smile.

"No doubt she'll pop in to tomorrow sometime," he said, grinning.

I grinned back. "I'd like that."

Mike smiled and patted me on the shoulder before turning toward Noah. "Noah, I'm heading home. You need a ride?"

"Nah, I'll find my own way, thanks," Noah replied, downing the last of his beer. "Who's for another drink? My round this time."

Bailey and Emily were the only ones to decline. Having to drive turned out to be a good excuse. I had no interest in making a spectacle of myself on my first night out. Not to mention, Noah Taylor was like quicksand to me—the last thing I wanted was to be seen throwing myself at him. Too much alcohol might give me the courage to try for a third attempt, but I wasn't ready for that kind of mess.

Mike said goodbye and left, walking with Noah to the bar.

From where I sat, I had a perfect view of the two of them. As soon as Noah approached, Whitney jumped to attention, flirting and pawing at him across the counter. Noah didn't seem to notice, glancing back toward the table, likely to check if I was watching. I didn't bother pretending like I wasn't. We both knew I was.

Whitney quickly filled a tray with full glasses. Noah grabbed two, while she carried the rest. I couldn't help but watch as they walked toward us. There was no doubt Whitney was into him, but Noah didn't seem so keen.

After handing out the drinks, Whitney returned to the bar, and the guys left the table to play pool.

"Good. Now that they've gone, why don't you tell the others about your business, Bailey?" Ali suggested, her voice full of enthusiasm.

I grinned, the excitement bubbling up. Talking about the retreats made it feel real, even though I was still waiting to talk to Cooper about the renovations. But the more I spoke about it, the more it felt like it would actually happen—someday. And that thought, for all its uncertainty, was exciting.

"It sounds wonderful. I might have to book in sometime to escape my madhouse." Emily laughed. "Who would guess two children and a husband could be such a handful?"

"You're welcome anytime, even if you just want to join in for the days," I offered. I couldn't imagine being a farmer's wife was any easier than being a farmer.

"I'd like that. Perhaps when the kids are at school. I love craft and sewing. I'd be happy to help if you need it," Emily said, a bright smile lighting up her face.

They were making this too easy for me. If Emily wanted to get involved, I was more than happy to have her. "Sounds good to me."

The conversation shifted to the wedding.

"Has Matt RSVP'd yet?" Ali lowered her voice. With the noise around us, it was unlikely anyone would overhear.

Sophie nodded. "Yep, he's coming. I thought Rick would've told you. They're making a holiday of it, and he'll even be here for the bucks night."

Cassie groaned. "And the witch, is she coming with him?"

"What d'you expect, Cas? Do you think she'd miss out on an opportunity to be the center of attention?" Emily jumped in before Sophie could respond. Disgust laced her voice, the words sharp and pointed.

I remained quiet, letting the conversation swirl around me. Cooper had mentioned Matt was Rick's younger brother, so the *witch* had to be Charlotte.

"No one will make a fuss of her, that's for sure. It's your day, Soph, and I'll do the maid of honor thing and make sure she remembers that." Ali's smile was thin, almost bitter.

It seemed Charlotte wasn't exactly the most popular person in this circle.

"We came here to relax. How about we change the subject, because even her name causes stress?" Sophie suggested, her voice carrying a hint of frustration.

"And if Noah overhears…" Cassie nodded in his direction, but didn't finish the thought.

I wasn't sure if she meant for the words to hang in the air like they did, but I could practically feel the tension surrounding us.

"Shall we join them? Anyone would think we're back in high school again, boys in one corner, girls in the other," Ali laughed, a carefree note in her voice that I appreciated.

The four of them were deep in a doubles game of pool—Noah and Rick against Cooper and Ben. Dan was off to the side, chatting with another farmer. Their accuracy surprised me, especially considering how many drinks they'd already consumed. It seemed they'd just been handed another round, with four fresh beers waiting in the middle of the table where the girls had settled.

"We're going to be carrying them home, you know that, don't you?" Cassie warned, her tone matter-of-fact.

"You say that like it's something new and different," Ali rolled her eyes, clearly unfazed.

"So another round isn't a good idea?" I was already feeling the buzz from my first beer. The meal I'd ordered had been so large I'd been waiting for a good moment to make room.

"Oh, believe me, they're far from finished." Emily gestured toward the pool table as Noah sank the black ball with surprising skill. "They'll quit when they stop sinking the balls."

I laughed. I'd never been to a bar quite like this where everyone was so laid-back, perfectly content to get absolutely blind drunk without the usual drama that followed.

Ali helped me with the next round of drinks. Whitney didn't spring into action like she had with Noah, and I couldn't help but notice it.

"She wants Noah, right?" I kept my voice low.

Ali glanced sideways at me, raising an eyebrow. "You think? Does that bother you?"

"No," I lied. I hadn't planned to feel anything

about it, but there it was—a small knot in my stomach.

Ali smirked, clearly amused. "Whitney's wanted Noah since we were in grade school. Noah has never wanted Whitney."

I couldn't help but smile at that. It felt good to know something that simple, some piece of their history. It almost made me feel like I wasn't entirely on the outside anymore.

We set the trays down on the table nearest the guys.

"Hey, who bought all these?" Cooper slurred slightly, his words a little more drawn out than usual.

"It was my turn." I handed him a glass, trying to keep the conversation light.

"Don't spend too much. I have a quote for you," he added, suddenly serious.

I grinned, ready to move past the tension I'd felt earlier. "I hoped you would. Do you have it here?"

Cooper nodded and retrieved a folded piece of paper from his wallet, handing it over. "Perhaps you should sit down."

"When do you start?" I was eager to move forward.

He laughed but shook his head, a hint of concern

crossing his features. "You didn't even look at what it'll cost you. You should before I give you a date."

I opened the paper, quickly scanning the price before shrugging. "Okay, now will you give me a day?"

Cooper hesitated, his brow furrowing as he studied me for a moment.

"What? You don't want to do it?" The tension crept back.

"No, nothing like that." He smiled, but it was a little forced. "Okay. Does Monday work for you?"

"Great." I folded the quote and tucked it into my purse for safekeeping.

Dan and Emily were the first to leave, heading toward the door with their usual ease. I was surprised when Noah didn't go with them. He was still deep into his game, unwilling to let his partner down.

"Bailey, would you mind giving him a lift back to Jack's for us, please? I'll sleep better knowing he's safe," Emily fussed, her concern palpable as always.

"Of course, no problem." The thought of disturbing Jack in the middle of the night didn't sit well with me, but I wasn't going to argue. Emily had already made her decision.

She wouldn't leave until Noah agreed to the

arrangement, and I honestly believed the only reason he caved was because he wanted to finish his shot, and Emily was in the way.

The bar closed at midnight, giving us no other choice but to call it a night. As we were heading out, Whitney's voice rang out.

"I'm happy to give you a lift home if you need one, Noah."

"I bet you are, Whitney," Cooper responded before Noah could even turn his head to look at her. "He's fine. Bailey's got him covered, haven't you, gorgeous?" Cooper draped his arm casually across my shoulders, the touch unexpected but welcome.

"And what about you? Do you need a lift?" I kept my tone playful but firm. There was no way I was letting him get behind the wheel after the way he'd been drinking.

"Although your offer is much more appealing, I came with Rick and Ali. We're neighbors," Cooper replied, a mischievous grin playing at the corner of his mouth.

"Hey, watch it or I'll make you walk," Ali teased, her voice light and the threat playful.

We walked to the car park together, the cool night air a welcome contrast to the warmth of the bar.

"Thanks for organizing tonight, Ali. I had a great time," I said, giving her a quick hug before she slid into the driver's side of the car. Rick and Cooper weren't quite as graceful, practically falling into their seats as they clumsily settled in. It made me laugh, their carefree energy contagious.

Sophie's car was parked on the opposite side of the lot, and after some quick goodbyes, the three of them pulled out, leaving me and Noah standing alone.

I glanced over at him. "You want me to take you home instead?" Not sure what he'd say.

"Nah, Jack's got a spare bed," he replied casually, but I could see the weariness in his eyes. It wasn't the kind of weariness that came from being drunk—he'd handled his alcohol well, almost too well—but there was something else. Maybe it was just the long day catching up with him, or maybe he wasn't the type to let his guard down easily.

We continued walking toward my truck, the gravel crunching beneath our feet, and I noticed something interesting. Noah didn't stumble like the others had. His steps were steady, deliberate, despite the amount he'd drunk. I knew he'd matched them drink for drink, yet he carried himself with that same composed, almost effortless swagger.

"You can stay in my spare room if you'd prefer not to wake Jack," I offered, not really expecting him to take me up on it. My spare room wasn't anything fancy, but it was clean and private.

To my surprise, he nodded. "That sounds good. Thanks."

It was unexpected—Noah, accepting my offer when he could've easily just crashed at Jack's without question. There was a brief moment of silence between us as we reached the truck. Maybe it was the alcohol still buzzing through me, but I couldn't help being a little surprised by how easily we were slipping into this new dynamic.

He was usually so aloof, so easygoing, but tonight there had been moments when I thought I saw something else—something softer, quieter. Something I didn't think I'd get to see from him.

CHAPTER 10

Bailey

Noah was quiet on the drive back to the farm. Whether it was from consuming too much alcohol or the prospect of staying at my house, I could only guess. The silence stretched out between us, thick and awkward, until I decided to break it.

"So, you never told me why you stopped by the other morning," I said, immediately regretting it. I could almost hear the tension in the air. A question like that was bound to bring up uncomfortable things—things I wasn't sure I was ready to hear, let alone discuss.

"Nothing important," he replied, his tone flat.

Well, that didn't help. Nope, silence was definitely more uncomfortable than anything I could've imagined. I didn't press the topic. Maybe his little speech the other night before dinner was all he had to say, and he didn't want to bring it up again. It wasn't my intention to bear all for him to see, and now things were awkward again.

I focused on the road, partly because I needed to, but also because the thought of hitting a wild animal made my stomach turn. With the bush thick right up to the edge of the asphalt, visibility was poor. I'd seen too many carcasses discarded amongst the scrub, and I didn't want to add another one to the list.

When I pulled up to the front gate, I turned off the engine and got out, the gravel crunching beneath my boots as Noah followed me up the path. As I fumbled with the lock in the dark, he spoke up.

"Most people don't lock their front door around here." There was the slightest slur to his words, but I didn't mind it.

"Most people don't live alone either," I replied, not looking at him.

"Jack wouldn't let anything happen to you," he said, his voice softer now.

I glanced over my shoulder, catching his eyes for a moment as I slid the key into place. "I know, but I feel better knowing there'd be no need for him to defend me."

The door creaked open, and I stepped inside, Noah following close behind.

"Are you sure you don't mind me staying here?" His voice low, almost uncertain.

I shrugged, trying to play it cool. "Why would I?"

No answer. Just that quiet hum between us again.

"Do you want something to drink before we go to bed?" I cringed as soon as the words left my mouth. My offer sounded too suggestive, like I was trying to push something that wasn't there.

Noah cocked his head, a smirk tugging at the corner of his mouth. "A cold drink would be nice, thanks."

"Lemon soda?" I suggested, trying to keep things casual.

"Great."

I poured two glasses and handed one to him. He took a mouthful before setting it down on the bench, taking a few steps closer to me.

"I came over the other morning because I wanted to apologize," he said, his voice unexpectedly serious.

"Things took me by surprise, and I reacted badly. I'm sorry for that."

I nodded, the tightness in my throat making it hard to speak. "Best we forget about it," I said quietly, trying to move past the awkwardness.

Noah's grin returned, and he let out a small laugh. "Kinda hard to wipe that one from the memory, and I'd prefer not to, even if I was an asshole."

I rolled my eyes. The alcohol was definitely talking now. There was no way Noah Taylor would admit to being an asshole without some liquid courage behind him.

He took another couple of steps, closing the distance between us, his hand reaching for my waist. Before I could react, he leaned in, capturing my mouth with his.

I wanted to protest. I wanted to pull away and tell him that this wasn't a good idea. But instead, I melted into the kiss, his hands roaming over my back as he pulled me closer. His touch was like a spark, reigniting something inside me that had been smoldering since the other night.

A low moan escaped me as he kissed a trail down my jaw and neck, his hands slipping under my top to roam over my skin. His touch was electric, leaving a path of fire wherever his hands went.

Then, his hands slid down to grip my ass, and he pressed himself against me, the heat of his body sending a rush of desire through me. His mouth found mine again, this time deeper, more demanding.

But I pulled away from him, taking a shaky breath. "You've had too much to drink, Noah. You might regret this."

"Should I take a hint?" His forehead pressed against mine, a teasing smile curling at his lips.

I brushed my lips over his lightly, feeling the coolness of the lemon soda on my tongue as I reached down to take his hand in mine. "Shall we go to bed?"

Noah grinned, the smile reaching his eyes as he followed me up the stairs. At the door, I stopped and turned around. "The spare room is made up if you'd prefer," I said, offering him an easy out.

But he didn't take it. Instead, he stepped forward, his arms encircling my waist, drawing me close. "Relax, will you?" His voice was soft, but there was a firmness in his touch that left no room for argument.

I resisted the urge to pull him inside the room

with me, though part of me wanted to. But I didn't, and I was glad I didn't. He took my hand and led the way to the bed.

The smell of alcohol on his breath reminded me that Noah might wake up in the morning with zero memory of what had just happened. As his lips met mine, I pushed that thought aside. What did it matter when the moment felt so right?

I ran my hands over his shoulders, feeling the muscles beneath my fingertips as I moved down his back. Gripping the hem of his tee shirt, I tugged it over his head and tossed it aside. My pulse raced in my ears, and I could feel his heartbeat matching mine as I traced my nails lightly up his sides. He flinched, obviously ticklish, and I smiled, deepening my touch. I gripped the firm flesh of his torso, pulling him closer.

Noah slid his hands up my body, taking my top with him as he did. His fingers worked swiftly, and before I knew it, one hand was reaching around me, releasing the clasp of my bra in one swift motion. Another moment, and it was discarded on the floor.

He kissed me again, claiming my mouth with his before dipping his head lower. I gasped as he took one taut nipple between his lips, flicking his tongue over the tip. He sucked it, then switched to the other, and my body arched instinctively to meet his touch.

His hands traced the muscles of my back, moving slowly, deliberately, down to the waistband of my jeans. His fingers found the button, unfastened it, and in a fluid motion, he unzipped them. The denim slid down my legs, leaving only the lace of my knickers between us.

Noah stepped back and swept his gaze over my body, his eyes dark with desire. My breath caught in my throat, and I felt a flush of heat creep across my skin. He removed his own jeans, his movements slow and deliberate, then stepped toward me. I took a step back, feeling the edge of the bed against the backs of my legs. I sank down onto it, and Noah, with a steady hand on each shoulder, eased me backward.

∽

I jerked awake by the sound of a knock at the door. My heart raced as I scrambled around, searching for clothes that had been discarded across the floor from the night before. I found my bra and slipped it on, snapping it into place just as Noah's eyes fluttered open.

"Pretend you're not home," he groaned.

"My car's out front," I hissed, running a hand through my messy hair. "It's probably Jack." I tugged on my jeans and glanced toward the door. Another knock came, louder this time. "Are you going to put your clothes on?"

Noah groaned but sat up, looking around at our discarded clothes with a confused expression. "What happened? Did we—"

I frowned as I pulled on my jeans, fumbling with the zipper in my haste. I was too frantic to answer, just trying to collect myself. "What?" Sitting up in bed, his gaze fixed on me, making no move to get changed.

I rolled my eyes. Leaving him to sort himself out, I rushed downstairs. I had given him more than enough time to get himself together. If he wanted to sit around asking questions while risking being caught coming out of my bedroom, that was his issue.

As I opened the door, I braced myself for the greeting of two overly excited pups, but what I wasn't prepared for was seeing Tracy standing there.

"Tracy," I stammered, unable to hide my shock.

"Oh, Bailey. Hi. I hope I didn't wake you. Mike said he'd mentioned I might pop over today, but I didn't think about the fact you were out last night and might still be asleep." She paused, clearly reconsidering. "I can come back if now isn't a good time."

I shook my head, forcing a smile. "No, I'm just about to make a coffee if you'd like one." I hoped, desperately, that Noah had slipped out the back door without me noticing.

"Oh, that would be lovely, thank you."

"Please make yourself comfortable," I said, gesturing toward the dining room table. "If you'd excuse me for just a moment."

"Of course, take your time." Tracy sat down, and I dashed upstairs to double-check Noah wasn't planning on surprising me—and her—by still being here.

I felt like the naughty teenager I'd never been. But when I walked into my room and saw Noah sitting on the edge of my bed, fully dressed and with his head in his hands, I knew my fears were valid. The wild bed hair he was trying to tame was a sure giveaway that he hadn't just stopped in for a friendly visit.

Closing the door behind me, Noah looked up, his eyes wide.

"Oh my goodness, it's your mother," I muttered. "How the hell do we get out of this one? She's going to think I'm a slut."

COUNTRY CHARM

Noah laughed, a loud, belly-deep laugh that I knew Tracy would hear. "Could this get any worse?"

I was too frantic to be offended.

"Bailey, settle down. It's no big deal, trust me," Noah said, standing up and walking toward me. He wrapped me in his arms, dropping a kiss on the top of my head. He stepped back, running a hand through his hair as he opened the door to leave. "I'll be back later. I think we need to talk."

I stood in the doorway, watching him go, my heart racing, still unsure of what to do.

"Hi, Mom."

I heard Noah's greeting as I stood frozen, waiting for Tracy's response.

"Noah, what are you—" she began, but didn't finish, leaving me to guess what kind of reaction she'd give once I returned. I heard the fridge door open and close again, the sound filling the silence as I made my way back downstairs.

As I stepped into the dining room, I found Noah standing in the kitchen, draining the contents of his glass.

"I'll see you after Jack's finished with me," he said, rinsing his glass before stacking it in the dishwasher as if he owned the place. "Have a great day, Mom," he added, kissing me on the cheek as he passed on his way out.

I stood there, a statue, unable to think of anything to say, even after the door clicked shut behind him.

"Well, that was awkward," Tracy said, breaking the silence before bursting into a fit of giggles.

I felt the heat rise to my cheeks, and I knew I looked as guilty as I felt.

"Nothing happened, just so you know. He was so drunk—" I trailed off, realizing there was no point in making excuses. The more I spoke, the worse it sounded. Besides, Tracy was laughing so hard she probably hadn't heard a word I'd said anyway.

∽

Noah

Outside, I ran my hands through my hair again and kicked at the gravel. "Damn." The cocky show I'd put on for my mother's benefit had been just that—a show. If only I could remember what happened. I cursed again as I headed toward the granny flat. No matter what I'd done, it didn't look good for either of us.

My mother wouldn't let up on the Bailey subject now. *What a mess.*

Jack was sitting in the lounge room with Isis and Zeus resting at his feet. As I slid the door open, the two pups lifted their heads, curious.

Jack smiled up at me. "I didn't hear your car."

"I didn't drive over, but I need to go home and change. Can I borrow the truck?"

"Sure thing. Not sure I'll be up to much today, I'm not feeling the best."

I nodded. Jack didn't want me to make a fuss, but when my grandfather said he wasn't well, I knew he meant it. "I won't be long. When I get back, we could take a drive and check the dams and water troughs, if you're up to it."

"That'd be fine. You know where the keys are."

I walked to the kitchen to grab the keys. "Be back soon." Jack barely lifted his head from his chair as I left.

I made a quick detour before heading for the truck.

Bailey answered the door moments after I knocked. "Hey, Noah, what's up?"

"Is my mum still here?"

Bailey held the door open, revealing my mum sitting at the dining table.

"Can you check on Jack before you leave, please? He's not well."

"He said that?" A frown crept onto her face.

"His words, I'm just going home to change."

"Okay. I'll give him a few minutes and then head over."

I glanced at Bailey, winked, and offered a smile before turning away. I wished I had the faintest idea what had happened between us. What if she decided she didn't want to be with me again? What then? The only time we'd been together was a black void, all blurred out by intoxication.

Coming to the end of the driveway, I slowed to a stop. Cooper pulled his car up alongside me and wound down his window.

"Hey, Noah. Good night last night." Cooper grinned.

I shrugged. "Not that I remember most of it, but yeah. We should organize nights like that more often." I tried to sound casual. "Are you starting the barn work today?"

"Nah, I have to go into the city for supplies. Thought Bailey might like to come for the ride. She has tiles and stuff to choose, so I thought it'd be the perfect opportunity."

I felt my jaw clench. "She's at the house having coffee with Mom. I'll see you later." I waved as I drove out of the driveway.

Cooper was one of my best mates. There was nothing going on between him and Bailey, right? I wanted to believe that, but what did I really know about her anyway?

∽

Noah

The traffic coming and going from my house that morning was more hectic than peak hour in town.

I rushed to open the door only minutes after Tracy had left to check on Jack.

"Hi Cooper, you're a few days early," I teased. After the night we'd had, I didn't expect he'd want to swing a hammer so soon.

"Actually, I've gotta go to the city to get some supplies and was wondering if you wanted to come for the ride. Thought we could hit the tile shops."

"Will we make it before they close?" The morning

was already slipping by, and I hadn't even had a chance to shower yet.

"If we leave soon, we'll have plenty of time."

"Do I have time to shower and change first? Oh, and I'll have to check on Isis and feed Freya. Tracy surprised me with an early morning visit." I hoped he didn't notice I was wearing the same clothes as the night before.

"No problem, I can wait outside."

"You're welcome to watch TV or hang out in here. Help yourself to a drink. I won't be long." I didn't wait for his reply before heading upstairs to the bathroom.

At least if I was off the farm, I wouldn't have to worry about running into Noah. Though I did hope he'd stay with Jack. I didn't like the thought of leaving him alone when he wasn't feeling well.

After a quick shower, I pulled on one of my dresses from the *not appropriate for the farm* section of my wardrobe, along with shoes that had the same status. I didn't have time to style my hair, so I just threw it up in a messy bun. A brush of mascara, pink gloss on my lips, and I was ready.

Cooper looked up from where he sat on the couch, an empty glass in his hand. Letting out a low whistle, he grinned. "You look more amazing than usual. So this is how city girls dress for tile shopping?"

I laughed. "This is how a country girl gets dressed up to visit the city. But first, this country girl has animals to tend to."

"I'll give you a hand." Cooper switched the TV off with the remote and stood. "That's a great TV, but I guess you know that."

I shrugged. "I don't really watch it. I thought I would, being on my own and all, but I don't." The truth was, I'd bought it in case the isolation became too much, but surprisingly, I enjoyed the silence.

I'd planned to spend the day with Freya, but the barn had to be done, and Cooper couldn't work if he didn't have the building materials he needed. I could make up for it the following day—it wasn't like my schedule was overloaded. Besides, the weather was warming up by midday, so a morning ride would be more pleasant for both of us.

I swapped my shoes for the cowboy boots I'd left outside the front door.

"That's more like it," Cooper teased. "Now you're half and half."

"I'll break my neck if I try to walk to the stable in those heels." The gravel could be slippery enough in boots. I guessed they'd be like walking on marbles in shoes designed for no real purpose other than ornamentation.

I set the pace, and Cooper fell into step beside me.

"So, any idea what color tiles you're after?"

"I'm open to suggestions, but I like white, and something that won't date. Clean and refreshing."

"Blue and white looks nice."

I glanced at Cooper. "Blue and white will work." Peaceful, very much like him.

"How'd Noah pull up this morning?"

I laughed. The image of Noah's face when he woke to his mother's early morning visit was still vivid. "I don't think he had time to think about whether he was hungover. Tracy turned up so early."

Cooper's frown turned to a smile as he tilted his head to look at me. "I thought Noah was staying at Jack's."

My cheeks heated. I walked right into that one. "I didn't want him to wake Jack. He's not well, so he crashed at mine." I kept my tone casual. There was nothing wrong with a friend staying over, though I wouldn't call Noah a friend. It seemed like the simplest explanation for our relationship. Giving it some thought, I wondered what category he actually fit into.

"What's wrong with Jack?"

His genuine concern touched me. But what impressed me more was the fact that it took priority over his interest in me and Noah's sleeping arrangements.

"Not sure, to be honest, but I need to pick up Isis so I'll check in on him then." Reaching the stable, I walked up to where Freya was waiting beside her feed bin. "You're a hungry girl, aren't you?" I rubbed her neck as the mare put her head over the fence to nuzzle me.

"You'll get all dirty. If you tell me the quantities, I'll feed her."

I grinned. Caring and old-fashionedly charming. Cooper was going to be quite a catch for someone, that was for sure. "Thanks."

We didn't talk much on the way back to the house, but it was a comfortable silence.

Noah drove into the driveway just as we reached Jack's door. Cooper glanced at me, raised his eyebrows, and grinned. "Your boyfriend's back."

I swatted him playfully on the shoulder. "Are you coming in to see Jack or not?"

"Of course, unless you're giving me permission to hassle Noah for the detailed report on last night."

"You'd be lucky. He was virtually comatose. I

doubt he remembers leaving the pub." I reached out and knocked on the sliding door. If I slipped inside before Noah caught up with us, I'd be able to avoid the embarrassing scene I expected.

Relieved when Jack called out for me to come in, I slid open the door. Two overexcited pups romped at my feet, rolling and nipping at each other, demanding my attention.

"Yes, you're both adorable." Bending down, I rubbed the top of their heads. "How are you feeling?" I straightened up and assessed Jack's appearance. He looked tired and a little off-color.

"Not the best, but I'll live." Jack dismissed my concern with the flick of one hand.

"Did these little terrors keep you up last night?"

"Not at all, they've been reasonably quiet today. Dogs are intuitive like that."

"I'm heading to the city for a few hours. Do you want me to put them outside in the yard while I'm gone?"

Jack nodded. "Thanks. It'll do them good to get some fresh air. Perhaps Cooper can do it. You look too fancy for getting around on the farm." His smile was genuine, but it didn't quite reach his eyes. "What's dragging you away from us so soon?"

"Cooper, actually."

Jack raised his eyebrows, but didn't say anything.

"We're going to choose tiles and pick up some building supplies."

"Ahh, very good." The effort of the conversation seemed to weigh him down, and he closed his eyes, resting his head back against the cushion of his armchair.

Noah entered as Cooper coaxed the pups outside.

"Nice boots." He looked me over like I was a specimen under a microscope, but that was all he managed.

"Thanks. How's your head?" I wasn't about to let him get to me.

"Full of questions."

I nodded, as if I sympathized, but really, he was just going to have to wait for answers. If that's what he was hinting at.

"Are you going to be here today?" I glanced over at Jack, indicating I was asking if Noah was staying to keep an eye on him.

"That was my plan. How long are you and Cooper going out for?"

I arched one eyebrow, sensing a hint of jealousy. "I don't know. How long does it take to drive to civilization, choose tiles, buy supplies, and return?"

Noah shook his head, ignoring my sarcasm, and

turned his attention to Jack, who had opened his eyes and was now watching us.

"How are you feeling?"

"I'd feel a lot better if you two would stop bickering like schoolgirls."

I hung my head, as though I were being scolded by the school principal. The poor man was sick, and here Noah and I were, at each other again.

"I'm sorry, Jack. I'm going now. Can I get you anything while I'm out?"

"No thanks, just tell Cooper to drive safely with you in the car."

I smiled. It felt good to know he cared. "Will do. I hope you feel better, and I'll see you when I get back." I glanced at Noah. "Bye, Noah."

He nodded once, his expression unreadable.

CHAPTER 11

Bailey

Cooper had little choice but to drive carefully. We were stuck behind a slow-moving vehicle pulling a caravan, which added half an hour to an already long trip. His country music played softly in the background, and by the time we reached the bathroom supply shop, I was fighting to keep my eyes open.

"We'll pick up the materials I need after you've picked out what you like," Cooper said as he parked the car. "The hardware is open until late, so we won't have to rush. There are other tile shops too, so don't feel like you have to buy from here. I just thought this one might be a good all-rounder."

Inside, the showroom gleamed with polished surfaces and neat displays. We browsed for a few minutes before a saleswoman named Jill approached us, all professional charm.

"Are you installing a shower unit, or tiling?" Jill directed her question at Cooper, who immediately looked at me.

"She's the boss," he said with a shrug.

I smiled. "I guess a unit would be easier to clean." I explained briefly what the bathroom would be used for, keeping it simple.

"If that's the case, I'd definitely recommend a shower unit," Jill said and gestured for us to follow her to the far corner of the shop. "Did you bring the floor plans with you?"

I frowned. Usually, I was the one who came prepared, but I hadn't even thought about bringing plans. "Ah, yeah. Sorry, I left them in the car. I'll be back in a minute."

Cooper gave me a small smile.

"Thanks, Cooper."

"Don't mention it. All part of the service," he said, heading for the exit.

Jill watched him leave with a raised eyebrow. "I guess he wasn't joking about you being the boss."

I laughed lightly. "I'm paying the bill, yes, but he knows what he's doing. I'm merely an amateur."

Jill nodded, though her smile didn't seem entirely genuine. I turned my attention back to the gleaming rows of shower units. The choice wasn't difficult. My eye was drawn to one immediately, and I pointed it out.

Jill chuckled. "I thought you said you were an amateur. That's the top-of-the-range unit. Lovely, isn't it? And it comes with a not-so-lovely price tag."

I arched an eyebrow. Wasn't it a salesperson's job to stretch my budget, not deter me?

"Perhaps we should wait for your friend," Jill added in a patronizing tone that grated on my nerves.

"If the unit fits, that's the one I'll have," I said evenly. "Thanks. Now all I need are the tiles and a vanity."

Jill didn't argue, though I noticed her tight smile as she led me to the vanities.

"Hey, did I miss much?" Cooper asked, returning with the plans and handing them to Jill.

"No. I told you, I know what I like. If it fits, I've chosen the shower unit. We're on to the vanity now.

Any of these jump out to you?" I'd already spotted my favorite but wanted to see his thoughts.

Cooper shrugged. "I don't know. What's your budget?"

My frown deepened. Why did cost always have to factor into the decision process? I caught a smirk on Jill's face, and all she needed to add was, *I told you so.*

"I don't have a budget. I want what I want."

"Don't we all." Cooper laughed, but stopped when he saw I wasn't joining in. "Okay, I like that one." He pointed to a sleek, shiny white vanity, which would've been my second choice.

"It's nice, but shiny will show every fingerprint. What about that one?" I pointed to a unit tucked in the back with a molded glass top, a white bowl basin, and matching white cupboards. "It fits the artsy theme, don't you think?"

Cooper nodded. "Yeah, it'd work."

"Great. Now for tiles and taps."

Cooper suggested plain white tiles, and I agreed. I could add color with towels and candles.

"Wow," he said, sounding impressed. "One store and done in an hour. I'll shop with you anytime."

Jill offered to write up a quote, adding, "You can

call back with payment after you've had time to think it over."

"That's fine, Jill. I've thought about it, and I'm happy with my choices. Can you include delivery to Bennett Springs in the price, please?"

Jill nodded, but the smirk was back. It was the last straw.

"Is there a problem?" I was unable to keep quiet any longer.

"Not at all." Jill laughed nervously, then began typing numbers into the computer.

I glanced up at Cooper, catching the crease in his brow. "Are you okay?"

He nodded and attempted a smile, but I knew him well enough to see that something wasn't right.

"That comes to thirteen thousand six hundred and fifty dollars," Jill announced, peering around her screen.

"Lovely. Thank you." I handed over my credit card, ignoring the tightness in my chest.

Once we were back in the car, I turned to him. "What's wrong? You've been off since we walked out of the shop."

"It's nothing. Let's drop it."

"How can I drop it when you look so annoyed? She was the one judging me, and it was frustrating."

He sighed, his hands tightening on the steering wheel. "I'll be honest, Bailey. Your blatant disregard for prices can be…a little intimidating. Most people don't get it. Hell, I know you, and even I don't get it."

"Oh." The words hit harder than I expected. "Sorry, I didn't realize."

∼

Noah

Jack wasn't in any shape to be driving the property, so after convincing him to stay indoors, I left him to rest while I handled the boundaries. The fences furthest from the farmhouse were the worst, barely holding together. We hadn't had the cash to expand in years, so fixing them had always felt like a waste of time and money.

Still, with Bailey insisting she'd cover the cost of replacing all the fencing if it came to that, I started thinking this could actually work. Maybe we'd finally be able to introduce those small breed Dexters to the herd. It'd be a much-needed boost to our dwindling stock.

For now, the arrangement with Bailey was

working well—at least when we weren't arguing. Damn, she was frustrating, though. Too independent for her own good, and stubborn as hell.

I couldn't stop thinking about her, about the night before. The fact that I had no memory of what actually happened between us ate at me all day, gnawing at the edges of my thoughts like a dog with a bone. Worse, knowing she'd been alone with Cooper for hours didn't sit right.

Cooper was one of my closest friends, a solid guy I trusted with a lot. So why did the idea of him and Bailey twist something sharp and uncomfortable in my chest? What right did I even have to feel that way? It wasn't like I'd made a commitment to her.

At least, I didn't *think* I had.

But the truth was, in the state I'd been in that night, anything was possible. I vaguely remembered her saying something about a rain check, but after that, my memory hit a wall. Just a big, blank void that left me guessing.

Shaking the thoughts loose, I forced myself to focus on the fencing again. A particularly battered section caught my eye, the wires sagging and splintered posts leaning at odd angles. I grabbed my notebook from the console and jotted it down as another repair to add to the ever-growing list.

After finishing my sweep of the boundaries, I turned the truck around and headed back to check on Jack.

~

Bailey

"All this shopping has made me hungry," I announced as Cooper pulled out of the hardware service area. My stomach growled, proving my point. "Do you want to get some food before we head home?"

"Sounds like a plan," Cooper said, glancing at the rearview mirror to check on the truck bed. "But it'll have to be somewhere I can keep an eye on the truck. I don't fancy having anything ripped off after all the drama we had finding it all."

I couldn't blame him. The building supplies took forever to gather, partially because Cooper wouldn't settle for anything less than the right stuff. I admired his dedication, though I couldn't help feeling a little drained after so much back and forth. At least we managed to arrange the rest as a bulk delivery for next week.

"Have you ever been to Alfreds? I hear they make the best burgers," he said, his tone brightening.

"Excellent choice," I replied with a grin. "Alfreds it is."

Cooper grinned back, and for a moment, he looked almost childlike—pure joy. It was rare to see that side of him, but it was infectious.

When we arrived, I insisted on paying for our meals. "You paid for petrol," I said, cutting him off before he could argue. "The least I can do is fuel the humans."

He chuckled but hesitated. I could tell he wasn't entirely comfortable with the arrangement, but eventually, he gave in.

We found a table near the door where Cooper could keep an eye on the truck. I'd suggested getting takeaway to save time, but he shook his head. "The truck's fine," he said. "Besides, it's good to sit down and relax for a bit."

He was right—after the chaos of the day, it was a relief to pause. The restaurant buzzed with quiet chatter and the occasional clatter of plates, creating a warm, lively atmosphere.

"So, are you looking forward to the wedding?" I picked at the edge of my napkin. Weddings always made me happy. The thought of Ben and Soph tying the knot put a grin on my face.

"Yeah, it'll be a good night," Cooper said, leaning back in his chair. "Ben's parents' place is amazing. You'll love it."

"Sounds fancy," I teased. "And the buck's party? I hear you're organizing it. Big plans?"

He shifted in his seat, and I noticed the change in his posture. Did I hit a nerve?

"Sorry," I said, holding up my hands in mock surrender. "You don't have to give away any boys-only secrets. But, just so you know, I'm not the type to get antsy over strippers or anything."

That got a laugh out of him. He shook his head, his shoulders relaxing. "Ahh, nah. It's not that. We're keeping it low-key. Soph and Ben aren't big on too much fuss."

"But you're going to anyway, right?" I leaned forward with a smirk.

His grin widened, and his eyes gleamed with mischief. "You bet we are."

I laughed, unable to help myself. "Good."

The easy banter between us settled the tension that had lingered earlier in the day. Cooper had a way of making everything feel lighter, even when the weight of the world seemed determined to drag me down. Around him, it wasn't hard let myself relax, and to savor the moment.

~

Noah

The headlights of Cooper's truck cut through the dark as we approached, the faint hum of the engine announcing my arrival. Noah, caught in the middle of tending to the dogs, looked up. His posture stiffened, though he managed a polite wave, his hand lifting briefly in acknowledgment. Of course, he continued with what he was doing, like refilling a water bowl for the pups at this hour was the most natural thing in the world.

Cooper stopped just long enough for me to hop out. He gave a quick wave before turning the truck around and heading off, his taillights vanishing into the night. Noah straightened as I approached.

"Hey," I said, my breath puffing in the cool night air. "You're still here?"

"Um, yeah," he replied, his tone clipped but not unkind.

"How's Jack?" I wrapped my arms around myself, partly for warmth and partly for comfort.

"Not so great," he admitted. "I'll stay with him tonight if that's okay."

"Of course," I said, shrugging, though guilt tugged at me for not being there earlier. "I'll take the pups inside with me after I feed Freya."

"You're going to the stable now?" A note of surprise crept into his voice.

"Well, I'm not going to let her go hungry," I snapped, sharper than I meant to. Exhaustion and worry had worn my patience thin.

"Want me to come with you?" he offered, his brow furrowed in concern.

"Nah, I'm good. Thanks for the offer." I flicked on the flashlight of my phone and started toward the stables. "Goodnight," I called over my shoulder, my voice softer this time.

"Night," he replied, his words carried on the crisp night breeze.

I could feel his gaze lingering as I walked away, the light from my flashlight guiding me down the familiar path. By the time I reached the stables, I was glad to be alone. The rhythmic sound of Freya's hooves against the stable floor was soothing, a stark contrast to the jumble of thoughts in my head.

Freya greeted me with a soft nicker, her large eyes watching me as I prepared her feed. "Sorry I'm late, girl," I murmured, brushing my hand along her neck. She leaned into my touch, her trust grounding me in a way nothing else could.

By the time I finished up and made my way back toward the house, the granny flat was in darkness.

As I let the dogs inside and locked up for the night, I felt the tension in my chest ease, just a little. But sleep didn't come easily. My thoughts kept circling back to Noah, to the awkwardness between us, to the night we never talked about. He probably thought it was Cooper creating the distance between us, but it wasn't. The walls I'd built weren't because of him. They were because of me—and everything I wasn't ready to face.

CHAPTER 12

Bailey

I couldn't shake the feeling that Noah was checking up on me. He claimed he was staying at Jack's to keep an eye on him, but I suspected there was more to it. Either that, or Jack was sicker than I realized, which I sincerely hoped wasn't the case.

I got it, though. Noah had his insecurities, especially after what Cooper told me about Rick's brother and his ex-wife. Betrayal like that would mess anyone up. But I wasn't Charlotte, and Cooper wasn't the type to hurt a friend—Noah, of all people, should've known that.

Jealousy wasn't something I'd dealt with in my past relationships, but to be fair, I hadn't had many. Sure, there were boyfriends before my six-year disaster, but most of those weren't real relationships. They were more like arrangements—convenient but hollow. I insisted on exclusivity, but they lacked any genuine emotion. They worked until they didn't, and I ended them before things got messy.

I'd never trusted anyone enough to let them in, and honestly, I'd been too busy to try. But moving to Bennett Springs had shifted something in me. I was ready to put my heart on the line for the right guy, and the only one who'd made any kind of impression was Noah.

Except he was so hot and cold, I couldn't figure out if he was interested or not. The ice wall he constantly put up between us wasn't doing much to help my confidence, either.

Once I had Isis and Zeus settled for the evening, I dragged myself upstairs for a much-needed shower. It always amazed me how sitting in a car for hours could make you feel so grimy

The hot water felt incredible against my skin. Tilting my head back, I ran my fingers through my hair, letting the water cascade over me. When I tipped my face into the stream, my mascara smeared and stung my eyes.

"Ouch." I rubbed my eyes with the backs of my hands, hoping the water would flush out the burn. The sting lingered, but there wasn't much more I could do.

Halfway through shampooing my hair, the water suddenly turned icy. I yelped and instinctively dodged the freezing spray, only to lose my footing and land hard on my left thigh. Pain shot through my hip, radiating like fire.

I groaned, my body trembling under the icy drizzle. I didn't dare move—every slight shift made the pain worse. Resting my forehead against the cold tiles, I tried to summon the strength to push myself up.

Eventually, I managed to get onto my good leg, but my left thigh throbbed with every movement. Glancing down, I saw the beginnings of a nasty bruise that would only get uglier by morning.

The hot water returned, mocking me.

I skipped the conditioner, rinsed the suds off as quickly as I could, and shut off the water. Shivering and annoyed, I grabbed my towel and dried myself off, careful not to put weight on my injured leg. Limping to my bedroom, I didn't bother with clothes. I just eased myself onto the bed and pulled the covers over me.

I'd barely got comfortable when I heard a door slam, followed by what sounded like soft, muffled crying.

I craned my neck, trying to make out the sound. It definitely sounded like someone crying, but I was too exhausted to investigate. Dragging a spare pillow over my head, I tried to block it out, hoping the noise would stop on its own.

Taking a deep breath, I caught the faint scent of Noah's aftershave on the pillow he'd used the night before. The familiar smell tugged at something inside me. I couldn't help but wish he were here, if only to ease my mind about the noise and whatever had made it.

When I woke the next morning, I felt as though I hadn't slept at all. The first thing I noticed was the ache in my left side.

I flipped the covers back and looked down. The bruising was worse than I'd thought—black and blue streaks stretched from my hip to my knee. Dropping my head back onto the pillow, I stared at the ceiling. At least the crying had stopped.

Sitting up, I swung my legs over the side of the bed, biting my lip as pain shot through my thigh. I tested my weight on it. It hurt like hell, but I could manage.

I slipped into a lightweight sundress, skipping underwear because I couldn't imagine bending down to put it on. Coffee and painkillers were the only things I cared about right now.

Leaning on the wall for support, I made my way to the staircase. This was going to be a challenge. I considered sliding down, but sitting wasn't an option, so I gripped the railing and hopped down, one step at a time.

By the time I reached the kitchen, I was drenched in sweat, my leg throbbing worse than ever. I opened the solid door to let the breeze in, standing there for a moment to cool down. It was going to be a long day.

After downing painkillers with a cup of coffee, I sat there waiting for them to kick in. Isis and Zeus needed to go out, but I couldn't let them roam free—they'd end up under Noah's truck if he drove by. I clipped their leads, struggling as they jumped around, too excited to sit still.

Walking them to the verandah was the hardest part. They pulled and lunged, nearly knocking me off balance more than once. I grit my teeth, determined to get it over with.

I had just about finished tying them to the post when Isis leapt onto my lap. Her paw slipped, claws raking down my bruised thigh.

I cried out, tears spilling before I could stop them.

And that's when Noah rounded the corner, catching me at my lowest yet again.

I clutched my side, trying to shield it from further assault as Isis reacted to Noah's presence, her tail wagging like mad.

"Hey, why don't you put them—" Noah started but stopped short, his expression shifting as he realized something was wrong. "What's up?"

I shook my head, knowing that if I tried to talk, the tears would flow faster, betraying me completely.

Noah leaned down, scooping Isis off my lap and placing her gently on the ground. Then he extended his hand to me. "Come on," he said, his voice softer now.

Grateful but reluctant, I gripped the railing with one hand and his outstretched hand with the other. Pain flared as I shifted, and I winced.

"What happened?" His brows knitting together.

I bit my lip. He was going to think I was ridiculously clumsy when he found out the truth, but I couldn't come up with a convincing excuse on the spot. "I...uh, I had a fall last night," I admitted reluctantly. "I'm a bit sore."

"Sore where?" His tone sharpened with concern.

I hesitated, suddenly wishing he'd just leave so I could lie down and let the painkillers work. "It's nothing."

"Bailey," he said firmly, "answer me."

I sighed, meeting his gaze. His eyes were full of worry, and despite my annoyance, I couldn't brush him off. "My leg," I muttered.

His gaze dropped, and his expression darkened when he noticed the bruise peeking out from beneath my dress. Without another word, he knelt down for a closer look.

"Is that necessary?" I clutched the hem of my dress self-consciously.

"You're hurt," he replied matter-of-factly, glancing up at me. "And for goodness' sake, after Friday night, maybe save the modesty." A grin tugged at the corner of his mouth.

I narrowed my eyes, annoyed despite knowing he was teasing. "That just shows how much you remember."

His smile vanished.

"Thought so," I said flatly. "Did you come here for

a reason, or are you just passing time? Because I have things to do."

He stood, raising his hands in mock surrender. "Just passing by," he said, turning to leave. But then he paused, glancing back over his shoulder. "I'll let you get back to it."

"Uh-huh. Have a nice day." I folded my arms, waiting for him to leave, but he didn't move.

Instead, he turned fully to face me again, his expression unreadable. "Walk inside, Bailey."

I blinked, caught off guard. "Excuse me?"

"You heard me. Walk inside."

He was smart. Too smart. He knew I'd struggle with the task, and he was clearly testing me. Taking a deep breath, I shifted my weight onto my good leg and stepped back. The pain flared immediately, stealing my breath.

He raised an eyebrow, a silent challenge.

"I never said I wasn't in pain, Noah," I snapped. "Can't you just go away?"

"Sorry for wanting to help," he shot back, turning on his heel again.

I took another step backward, more out of stubbornness than anything else. That's when Zeus, clearly thinking it was playtime, lunged at me. His sudden weight knocked me off balance, and instinctively, I shifted my weight onto my injured leg. The sharp pain was too much—I cried out as I collapsed onto the top step, Zeus happily perched on top of me.

Noah was at my side in an instant, prying Zeus off me with surprising gentleness. Without hesitation, he scooped me up, cradling me against his chest like I weighed nothing.

I didn't resist. At that moment, I couldn't. The pain and the humiliation of it all had drained me of any fight. He carried me inside and carefully laid me down on the couch, his jaw tight with unspoken concern.

"Now," he said, standing over me with his arms crossed, "how about we start over?"

I sighed, propping myself up on my elbows. "Fine." Gripping the hem of my dress, I lifted it just enough to reveal the ugly bruising on my thigh.

"Shit, Bailey." Noah crouched beside me, his fingers brushing the edge of the bruise as he pushed the fabric aside to see the full extent of it.

I slapped my hand down to keep the dress from riding up too far. "Watch it," I muttered.

"Did you put ice on this?" His eyes met mine, concern etched into every line of his face.

"No," I admitted. "After the shower ran ice-cold, I didn't bother."

He frowned but said nothing. For once, I was grateful for his silence.

"Weird things keep happening. The shower runs hot and cold, doors slam shut on their own, and sometimes I hear what sounds like a child crying." My voice wavered as I spoke, the words tumbling out before I could second-guess myself. Taking a shaky breath, I braced for Noah to laugh or tell me I was imagining things.

Instead, his frown deepened. "I guess you haven't fed Freya this morning."

Tears stung my eyes. Lack of sleep, the pain, and the growing weight of handling everything on my own were catching up to me. I felt like a burden, and I hated it.

"I was waiting for the painkillers to kick in," I admitted, my voice quieter now. "I'll go in a minute." I didn't need him judging the way I cared for my animals.

"Don't be ridiculous. I'll sort her out. I'll feed her tonight, too." He paused, his sharp gaze scanning my face. "But before I do anything, have you eaten?"

I shook my head. Stubbornness would have been my usual response, but I didn't have the energy to argue. Maybe I could buy him a gift later—an offer of payment probably wouldn't go over well.

"I'm a whiz in the kitchen," he said. "You rest."

"Only if you eat too," I countered. The thought of eating alone in front of him was worse than his fussing.

To his credit, Noah didn't argue. He headed to the kitchen, and within minutes, the sounds of clattering pans and muttered curses drifted toward me. I couldn't help but smile faintly, curiosity replacing my earlier gloom.

Closing my eyes, I tried to get a grip on my emotions. Accepting help felt so unnatural, like admitting some kind of failure. It was hard to reconcile—being isolated out here meant I'd had no choice but to be self-reliant.

My thoughts drifted to my mom. Memories of her came flooding back, uninvited and bittersweet. I missed her so much. The ache of abandonment was sharp and raw, even after all these years. What had I done to deserve her leaving? And worse, I feared the resentment creeping in would tarnish what few good memories I had left.

"Here you go."

Noah's voice pulled me back to the present. I opened my eyes to see him standing over me, a wide grin lighting up his face. Despite myself, I smiled back.

Sitting up was a struggle. Pain shot through my side, and I grimaced as I tried to get comfortable.

Noah placed two plates on the coffee table and gathered some cushions from nearby chairs, tucking them behind me before handing over the food.

Scrambled eggs on toast—my favorite. "Thanks, Noah. I appreciate it."

He reached out, his fingers lightly brushing the side of my cheek. "Coffee or juice?"

"Juice, please."

Moments later, he returned with two glasses, setting them down beside the plates. He sat down at the end of the couch where I was stretched out. When I tried to move to give him more space, he gripped my ankle gently.

"Relax," he said, his tone amused. "I've got room."

He started joking and teasing, something he didn't often do, but I liked this side of him. It made me feel... lighter somehow.

"How's Jack feeling?"

"Better than you, that's for sure."

I grinned. "What are you talking about? I'm fine."

"Compared to what?"

I could have joked with him all day, but it didn't

change the fact that I was going to need help for the next few days. I hated the thought of being dependent on anyone, but Freya was another story. There was no way I could make it out to the horse yards like this.

A familiar pang of longing hit me. I wished my dad were still alive. Not that I would have burdened him with my problems, but just knowing he was there would have been enough. A mother would've been even better.

"Hey, Bailey." Noah waved a hand in front of my face. "Where'd you go just now?"

I frowned, caught off guard.

"I'm boring you, huh?"

"Not at all," I said quickly. "But don't stop work for my sake. I'm fine, really."

"I can take a hint," he said with a smirk, standing up. He leaned down so close that for a split second, I thought he might kiss me. Instead, he just grinned.

"Don't worry about Freya," he said. "I'll take care of her for the next few days, or until you feel better." He winked, collecting the dirty dishes from the table as he went. "Call me if you need anything." I didn't offer to pay him at risk of offending him.

"Thanks for breakfast," I said. "It was really good."

Noah scoffed as he disappeared toward the kitchen. "What'd you expect? I'm a farm boy."

A moment later, I heard the kitchen door open and shut behind him.

And just like that, the house felt too big again.

CHAPTER 13

Bailey

True to his word, Noah fed Freya morning and night. I offered for him to ride her if he wanted to, but he declined, promising instead to lunge her if he got the time.

On top of that, he'd brought over arnica ointment to help break up the bruising. His thoughtfulness wasn't lost on me, though I wasn't sure how to express my gratitude without sounding overly sentimental.

Monday morning, Cooper turned up as promised. I desperately wanted to head out to the barn to help him, but my body wasn't cooperating. Instead, I propped my laptop on my stomach and worked from the couch, trying to keep my restlessness at bay.

By Tuesday, I couldn't stand being idle any longer. The bruises had turned into a kaleidoscope of colors—angry reds fading into yellows and purples—and while they were still tender, I could move around with a little more ease.

"Hey, can I come in?" Cooper's voice called from the kitchen, his tone cheerful.

"Yay, a visitor. Of course, you can." I answered, eager for company.

Cooper strode into the living room, his footsteps echoing against the wooden floors. He stopped at the coffee table and perched on its corner, holding out his phone.

"I took some photos so you don't miss out on the progress," he said, his grin as wide as his shoulders.

I took the phone from him, and my smile stretched even wider. "Has anyone ever told you that you're wonderful? Because you are."

As I scrolled through the photos, the transformation of the space amazed me. My meditation room was coming together beautifully.

"You've done so much already, and it's only been

two days. I'm impressed," I said, scrolling through the pictures again before handing the phone back.

"I'll send them to you," he offered.

"Thanks, that'd be great." Leaning forward, I kissed his cheek in a moment of genuine appreciation.

"Finished for the day already?"

Noah's voice cut through the air like a blade, and my head snapped toward him. I hadn't heard him come in, too caught up in Cooper's updates.

His tone wasn't just curt—it was cold—and the way he stood, arms crossed and frowning like he was auditioning for a thunderstorm, only made it worse.

"Hey, Noah," Cooper said, unfazed. "Just showing Bailey the job so far, seeing as she's stuck in here."

Noah barely acknowledged him, his glare fixed on me. "Do you need anything from town? I've got to pick up more feed for Freya."

I frowned, thrown off by his attitude. "Oh, yeah. Sorry. Thanks for that. Could you ask Mel to put it on my account, please?"

Noah nodded stiffly. "If that's all, I'll leave you to it."

I swallowed back the urge to snap at him. I knew he'd been hurt in the past—hadn't most people?—but his behavior was out of line. Still, he was the one helping me, and I wasn't sure if I should call him out or just let it slide.

"Before you go, how's Jack? I haven't seen him around, and he usually calls in for a chat," I hoped to soften the tension.

Noah's gaze flicked briefly to Cooper before settling back on me. "He's on the mend."

I nodded. I was on the mend too, and I hoped by tomorrow I'd feel well enough to drive out to the barn for a proper look at the progress.

"I'd better get going, too," Cooper said, rising to his feet. "See you tomorrow, Bailey. Take care of yourself."

"Thanks, Cooper. See you tomorrow."

Noah gave me a quick nod before following Cooper out.

The house felt quiet again, but this time the silence left me simmering. Noah was being ridiculous. There was no rule saying Cooper and I couldn't be friends. Just because Noah's ex-wife had cheated didn't mean every woman was the same—and I certainly wasn't

I exhaled heavily, trying to shake the irritation. Maybe tomorrow, I'd set him straight. Or maybe I'd let him stew in his own nonsense for a bit longer.

Noah

I didn't have time to stand around and chat with Cooper, nor did I want to. For the first time I could remember, his carefree nature actually grated on my nerves.

"Look, mate," Cooper said, running a hand through his hair. It was a nervous gesture he'd never grown out of. "I know you've had a rough trot in the past, but you're like a brother to me, and I'd never do anything to jeopardize that."

I didn't respond, just shifted my weight from one foot to the other.

"She's not like that, mate," he added, jerking his head toward the front door. "Just because Charlotte was a bitch—don't screw this up. She likes you."

His words landed like a punch, and I couldn't think of anything to say. My behavior must've been painfully transparent if even Cooper—who never cottoned on to much—had figured out I wasn't thrilled about how close they'd been.

Deep down, I knew Cooper wouldn't betray me. But that didn't stop the image of Charlotte and Matt from creeping into my mind. It was like a scar I couldn't stop picking at, no matter how much it bled.

I clapped Cooper on the shoulder. "I know you wouldn't do that to me, but there's nothing going on between us." The words felt heavy, hollow. Part of me wanted to tell him to go for it if he was interested in her, but I couldn't bring myself to say it.

Cooper shook his head, a grin tugging at the corner of his mouth. "Whatever you reckon, Noah. I've gotta get back to it, but stop in and check it out sometime."

I nodded, not trusting myself to speak. I'd been avoiding the barn, and I wasn't sure I was ready to face it. It had been Maggie's dream, and seeing it come alive felt like a ghost haunting me. The guilt of her not being here to see it through was still fresh.

"Will do," I finally said, pulling the keys from my pocket to signal that the conversation was over.

The drive into town wasn't long enough. I needed more time away from the farm, but things had been too quiet lately. Between my parents, Jack being laid up, and Bailey hobbling around, I didn't have much choice but to help out.

Even so, the farm stirred up too many memories. I told myself reliving the past was a waste of time, but no matter how hard I tried to redirect my thoughts, they wouldn't stop tormenting me.

When I pulled into the stock feeders' car park, I had to hit the brakes to avoid Whitney prancing out of the shop like she was on a runway. She crossed in front of me, all blonde curls and swaying hips, and I prayed she hadn't seen me.

Parking as far from her as possible, I leaned across the seat to grab my wallet from the glove box, stalling longer than necessary.

Of course, she waited for me. "Hey, good looking," she purred. "I was just thinking about you."

I cringed inwardly. Cartwheels naked in the street would've been subtler than the way she said it.

"Hi, Whitney. How are you?" I kept my tone flat.

"Better now that you've stopped by. What are you doing?"

"Buying feed."

"Oh, of course. How are the cows?"

I raised an eyebrow. Since when did Whitney care about cattle—or any animal, for that matter? "Fine," I said shortly. The less I said, the quicker this would be over.

"I must come over sometime so you can show me around. Maybe we could go out riding together." She twirled a curl around her finger, her attempt at being endearing only irritating me further.

"It's not my farm, and I don't have a horse."

I turned to leave, but her claw-like nails dug into my arm, stopping me.

"It's terrible what she's done to you and Jack," Whitney hissed, her voice dripping with venom. "I don't like her. Too rich and pretty in her fancy gear. She gets around town like she owns the joint. It's probably just a show. I bet she has debt up to her ears like the rest of us."

"Which is why I have to get back to work. See you," I said, shrugging her off and stalking into the shop.

Rick was waiting for me just inside, laughing as he nodded toward the parking lot. "Mel said Whit bailed you up out there."

"Yeah, right," I shot back, grinning despite myself. "You just wanted to watch me squirm, you bastard."

Rick laughed again. "Why she didn't leave with the rest of the girls out of high school, I'll never know. Maybe she likes the isolation."

"Doubt it," I muttered.

"What brings you in? Jack ordered grain last week."

"Freya's almost out of feed. Bloody horse eats like no other I've ever had."

Rick frowned. "You're looking after her now, too?"

"Bailey had a bit of an accident and can't walk. Thought the whole town would know by now."

"Ali didn't mention it, so your secret's safe. Must suck to have no one. Good thing she has you, huh?"

"She doesn't have me. I'm just feeding her horse."

But his words stuck with me. Bailey didn't seem to have anyone who really cared about her. I wondered, for a moment, if bringing up her mother again would be such a bad idea. Maybe she had a reason for walking out—and maybe there was one stopping her from walking back in.

∼

Bailey

I was bored. Daytime soaps were mind-numbing, and I missed the fresh air I'd taken for granted since moving in. Staring at the screen, I couldn't stop thinking about the barn. If I could just make it out there tomorrow, I'd finally get to see Freya and break this monotony.

The sound of a car pulling up had me perking up, hopeful it might be Cooper swinging by to talk about the barn. But then came the unmistakable sound of female laughter, and I immediately guessed it was Emily and Tracy. My excitement dulled. Sitting still hurt, but if it meant breaking up the day —even with them—I'd make the effort. Tomorrow was barn day, no matter what.

The kitchen door creaked open, followed by a knock. "Hey, Bailey, can we come in?" Ali's familiar voice broke the silence, and despite myself, I grinned.

"Of course. I'm in the lounge room." I figured Ali must've been to the house before, if Cooper's stories were anything to go by.

Ali appeared first, followed by Sophie and Cassie, each carrying something. A bottle of soda, two pizza boxes, and what looked suspiciously like a cake box made their way into the room.

"We hope you're hungry," Cassie said as she set the pizza on the coffee table, only to lift it again. "Do you have a cloth or something to put under this?"

"No, it's fine as is." Tears prickled my eyes, and I blinked rapidly to keep them from spilling over. It had been a while since anyone thought to stop by just to keep me company.

"Now, what have you gone and done to yourself?" Ali rolled her eyes as she set her box beside the pizza. "Rick said you had an accident but didn't elaborate. Typical male."

"It's a bit embarrassing. I slipped in the shower." My cheeks burned as I admitted it out loud. To prove my case, I lifted my dress slightly to show the enormous bruise on my thigh. "It's getting better," I added quickly when they all cringed.

"Thank goodness Noah was here to help," Sophie said matter-of-factly.

"Oh, he wasn't here when it happened," I corrected. "He saw me limping the next day when I was trying to sort the dogs out." Noah hadn't gone into details, thankfully, but I could already imagine how colorful the story must sound. Him *rescuing* me from the shower? It implied far more than I'd ever want anyone to believe.

"Well, thank goodness he's been taking care of you," Ali said, taking the soda from Sophie. "Now, where are your cups and plates? I'm starving."

"Oh yeah, sure. Cups are in the top drawer by the microwave, and plates are in the one below."

Ali disappeared into the kitchen, Sophie following close behind. They returned a few moments later with four glasses and a plate for each of us. Cassie opened the pizza boxes, positioning them side by side.

"We got one feta and spinach with creamy garlic sauce—my favorite—and satay chicken. Hope that's okay," Cassie said.

"Sounds wonderful. Thanks, guys." Tears threatened again, and I forced a smile to hide how much their thoughtfulness meant to me.

"You want one of each?" Cassie was already placing a slice from each box onto a plate and handing it to me.

The conversation quickly shifted as Ali steered us toward Sophie's upcoming hen's night. "What do you mean, hire a hall? Why can't we have it here?" I was determined to be part of the planning.

"Oh no, thanks, but we can't," Sophie said, shaking her head.

"Why not? If the boys are at Ali's, we won't get in the way, and anyone who wants to stay can. It makes sense to me."

Ali grinned. "Okay, wonderful. You don't have to worry about a thing. Cassie and I will take care of it all."

"I'd be happy to help if you need me. I've got plenty of time on my hands until the barn's finished."

"We'd like that," Ali said, her tone suddenly cautious. "But there's something you should know before you agree to anything." She paused, clearly searching for the right words. "Charlotte will most probably be coming." Her lopsided smile showed she wasn't thrilled about it either.

"Does that matter?" I couldn't help my curiosity. Meeting Noah's ex-wife before the wedding didn't seem like the worst idea. At least here, in my own house, I'd be on familiar ground.

"Not to us," Cassie chimed in. "She's an obligatory invite only. Pity she didn't have an affair with someone else so we could be rid of her." Cassie glanced at Ali, who frowned and subtly shook her head, effectively ending the topic.

The conversation shifted again, bouncing from topic to topic, though Sophie's hen's night took center stage. Laughter filled the room as we brainstormed wild ideas to make it a night to remember.

By the time they decided it was time to leave, I couldn't stop yawning. Despite doing nothing for the past few days, the noises at night kept me awake.

"Is there anything I can get you before we leave?" Ali fussed over me.

"I think I'm good, thanks."

"You look exhausted. You sure you don't want painkillers or anything?"

"Sleeping tablets strong enough to drown out the ghosts would be good," I joked, laughing softly.

"What ghosts?" Sophie glanced around as though expecting one to materialize. "Is this place haunted?"

"With all that's gone on in this house, anything's possible," Cassie said, shuddering dramatically and rubbing her arms as though warding off a chill.

"And exactly what has gone on?" Cooper had been frustratingly tight-lipped whenever I tried to pry.

"Nothing worth freaking out about," Ali said quickly, glaring at Cassie. "Just the usual old farmhouse stories, you know."

I recognized a deflection when I saw one. Ali clearly didn't want to elaborate, but I knew better than to push. If there was one thing I understood about small towns, it was that someone, eventually, would spill the tea. It was just a matter of time.

CHAPTER 14

Bailey

Noah insisted he could keep feeding Freya for a few more days, but I couldn't stay away any longer. Even when I lived in the city, I'd never gone this long without seeing her.

My leg was still tender, and the bruises were an unpleasant shade of mottled purple and yellow, but I refused to let them keep me confined to the couch. Sitting around only left me stewing over everything wrong in my life or what wasn't getting done—a vicious cycle that helped no one.

My mother's absence loomed larger with every

passing day, stirring a resentment I hated acknowledging. I couldn't let bitterness taint the memory of what had once been the closest relationship I'd ever known, apart from the bond I shared with Freya.

Not trusting my leg to carry me that far yet, I drove to the stable instead of walking. There was no point proving I could make the trek only to collapse halfway there—not exactly the kind of behavior that would win admiration from Noah.

Freya greeted me with a soft whinny, and guilt twisted my chest. I'd brought a handful of carrots as a peace offering, and as she munched them, I brushed her coat with slow, soothing strokes.

The simple routine brought a sense of peace I hadn't felt in days. I could've stayed there forever, watching the play of light on her dark coat and listening to her gentle breathing.

After a while, I sat on an old bench that had probably been Maggie's. I could picture her sitting right here, keeping an eye on her horses the way I was now. Just being in the stable, with Freya so close, was almost as satisfying as galloping through a paddock on her back. Almost.

I couldn't wait for my stallion to arrive—and one day, a foal. The thought warmed me as I leaned back against the wall. Rob had explained the long process of bringing a horse over the border, and while it wasn't as simple as I'd hoped, I understood the need for patience.

With so much work to do on the barn and the retreat, maybe it was better that my new addition wouldn't arrive anytime soon.

That decision was easy compared to the one that kept gnawing at me: whether or not to reach out to my mother. Writing a letter felt safe enough—it wasn't like I had to face her rejection in person—but the thought of her ignoring it, or worse, telling me to go away, was enough to stop me in my tracks.

Not knowing meant I could still hold onto hope. Maybe she missed me. Maybe she wanted her daughter back and didn't know how to reach out. I shook my head, forcing the thoughts away.

This wasn't getting me anywhere.

Freya nudged my shoulder, her warm breath breaking the spiral of worry. I smiled at her and stood, my leg protesting as I stretched. Cooper would be at the barn by now, and I wanted to see how much progress he'd made.

The pictures he'd sent were great, but they didn't compare to seeing it all in person. Watching the transformation from the dusty storage space it'd become to a tranquil retreat was one of the few things keeping me grounded.

I glanced at the time. If I left now, I'd get there right around morning tea. Perfect. On a whim, I'd packed a picnic basket, along with the new coffee machine I'd bought on our last trip to the city. If Noah or Jack happened to drop by, there'd be plenty to share.

The weight of the coffee machine and the awkward limp I couldn't hide had Cooper grinning as soon as he spotted me.

"I'll get that for you," he said, dropping his screwdriver and rushing over.

"Thanks. And wow—this looks amazing. Even better than the pictures." I gestured at the barn, which was already beginning to resemble the vision I'd carried in my mind for months. "I'm sorry I haven't been much help, but after morning tea, I'm all yours."

"Deal. Is there more in the car?"

"Just a picnic basket in the front seat. I thought you could use a break."

"If coffee's involved, I won't say no." He disappeared and returned moments later, hefting the basket with ease. "How many people are you expecting? This thing weighs a ton."

I laughed. "You never know who might show up."

Cooper set the basket down, and we unpacked it together. I'd brought chicken and salad wraps, fruit salad, and cooler blocks to keep everything fresh. It felt good to do something small for him after all his hard work.

We spent the afternoon working side by side. I measured, held boards steady, and swept up the endless sawdust. By late afternoon, my leg throbbed relentlessly, and walking was becoming unbearable. If it didn't improve soon, I'd have to see a doctor—not that I was in any rush to admit defeat.

Cooper wiped the sweat from his brow and grinned at me as we wrapped up for the day. "We make a good team. You sure I can't steal you away from Noah?"

I glanced sideways at Cooper, his grin making his dimples stand out. "You know as well as I do there is nothing going on between Noah and me. He can barely be in a room with me for five minutes without hurling some sort of offensive comment."

"Didn't they teach you anything in primary school? Boys are only mean to girls they like."

I laughed, shaking my head. "It would've been so much easier if I fell for someone like you, Coop. You're easy to talk to, you make me laugh...but you're more like a brother to me. And let's face it—that's not the kind of feeling you start a relationship with."

He smirked. "Well, that's a relief. I'm not sure I'd survive you bossing me around all the time."

Nighttime was when the loneliness crept in the most. Every sound seemed amplified in the quiet, echoing as though it were right outside my window. Too often, I felt chills rush over me, leaving me clutching my blanket like it was the only barrier between me and whatever might be lurking in the shadows.

Jack hadn't been around much lately. First, he'd been sick, and then I hurt my leg. I missed his company more than I wanted to admit. Maybe he thought he'd be imposing if he came by too often, though his presence was never an imposition to me. If anything, it felt comforting.

After an hour of attempting to concentrate on paperwork and failing miserably, I gave up. I needed a break, and I figured Jack might, too. I cut two generous slices of the sponge cake I'd baked earlier and placed them on plates, covering each with a serviette to keep the bugs away. Grabbing the plates, I made my way to the granny flat as best as my leg would allow.

Jack greeted me with a warm smile when he opened the door. "Hello, what a lovely surprise."

"I thought you might like some dessert," I said, stepping inside and setting the plates on the table. I removed the serviettes, revealing the cake.

Jack's gaze softened. "You've been busy. Sponge cake was Maggie's specialty."

Though he didn't say it to make me feel bad, I couldn't help but regret my choice. "I wish you'd told me that after we'd eaten," I said with a laugh, trying to lighten the moment. "Maybe I should've brought coffee, too. You know, in case you need to wash it down."

Jack's smile returned. "That wasn't very tactful of me. I'm sure it'll be delicious."

He seemed a bit off, though, missing some of his usual spark. I wondered if he still wasn't feeling well. "I'll put the kettle on," he said, heading to the kitchen. "I make a mean hot chocolate. Interested?"

"Sounds good to me." I followed him into the small, impeccably tidy kitchen. Everything had its place, just like in my own. It wasn't easy keeping a space this small organized, but he managed it.

"Noah tells me the barn's coming along," he said, opening a cupboard to grab two mugs. "I should head up and take a look soon."

"Cooper's been keeping me updated with photos, but I saw it in person today. It looks amazing. He's done such a great job, and so quickly, too." I realized I was babbling but didn't care. Talking about the barn excited me, and talking to Jack felt easy.

Jack listened, spooning hot chocolate flakes into the mugs as the kettle boiled. "I'm glad to hear it. I'll definitely make my way up there sometime this week."

He finished the drinks, adding milk and water before handing me a mug. "Would you mind grabbing a couple of spoons for the cake? Or forks, if you'd prefer."

I grabbed two spoons from the drawer and joined him in the lounge room. The smell of the hot chocolate filled the air, rich and comforting.

We didn't talk much as we ate. I watched Jack's face as he took his first bite of cake. He closed his eyes briefly before looking at me. "Did Tracy give you this recipe?"

I grinned. "I'll take that as a compliment. No, it's my mum's recipe."

Her recipes were the best. She'd tweaked them until they were perfect. I was just grateful she'd written them down. It was one of the few things she'd left me that felt personal.

Jack set his plate down and gave me a thoughtful look. "Have you thought about contacting her?"

"Constantly," I admitted, surprising myself with the honesty. Sharing it with Jack felt cathartic, as if I were just realizing how much I'd been dwelling on it.

"Then do it. What have you got to lose?"

"Hope." The word slipped out before I could stop it. I rushed to explain. "Until I contact her, there's always hope she'll come back. Once she says no, that hope is gone." I shrugged and took a large bite of cake to avoid saying more.

Jack nodded, his expression kind but firm. "And if she responds, which I'm sure she will, you won't need to hold on to *what if* anymore."

He was wise but never condescending, and his words lingered long after we'd finished dessert. As I sipped my hot chocolate, Jack gave me a small smile. "Miss Bailey, has anyone ever told you what an amazing cook you are? You'll make some guy a very lucky man someday."

Later, lying in bed, I replayed our conversation over and over. Jack was right. The only way to move forward was to take the plunge and find out the truth. Making up my mind to deal with it in the morning, I finally drifted off to sleep.

Somewhere in the distance, I heard a faint cry, like a child's. I pulled the blanket tighter around me, willing the sound to stop. But it didn't. My heart raced as ice-cold chills washed over me. This was getting beyond a joke. It wasn't just unnerving me anymore—it felt like whatever was out there was as distressed as I was.

Slipping out from under my blankets, I turned on my bedroom light and stepped into the hallway. The sound I'd heard just moments ago had stopped, but I followed the direction it seemed to come from. My heart pounded as I approached the door at the end of the hallway.

Pushing the door open, I reached inside and felt along the wall for the light switch. Flicking it on, I was met with nothing but silence and an empty room. Goosebumps prickled my skin, and I hurried back to my bedroom, hoping that would be the last of it for the night.

Even after I'd been back under my blankets for a good five minutes, with the house silent around me, my heart was still racing like a drumline in a marching band. I pulled the covers tighter around me and tried to focus on my breathing.

By the time Noah arrived the next morning, I was already on my second cup of coffee. After the night I had, I doubted even two cups would be enough.

"Hey, are you okay?" he frowned as he took in my expression. "What's up?"

"I think this house is haunted," I said, watching him carefully for a reaction.

I didn't expect him to burst out laughing.

"It's not funny. I'm seriously freaked out, and all you can do is laugh," I snapped. "You badger me to tell you what's wrong, but you won't even tell me who died in this house." I crossed my arms and pouted like a petulant child, realizing too late how ridiculous I must have looked.

He stepped forward and wrapped me in a tight hug. His mood swings were wilder than a menopausal woman's. "I didn't hear anything the other night," he said.

"Noah, you were practically comatose. Of course, you didn't hear anything. Besides, it didn't happen when you stayed."

"Do you want me to stay tonight so you can get some sleep?"

"Smooth, Noah," I muttered.

"I'm serious," he insisted. "I can sleep on the couch if it'd make you more comfortable."

"I can just leave the lights on from the moment I

go to bed," I said, mostly to myself. "The crying stops when the lights are left on—maybe the ghost is afraid of the dark." My attempt at humor fell flat when I felt his body tense. What was he hiding?

"The offer's there if you need it," he said. "Or call me if it happens again, and I'll come over."

"Did you dream of being a Ghostbuster when you were a little boy?"

Noah laughed, and I felt the vibration as it rumbled through his chest against mine. His embrace was warm, comforting. For a moment, I considered saying yes to his offer. But before I could make up my mind, the sound of Cooper's car pulling up had me stepping back. No need to feed the small-town grapevine with unnecessary gossip.

"So, do you want coffee?"

Noah glanced toward the door. Cooper waltzed in without knocking.

"Sorry, I should've knocked. Habit, you know," Cooper said, sheepishly.

"Perhaps try next time," Noah replied, his tone sharp. Then, turning back to me, he shook his head. "No thanks. Jack gets antsy if I'm late. I'll talk to you later."

Still too tightly wound from the night before, I decided to let Cooper work on his own and headed into town instead. Eating alone wasn't my favorite, but it beat dining with a ghost. Besides, supporting the local businesses fit with my plan to keep produce as local as possible. Maybe I'd make a collage of business cards and menus to include in my venture.

Carefully sliding out of my truck, I avoided banging my leg on the door. Any knock or awkward movement still made me wince. With only one café on the main strip, it wasn't hard to choose where to eat. The retro style of the dining area felt both homely and stylish, with mismatched furniture in shades of black, cream, and taupe. The smell of something delicious teased my senses as I walked up to the counter.

"Hi, what can I get you?" The woman behind the counter smiled, though curiosity gleamed in her eyes.

"Hi, whatever's cooking at the moment, please," I said with a laugh. The woman frowned, tilting her head. "Sorry, it smells amazing in here."

Her smile widened with pride. "My son's trying a new dish. Not sure what he calls it, but it does smell good, doesn't it?"

"It does," I said, nodding.

"I'm sure he'd love a second opinion if you're

interested. If you don't like it, I'll make you something else from the menu."

"I'd love that, thank you."

"Great. Have a seat, and I'll bring it out to you."

I chose a table in the corner, leaving the booths for larger groups. Pulling a notepad from my bag, I began sketching my idea for the restaurant, incorporating a collage style with menus and business cards.

The food arrived just as my drawing started to take form.

"Hey, that's fantastic," the woman said, setting the plate down.

"Thanks," I replied, glancing up. The smell up close was even better than I'd imagined.

"You're not from around here, are you?" Her curiosity was evident again.

"I'm newish," I said, hesitant to share too much. "Bailey Cooper."

"Ah, Jack's Bailey. I should've guessed." She smiled warmly. "I'm Trish. Nice to finally meet you."

Her welcome put me at ease. "Likewise. So, *Jack's Bailey*?"

Trish chuckled. "He always wanted another granddaughter, and I think he's adopted you. He's always raving about you. Bailey this, Bailey that. He's so proud of you."

Warmth filled me at her words. "That means a lot. He's been wonderful."

"Don't be shy. Tell us what you think of your lunch," Trish said, moving off to tend to another customer.

I took a bite, and each mouthful was better than the last. By the time I'd finished, I was in awe of whoever had made the dish.

"So, what did you think?" Trish waited until she was clearing my plate to ask.

"I've never tasted anything better in all my life. Where did he learn to cook like that?"

Trish beamed with pride. "Maggie."

CHAPTER 15

Bailey

Ali, Emily, and Cassie burst into the café, their laughter and chatter cutting through the hum of the small dining area. Ali didn't even wait until she reached the table before calling out, "Oh wow, this is freaky. I just tried to call you to see if you were interested in meeting us for lunch, and here you are."

I frowned, pulling my phone out of my bag. I hadn't heard it ring and was half-worried I'd left it at home, but there it was. Silent. Apparently, I'd switched it to silent without even realizing.

"Hi, Trish," Emily greeted warmly as she gave me a quick hug. The others chorused their hellos.

"We're having a last-minute hen's night meeting and thought you might want to join us," Ali explained.

"Sounds good to me, but I've already eaten," I admitted, leaning back in my chair.

"Cal's been trying out new recipes," Ali said as she slid into the booth closest to my table. "Do you mind if we join you? There's more room over here."

"Not at all," I said, gathering my notebook and bag before sliding into the booth with them.

Cassie and Emily ordered their usual, which Trish obviously understood since she didn't need any further explanation. I couldn't help but smile as I watched her retreat to the kitchen. Small-town life had its charms.

"We have a lot to get through, and I have to be back for Mrs. Elliot's bikini wax," Ali said absent-mindedly, flipping through her notes.

Cassie grimaced and held up a hand. "Spare us the details, please. That's enough to put anyone off their food."

"Whoops. Sorry," Ali said with a sheepish grin.

"So, we've agreed on the color theme matching

the wedding," Cassie said, opening a file Ali had brought with her.

"I have the pearly balloons and helium tank ready to go," Emily added, her voice quieter but no less efficient.

Ali turned to me. "Bailey, what do you need us to bring besides food and drinks? Tables, chairs, a barbeque? We know you've just moved in, so don't hesitate to ask."

I'd been mulling over the menu for days and finally had an idea I hoped they'd like. "Well," I started hesitantly, "I've been thinking. If you're open to it, I'd love to use this as an opportunity to test out the menu I've planned for the retreats. It'll give me a chance to get used to cooking for a crowd of about twenty. What do you think?"

Cassie's face lit up. "Sounds good to me. I'm a terrible cook, so it's a win-win."

Emily nodded, though it was hard to tell if she was agreeing with the plan or Cassie's confession. Either way, the idea was approved.

Ali's organizational skills shone as she went over the finer details. She was efficient and warm, her confidence making the whole process feel easy. Cassie, on the other hand, wouldn't let go of her insistence on hiring a stripper.

"Do you really think Sophie would want that?" Emily frowned, her voice filled with doubt.

Cassie shrugged. "Honestly, Em, think of the stories she could share with her kids one day."

Emily rolled her eyes. "Tell me, would you want to hear a story about your mother and a stripper?"

Cassie shuddered. "Okay, fair point. But it would be a good laugh on the night."

Ali grinned. "Maybe we should make a rule: what happens at Bailey's stays at Bailey's."

"Good plan," Cassie said with a smirk. "Means we can talk freely about Whitney going home with the stripper afterward."

"Oh, Cassie, don't be a bitch," Ali chided, but her laughter took the sting out of the words.

I found their banter entertaining. It reminded me of work colleagues, but with a sharper edge. Cassie's judgmental streak was as clear as Noah's, though her delivery was more playful. Ali was confident and competent, while Emily acted as the group's conscience. I realized how much I missed having female friends like this. Their dynamic made me feel part of something, even if it was just for a little while.

The conversation eventually shifted to the wedding. "I wish they were going on a honeymoon,"

Emily mused. "You only get one chance, and I think they'll regret it later."

"I don't think their kids will want to hear about that milestone either," Cassie teased. "The wedding's costing more than they expected, and with buying a house, going away would just add financial pressure."

"Fair enough," Ali said, standing. "On that note, I have to get back. Mrs. Elliot doesn't like to be kept waiting."

Cassie groaned. "Enjoy."

Later that evening, as I returned from feeding Freya, I caught a glimpse of Noah's truck disappearing down the driveway. Disappointment settled over me like a heavy cloak. If I hadn't lingered so long, we might have bumped into each other. Even to myself, I sounded desperate. We weren't teenagers, for goodness' sake.

But there was no denying I'd started to enjoy the time we spent together after he and Jack finished for the day. It hadn't occurred to me that those moments would end once I was back on my feet. Maybe his attention had been out of pity—a way to repay me for all I'd done for Jack.

Shaking off the thought, I took my time walking back to the house. It was probably for the best.

Getting attached to someone like Noah would only lead to heartbreak. I had more important things to focus on anyway, like deciding on outdoor furniture for the hen's night. With twenty guests confirmed, I'd need two large settings to ensure everyone had enough space.

The outdoor entertaining area had plenty of room, and I wanted it to be perfect. Even if Noah's absence left a void, I could at least pour my energy into something productive.

This was Sophie's special night, and I wanted to make it as memorable as possible. A cozy, intimate celebration for the bride and her closest friends. No pressure, right?

After setting the pasta sauce to simmer, I carried my laptop to the table and turned it on. Honestly, I didn't know why I bothered putting it away. I never worked in my study anyway.

Not in the mood to browse aimlessly, I opened my favorite furniture store's website. They prided themselves on quality customer service, and I knew they'd deliver on time. I scrolled through the options, stopping the moment I saw it. Perfect. A white wicker table with a glass top, surrounded by elegant yet comfortable chairs. It looked like it had been made for this occasion.

I added the matching outdoor daybed and coffee table to my cart, along with two barbeques—one large for entertaining, the other smaller for when I was just cooking for myself. As I headed to checkout, an option to add outdoor gas heaters popped up. Nights could still be chilly, and with twenty guests confirmed, I figured four heaters would do the trick. Delivery costs were steep now that I lived so far out, but getting everything in one order would save me in the long run.

Satisfied with my progress, I closed the laptop. After turning the stove to a low simmer, I put the spaghetti on to cook. A quick glance at the clock told me I'd have time for a shower before settling in front of the TV. Maybe a movie would help drown out the strange noises I'd been hearing at night.

Later, I curled up on the couch with a bowl of pasta and a beer, scrolling through movie options. A romantic comedy was exactly what I needed. I flipped my notepad to a fresh page and wrote *menu* at the top. I was just about to jot down ideas when a loud knock at the door startled me. My spoon clattered into the bowl as my heart jumped into my throat.

Peeking through the curtains didn't seem smart, and I still didn't have a peephole installed. What was

I thinking, living out here alone? I cracked the door open, relief washing over me when I saw Noah on the other side.

"If you're nervous about opening the door, maybe ask who it is first. Could save you the adrenaline spike," he said, smirking.

I laughed, pushing the door wide. He wasn't kidding about staying over. A sleeping bag hung from one hand, and a six-pack of beer dangled from the other.

"Figured all Ghostbusters should travel with essentials," he said, stepping inside.

"I didn't think you were serious. You don't have to stay if you don't want to."

I closed and locked the door behind him, suddenly aware of how underdressed I was. But given what he'd already seen—more than I was comfortable admitting—it probably didn't matter.

Noah dumped his sleeping bag on a dining chair and set the beers on the kitchen counter. "You hungry? I'm just having dinner."

"What's on the menu?"

"Spaghetti bolognaise."

"I've eaten, but I never say no to spaghetti bol." His grin widened as I handed him a bowl.

"Want cheese on top?"

"Is the pope Catholic?" He accepted the bag of grated parmesan I held out, sprinkling it generously. "Thanks. Want a beer?"

"I already have one, but thanks."

He glanced toward the dining room table. "You don't eat in here?"

I shrugged. "It feels... lonely when it's just me."

"Point taken. Couch it is."

We sat together, eating in comfortable silence for a few moments before Noah broke it. "This is good. Who taught you to cook?"

"My mom, at first. Then years of trial and error."

He hesitated. "Why'd she leave?"

I froze, the question catching me off guard. Shoving a forkful of pasta into my mouth, I chewed slowly, buying time. "Your guess is as good as mine," I said finally, keeping my tone casual. "She said my grandfather was ill and she needed to be with him. She left, and I never heard from her again."

The silence that followed felt heavier than before.

"I could help you find her," Noah offered, his voice quiet. "If you wanted to."

It was a generous offer, but I couldn't take it seriously. The only reason I'd consider it would be to spend more time with him. "How about you tell me who—or what—could be lingering in my house? And why they're so sad."

Noah's head snapped up. His fork hovered in midair as he stared at me. He knew something, or at least suspected it.

"I don't know what you're talking about," he said, shoving another bite into his mouth. His sudden focus on eating was a clear attempt to avoid the topic.

"Come on, Noah. You said yourself this house has a history. What aren't you telling me?"

He leaned back, grabbing his beer. "There's no mystery here. It's an old house. People die. There are always ghosts from the past—literal or otherwise. It just depends on how many you bring into your future."

His tone was sharp, and I got the feeling he wasn't just talking about my house. Sensing I was treading on sensitive ground, I shifted gears.

"So... have you thought more about building the stables for me?"

His shoulders relaxed slightly. "Ah, huh," he said, finishing the last of his food.

I watched the muscles in Noah's jaw clench as he chewed, a slight frown creasing his brow. He seemed to be mulling over something, his thoughts deep and unreadable. Was it wrong that I found him completely irresistible, even while he was doing something as ordinary as eating? The chewing stopped, and he swallowed. I'd already finished my own meal, but I couldn't stop myself from following the movement of his throat.

"In what way were you meaning, though?" His voice broke through my thoughts. "Style, or whether or not I'd do the work?"

"Style, providing you think the existing area is adequate to house my stallion when he arrives, too. Because, if it's not, then when can you start?"

"You have another one?" His head shook slightly as he spoke, dismay flickering across his face. "You're not going to ride him, I hope."

The way he said it, implying I couldn't handle myself without actually saying so, grated on me. "What, you think I can't handle myself on a horse, Noah? I've been riding most of my life, and I'm not about to limit myself now just because you think I'm not good enough."

"You said that, not me," he replied, his tone maddeningly neutral as he stood. Picking up both our bowls and empty bottles, he carried them to the kitchen without another word.

I slumped back against the couch, my arms

crossed. I'd never met anyone so frustrating. Noah managed to provoke my most fiery reactions—positive and negative—and I didn't like it. Maintaining control had always worked well for me, much better than this constant whiplash of emotions. Just moments ago, I had barely resisted the urge to lean over and indulge in him for dessert. Now, I felt like the flame to crème brûlée, trying not to scorch something delicate and sweet.

Was there any topic safe to approach?

Noah returned, two beers in hand, and passed me one as he sat back down. "So tell me," he said, his eyes glinting with humor, "how many more of those beauties do you plan to buy?"

I grinned. "I don't. I want to have babies." Realizing how that sounded, I quickly added, "Foals."

He laughed, the deep sound warming me in ways I wished it wouldn't. "I knew what you meant. So you want to start up a Friesian stud?"

"A small one. Eventually, I'd like to get another mare. I wouldn't want Freya in foal all the time. That's just cruel."

To my surprise, once Noah got over his initial shock at my plans, we actually managed a civilized conversation. His ideas for the stables were thoughtful and detailed, revealing a depth of knowledge I admired. "If I had the money to build anything," he said with a wistful smile, "that's what it'd be like."

"Maybe you should save the design, and we could look into something a bit different for me," I suggested. It didn't seem fair to expect him to build his dream structure on my property, knowing it might have been what he'd envisioned for himself one day.

"Come on, Bailey, be real," he said, brushing off the thought.

Not wanting the conversation to veer into financial territory, I stood and grabbed his empty bottle. "Want another?"

"Thanks," he said, handing it to me with a small smile.

Two beers were usually my limit, but tonight, they went down easily. I wasn't ready for this relaxed mood to end, even if it was dangerous territory.

Settling back onto the couch, I tucked one leg under me and angled my body toward him. "So, how does Trish fit in?"

Noah raised an eyebrow, amusement dancing in his eyes. "You went into the café, huh? She's been itching to meet you." He reached out, toying with the scalloped edge of my dress as he spoke. "She's my mum's cousin."

His hand brushed against my thigh, and his expression shifted. "How's your bruising?"

I barely had time to answer before he pushed the fabric of my dress up enough to reveal the still-tainted skin beneath. "It's still a bit sore," I admitted, grabbing his wrist when his fingers traced the outline of the bruise. "But I'll live. And I can assure you it extends higher than you need go."

Looking up through my lashes, I caught the way his gaze darkened. "Sometimes needs differ from wants," he said, his voice low and husky. "But I like to think they're both important."

The air between us thickened, and I held my breath, willing him to lean forward and claim my mouth as he had on other occasions.

"I don't think it's fair that you're the only one who remembers what happened after the pub," I teased, trying to break the tension.

His lips quirked into a half-smile. "That's what you get for drinking too much. How much do you remember?"

"Up to you suggesting I take a rain check," he admitted, his knuckles brushing against my cheek in a tender gesture that left me breathless. "I'd like to take you up on your offer, thanks."

My pulse quickened at his words, and I knew I was in trouble. This man could undo me with a single look, a simple sentence. It should have been enough of a warning to stay away, but I couldn't.

Slowly, I took his beer from his hand and placed it alongside mine on the coffee table. Leaning back into the cushions, I met his gaze, my heart pounding. Did I dare kiss him?

The space between us was charged, the question hanging in the air unspoken. Whatever happened next, I knew it was a line I couldn't uncross—and I wasn't sure I wanted to.

CHAPTER 16

Noah

I was starting to think I'd made a mistake volunteering to stay the night with Bailey. The attraction I felt toward her wasn't in question. Hell, anyone would be drawn to her. Even my grandfather couldn't hide how smitten he was with her.

But physical desire was a double-edged sword. It muddled my judgment, made me act out in ways I only regretted later. She didn't deserve that—not when she'd been kinder to Jack than anyone else would've been under the same circumstances. It'd been a long time since I'd seen Jack so happy. I hadn't realized how much the money issues had weighed on him, but now that burden was gone, and he was almost as lively as when Maggie was around.

The horses, and Bailey's passion for them, only fed the guilt I carried over Maggie's death. People I loved always seemed to get hurt. I couldn't let Bailey become one of them.

She met my gaze, and in that moment—when she took the beer from my hand and placed it on the coffee table—I remembered why I'd come. Seducing her wasn't part of the plan. But the longer I was with her, the harder she was to resist, especially when she looked up at me through her lashes like she was now.

"You never told me what you're going to do about the situation with your mum," I said, shifting in my seat, hoping to steer the conversation somewhere safer. The rain check I'd asked for earlier hovered between us, and I wasn't ready to face it yet.

Bailey sighed. "Even if I contact her, I don't know if I could trust her again. It's hard to invest in someone who's turned on you so dramatically. Surely you understand that."

Her words hit their mark, though I wasn't about to let her know it. "So you know where she is then?"

"I have a fair idea. That is, if my grandfather's still

alive. You'd think someone would've told me if he'd died."

"Who, your mum?" The words were out before I could stop them, and the look on her face was like I'd slapped her. "I'm sorry, Bailey. That wasn't fair."

She shrugged, but it was all for show. I recognized the expression; I'd seen it often enough in the mirror.

Bailey stifled a yawn, and I took the hint. "You're tired. I should let you go to bed."

She didn't argue, and I couldn't help but think it was an escape tactic, a way to avoid the growing tension between us. I'd been hoping for a different reaction—anything but the chill she sent my way.

"The spare room's made up if you'd prefer it to the couch," she said as she stood.

"The couch is fine, that is, if you don't mind me sleeping on it."

She shrugged again. "Why would I?" Her tone was colder than a blizzard.

"Goodnight."

"Night."

I half-expected her to offer a hug or at least a glance back, but she didn't. She walked upstairs, leaving me feeling like a fool for hoping.

Pulling my tee shirt over my head, I didn't bother

taking off my jeans. It wouldn't be the first time I'd slept in them, though it was usually after one too many beers at the pub. Stretching out on the sleeping bag, I stared up at the ceiling and let my mind wander.

What if Bailey had come into my life before Charlotte? How different would things have been? Maggie had told me from the beginning that Charlotte wasn't right for me. "She doesn't like to work, yet she wants the life of an heiress," she'd said. Maggie had been right, of course. She always was.

Pity she wasn't around to comment on Bailey. Not that I needed her here to tell me Bailey was different. Bailey reminded me so much of Maggie that it scared me. I hadn't been there for Maggie when she needed me most, and nothing would convince me it wouldn't end the same way with Bailey.

A soft whimper interrupted my thoughts. The sound was faint but unmistakable, and it came from upstairs. Was Bailey crying?

I hesitated. What should I do? Go up and see if she wanted company, or leave her to cry alone? Either way, I'd regret it, but knowing I was the reason for her tears was worse than any outcome.

I climbed the stairs, careful to avoid the creaky

ones. If the crying stopped before I reached her door, I'd turn around and leave her be. But it didn't. It grew louder, pulling me toward the end of the hallway. A cold sensation rushed through me, like ice water in my veins. The sound wasn't coming from Bailey's room but from the one at the end of the hall.

Bailey stepped into her doorway, her expression a mix of confusion and concern. "You hear it too?" she whispered. Her eyes flicked over me, probably wondering why I was standing in the hall shirtless.

"I thought it was you," I admitted. My voice sounded as shaken as I felt. "What do you usually do now?"

The crying stopped abruptly.

Bailey held out her hand. Without hesitation, I took it, and together we walked to the end of the corridor. The door was ajar. That part was unpredictable. Usually, she said, she heard it slam. But tonight, it hung open, daring us to step inside.

"This is the room where the door slams even when the windows are closed, and the crying always comes from in here."

Bailey

Noah nodded but didn't speak, his silence heavy with skepticism.

I reached inside and flicked on the light. The air, sharp and icy only moments ago, warmed slightly. "I think she's scared of the dark, so I leave the light on."

"All night?" His tone was unreadable, hovering somewhere between curiosity and incredulity.

I glanced up at him, arching an eyebrow. "I was scared of the dark when I was a little girl, and I can't bear the thought of my little ghost girl going through that."

A smirk tugged at the corner of his mouth. "Your little ghost girl, huh?"

"Well, yeah. I bought the house, so I get the ghost too." My eyebrow arched higher, daring him to challenge me.

Instead, he tipped his head down, his lips finding mine. The kiss was soft at first, his warmth spreading through me, but then I cupped his cheek and deepened it, letting myself drown in the moment. Too soon, I pulled away, regret settling in almost immediately. "I don't feel right about staying in here."

Noah blinked as though waking from a trance, his eyes softer, more vulnerable. For a fleeting moment, I thought I saw tears glistening there, but I didn't dare ask. Maybe he felt the same tenderness I did, or maybe he was haunted by something entirely his own.

"You're right," he said quietly. "Do you leave the door open or closed?"

"Open," I replied, stepping back. Despite the odd occurrences, the presence in my house wasn't malicious. She didn't frighten me, not like the stories I'd read online of violent hauntings. No, this felt different—sad, even.

We walked back to my bedroom, still holding hands. His warmth lingered in my palm, grounding me in a way I hadn't felt since my mom was around When we reached my door, I hesitated. "Do you want to stay with me tonight?" My voice wavered, betraying my nerves.

He looked down at our intertwined hands before meeting my gaze. "Do you think I'd be able to sleep otherwise?"

His answer sent a shiver of relief through me. Noah wasn't just beautiful on the outside; moments like this reminded me there was depth beneath his rough edges.

Without waiting for an invitation, he walked around to the side of the bed he'd slept on after that night at the pub. He pulled back the sheets and laid down like it was the most natural thing in the world.

"You're sleeping in your jeans—really?" I was unable to hide my amusement.

"Well, I—"

"Are you planning on building a pillow wall down the center of the bed? Because if so, the scatter cushions are on the chaise over there." I pointed to the corner of the room.

Noah stood, his movements deliberate, and turned to face me. His eyes met mine, steady and intense. Then, without a word, he undid the button of his jeans and slid the zipper down. My breath caught, and I tried not to look, but my traitorous eyes followed his movements.

He parted the fabric slightly, his gaze dipping down before flicking back up to mine. Was he teasing me? If so, it was working.

"Didn't anyone ever teach you it's rude to stare?" he teased.

I shrugged. "I appreciate beauty in all its forms. If you were a painting, I wouldn't look away just because it was considered bad manners."

"But I'm not a painting."

"You could be. Let me paint you, and I'll even let you wear the jeans." There was something intoxicating about a man dressed down to the point Noah had reached—exposed enough to spark curiosity, yet covered just enough to leave me wanting more.

I didn't waste time walking around the bed. Instead, I crawled across it on all fours until I knelt in front of him. My hands found his shoulders, tracing firm, slow lines down his chest. His skin was warm under my touch, his muscles taut beneath the rough pads of my fingers.

Noah's hands found my waist, pulling me flush against him. One hand slid into my hair, tilting my head up as he lowered his mouth to mine. His kiss was searing, his tongue tangling with mine as he pressed me closer. My body responded instinctively, craving more, needing more.

But then, he pulled back. "I can't do this, Bailey," he said, his voice hoarse. His hands loosened their hold but didn't let me go entirely.

"What's not right? You don't want me?" I hated how small my voice sounded, but I couldn't stop the words from spilling out.

Noah stepped away, running a hand through his hair and laughing bitterly. "Oh, Bailey, you have no idea what you do to me. You tie me up in knots—so many mixed emotions I feel like I'm going to explode, and not always in a good way. You frustrate me like no other woman ever has."

He turned his back to me, staring out the window. The tension in his shoulders was palpable, a silent battle raging within him.

I sat back on my heels, my hands resting on my thighs. His words stung more than I wanted to admit, cutting deeper than they should have. "I'm sorry, Noah," I whispered, my voice barely audible.

He turned, his eyes locking onto mine. In two strides, he was back at the bed, his hands cradling my face. He kissed me hard, his lips speaking the words his voice couldn't.

My head spun. His actions were a whirlwind of contradictions, pulling me closer one moment and pushing me away the next. "You're like an addiction I don't want, but can't kick either," he murmured against my lips.

I stiffened, his words hitting me like a slap. There it was—raw and unfiltered. I was something he didn't want but couldn't let go of.

I swallowed hard, pushing back the lump in my throat. "Then I'll make it easy for you—go home, Noah."

CHAPTER 17

Bailey

"I didn't mean it like that. Come on, Bailey, please."

I didn't want to hear another word. "I'm tired, Noah. I just want to go to sleep." My voice sounded steadier than I felt. Turning away, I eased myself from his touch, my heart heavy with the ache of disappointment.

I moved to my side of the bed, the place I always slept when I was alone. Slipping beneath the covers, I lay facing the doorway, my eyes stinging as tears finally began to gather. I was glad they had waited until now to fall. At least he couldn't see them.

"Do you want me to sleep on the couch?" His voice, so hollow and uncertain now, was a far cry from the heated edge it had carried earlier.

"Sleep where you like." My words came out clipped, impatient. I didn't care how it sounded.

The room fell silent except for the soft rustle of fabric. The sound of denim being tugged from his body reached my ears, and I bit my lip to stop myself from turning to look. Moments later, the bed dipped, and cool air rushed over my back as he slid in beside me.

How easy it would have been if he'd just done this from the start—if he'd let himself be vulnerable, stripped away the barriers between us. How different our night might have been. Perhaps, though, this was for the best. I shouldn't want him if he didn't feel the same for me. And yet, no matter how hard I tried to convince myself, I couldn't stop wanting him.

Hot tears slid down my cheeks, soaking into the pillow beneath me. My chest ached, heavy with the weight of unspoken emotions. Why did life have to be so cruel? Why couldn't I have just one person I cared about feel the same way for me?

I was feeling sorry for myself, I knew that. Somewhere deep down, I understood I had more than some people ever would—a roof over my head, a life I could call my own. But that didn't make it hurt any less.

The silence stretched between us, thick and suffocating. I kept my breathing slow, even as my tears continued to fall. I didn't want him to know how much his words—or lack of them—had affected me.

I indulged the low moment, letting myself sink into the sadness. Maybe I needed to feel it, to let it wash over me until there was nothing left.

Eventually, sleep found me, pulling me under with its heavy, numbing embrace.

Light streamed through the window, heating the room and coaxing me into consciousness. I tried to move but found myself tangled in a mess of bed linen—and Noah. His body pressed against mine, warm and solid, his arms wrapped so tightly around me that escape without waking him was impossible.

I closed my eyes again, letting myself pretend, just for a moment, that everything between us was perfect. That he hadn't made his feelings—or lack thereof—painfully clear last night.

There was no going back now, no undoing what he'd said. Maybe it was for the best. With the barn nearing completion, the hen's night, and the wedding coming up, I had enough to keep me busy. Too busy to waste time wondering if Noah might change his mind about me.

Noah stirred behind me, stretching lazily as his hand ran the length of my body. He groaned into my hair, the sound deep and unguarded, before his palm slid upward, stopping to cup my breast. A sharp intake of breath escaped him as he pressed his unmistakable growing desire against me.

I squeezed my eyes shut, trying to ignore the rush of heat his touch sent through me. Even if he didn't want me, my body betrayed me, responding to him far more than I wanted it to.

A sudden knock at the front door shattered the moment. Noah jerked against me, his reaction so abrupt I felt the jolt through his entire body.

"Shit, sorry," he muttered, pulling his hand from under my shirt and releasing me.

I didn't bother acknowledging his apology—or offering a morning greeting. Without a word, I flicked the blankets off, climbed out of bed, and made my way to the door.

"Hey, Cooper," I said, stepping aside to let him in. "Come in. I was just about to make coffee. You want one?"

"Sure," Cooper said, his brows lifting as his gaze flicked over my pajamas. "Did I wake you?"

"Ah, sort of. Late night." I shrugged.

Noah walked into the kitchen as I pulled the milk from the fridge. "Hey, Cooper. Here, thought you might want this," he said, holding out my dressing gown.

I turned to face him, placing my hands on my hips. "Really? Sorry, Cooper, does my outfit offend you?"

Cooper flushed, looking more uncomfortable by the second. "Nah, I'm good," he said, grinning awkwardly. The grin vanished when Noah shot him a glare.

Not wanting to make Cooper feel any worse, I snatched the robe from Noah's hand and threw it over my shoulders without bothering to tie it. "Happy?" I snapped.

I handed Cooper his coffee before making one for Noah, who had taken a seat at the table beside him. Tempted to curtsy as I set Noah's mug down, I thought better of it and returned to the kitchen to make my own.

The tension in the room was thick, the silence awkward and oppressive. The hum of the coffee machine was the only saving grace, a distraction from the weight of unspoken words.

"So," Cooper said once the machine quieted. "Good night last night?" His grin returned, laced with mischief.

"Don't even go there, Cooper," Noah barked, his tone sharp enough to make Cooper's smile fade instantly.

"I was wondering if you could come up to the barn sometime today," Cooper said, wisely steering the conversation toward work. "I wanted to ask your advice on something, if that's okay."

I nodded, grateful for the shift. In truth, I couldn't wait for them to leave so I could get on with my day. Waking up next to Noah, knowing he'd stayed out of obligation, had done little to improve my mood.

There was only one thing I could think of to turn it around, saddling up Freya and disappearing for a few hours.

But first, I had something else to do. For years, I'd put off contacting my mother, fearing her rejection. If I was enough as I was—just Bailey—then she'd welcome a reunion. I didn't want the news of a wedding or a baby someday to cloud her reaction. That wasn't too much to hope for, was it?

Now I just had to decide if I trusted the email address I had for her, old as it was, or if I should try a letter instead. As the boys chatted about the barn, I started planning what I might write.

"Earth to Bailey," Cooper said, breaking my thoughts.

"Sorry, what?" I asked, blinked away my daydream to focus on the conversation Cooper was trying to have with me.

"I wanted to know if you guys are planning a stripper for the hen's night."

I frowned, crossing my arms. "What, you think just because I'm the new girl on the block, I'm going to spill the beans? Sorry, but my girl's privacy comes first."

I wasn't about to give them any answers, but I couldn't resist throwing the question back at him.

"You can keep your secrets, but come on, Bailey, it's a buck's party—what do you expect?" Cooper leaned back against the counter with a cheeky grin.

"To be honest, nothing less," I said with a shrug. "Strippers don't do much for me personally, and if I had a boyfriend who went to an event where one was performing, I wouldn't be jealous. Marriage is supposed to be a celebration of two people. Sharing it with friends is only half the fun. People who think of it as their *last night of freedom* probably shouldn't be getting married in the first place."

Cooper slapped Noah on the back. "See, mate? You're made for each other. Who else looks at it that way? She just summed you up perfectly."

Noah didn't laugh. He didn't even crack a smile. Instead, he drained the last of his coffee and stood, holding his hand out for Cooper's mug. "You finished?"

"Yeah, thanks," Cooper said, handing it over.

They both stood at the same time, and I couldn't help but feel relieved.

"Thanks for the coffee. I'll see you later," Cooper said, heading for the door.

Noah rinsed the mugs and stacked them in the dishwasher. For someone who'd been in such a rush to leave, he suddenly didn't seem in much of a hurry.

"Look, Bailey, about last night—"

"You know what, Noah? Just don't. Okay?"

He nodded once, his expression unreadable, and disappeared into the lounge room. When he came back, his sleeping bag was slung over one shoulder. "See you 'round."

"See you," I said, the words barely audible over the sound of the door closing behind him.

I stood there for a long time, staring at the empty

space where he'd been. How had the night gone so wrong when it had started out so fun?

My laptop sat on the table, untouched since the day before. Sitting down, I stared at the screen for a few minutes before opening it. The worst thing that could happen was that my mother wouldn't reply. It wasn't like she could slam the door in my face or hang up on me. For all I knew, she might just hit delete.

Straight to the point, no pressure—that's what I told myself. All she needed to know was that I'd moved and would like to have contact with her. That was it. Simple.

Before I could overthink it, I pressed send, shutting the laptop down immediately afterward. No going back now.

I went upstairs to change. Freya would be a good distraction. I needed one.

By the time I returned, saddled Freya, and rode out, the morning had given way to a warm, golden afternoon. The forest enveloped us in dappled light, the breeze lifting my hair and cooling my skin. It had been a while since I'd taken the time to appreciate nature like this. Usually, I wore long sleeves when riding, but today the heat had convinced me otherwise.

When I finally made my way back to the farm, the barn caught my eye. I hadn't checked on its progress in weeks. Now seemed as good a time as any, though I couldn't stay long. Freya had worked hard, and it wasn't fair to leave her tied up, even in the shade.

As I walked toward the open barn door, raised voices stopped me in my tracks.

"For Christ's sake, Noah, you have to tell her. It's her house—she has a right to know," Cooper said, his frustration evident.

I froze. They were talking about me.

"Know what?" I interrupted as I stepped around the corner.

Cooper glanced at me, then back at Noah, who looked like he'd rather be anywhere else.

"Nothing," Noah said, his jaw tightening.

Cooper swatted the air in Noah's direction, muttering, "For fuck's sake, man," before grabbing a screwdriver from his toolbox and stomping up the stairs two at a time.

"What's going on, Noah?" I crossed my arms over my chest.

He didn't look at me. "I thought you didn't want to hear it, Bailey. Go hang out with Cooper. Let him give you a tour of your precious barn."

His words stung, even if I didn't entirely understand why. I'd come to check on the barn, but the tension between them bothered me. I didn't want to be the reason for their argument—especially when I had no idea what it was about.

"Hey, Cooper," I said as I climbed the stairs. "How's it going?"

"Getting there," he said, not bothering to stop working as he usually would have.

"How long until the first retreat?"

"The weekend after the wedding, I'm afraid. Do you think we'll make it?" I asked, glancing around at the unfinished space.

Cooper shrugged. "We've got a lot to do, but I think we'll pull it off. Somehow."

I nodded, trying to focus on his words instead of the unease curling in my stomach. Whatever Noah and Cooper had been arguing about, I couldn't shake the feeling it was something I wasn't going to like.

"Yeah, we'll make it, with days to spare." Cooper turned his head toward me and flashed one of his killer smiles.

I couldn't help but think, yet again, that it would've been so much easier if I'd developed feelings for Cooper instead. But life didn't work that way.

"Have you had many calls?" he tilted his head slightly to look at me as he continued to work.

I didn't want to think about the guest issue right now. Maybe I'd been overly ambitious, trying to pull off the first retreat so soon after the renovations were finished, with barely any advertising. Still, if even a small group booked, I'd be satisfied to work out the kinks for the future.

"Not so far," I admitted, "but I don't want to flog the advertising until we're closer to the finish line here."

Cooper nodded. "Makes sense."

"Can I get you a coffee?" I offered, hoping to break the train of thought I didn't want to dwell on.

"You're a gem, you know that. I'll be down in a few minutes."

Noah was still drilling, so I decided to wait until he was done before approaching him. In the meantime, I got started on Cooper's coffee.

"I can get you a crate to sit on if you'd be more comfortable." Cooper offered when I handed him the cup.

"No thanks," I replied, shaking my head. "I've been sitting all morning. Standing will do me some good."

Noah wandered over to join us. He didn't meet

my eyes when he took his cup, but at least he spoke this time. "Cooper was wondering if you could show him how to order online. He hasn't gotten his best friend a wedding gift yet."

"Thanks, mate. And you have?" Cooper shot back.

"Yes, as a matter of fact. I bought it the other day."

Cooper shook his head. "Only because your mother chose it for you. What'd you end up getting them, anyway?"

"Ahh, you'll have to wait and see."

The earlier tension between them seemed to have dissipated, which was a relief.

"What about you, Bailey? You got yours yet?" Cooper turned his attention on me.

I nodded, hoping he wouldn't press for details—at least not with Noah in the mood he seemed to be in.

"Well, don't hold out on me. Spill."

Noah's gaze landed on me, and I felt my stomach tighten.

"I opted for a couple of vouchers," I said with a shrug, trying to play it off like it was no big deal.

"Oh yeah? Good idea. Where from?" Cooper seemed genuinely curious.

I knew he was only being polite by including me in the conversation, but I wished he'd let it drop.

"Angel Cove Country Club."

"*What the*—but you barely know them. A salad bowl would've been sufficient," Noah blurted out before Cooper even had a chance to react.

I opened my mouth to respond, but no words came. The way Noah was glaring at me made it feel like I'd committed some heinous crime.

"Well fuck, you've just blown it for the rest of us." Cooper tried to lighten the moment with a chuckle. "Noah, come on, mate. Give it a rest," he added when Noah's expression didn't change.

Noah's voice sharpened. "Even you have to admit it's excessive. Not to mention how embarrassed they'll be when they open it."

"I'm not getting involved in this," Cooper said, raising his hands in surrender. "Honestly, man, you need to get a grip and stop acting like an asshole. Sorry, Bailey." He turned and retreated to the second floor.

I crossed my arms, looking directly at Noah. "What is your problem?"

"In the country, we keep things simple. Throwing money around isn't taken kindly when we work so bloody hard to earn it. People are wary of extravagant gifts. They feel obliged to give equal in return."

"I don't buy a gift thinking about what they might get me," I said evenly. "I buy it because I want to brighten someone's day."

Noah shook his head. "You're too much." Picking up his keys, he started toward the door.

"What's that supposed to mean?" I demanded.

Noah stopped but didn't turn to face me. "It means you have too much money, and I don't want to be part of a world that's so far out of my league. You're generous, and now that I know you, I trust you don't have an ulterior motive where Jack is concerned. But the money thing? It's a problem for me."

"So what if I donated it all to charity?" I shot back, desperate to understand.

"Then I'd say you were a bloody fool."

"But you wouldn't change your mind about us?" I pressed, needing to hear him say it.

"No, I wouldn't."

He turned to leave again, but I wasn't letting him have the last word.

"My money didn't seem to bother you yesterday when you were asking for a ticket to my bed."

Noah stopped in his tracks and slowly turned back to face me. "I had nothing to lose, Bailey. So yes, I would've enjoyed having sex with you. But it was a mistake. I knew that soon after I said it. It'll never work —especially when you broadcast how much I have to gain by being with you. I don't want to be some rich city chick's pawn, no matter how much I care about you. I've been the talk of the town enough already, and I don't intend on offering them the pleasure again."

He walked out, leaving me standing there, stunned and furious, my emotions a tangled mess I couldn't begin to unravel.

Noah's words cut deep, each syllable like a jagged edge tearing at me. I prided myself on keeping my emotions in check, but the tears came anyway, sliding down my cheeks in hot, silent streaks. Hearing the thud of Cooper's boots on the steps, I quickly turned my back, angling my face away. The last thing I wanted was for him to see how much Noah's rejection had gutted me.

But Cooper wasn't the type to let things slide. He stopped right in front of me, his presence steady and grounding. With a gentleness that caught me off guard, he brushed a few stray strands of hair from my face.

"Are you alright?" His voice was low and full of concern.

I nodded quickly, unable to trust my voice. My bottom lip trembled, and I felt seconds away from dissolving into a full-blown sobbing mess.

Without a word, Cooper pulled me into his arms. His embrace was warm and firm, and he smoothed my hair in a way that reminded me of how my mom used to comfort me when I was a child.

"I'm sorry you've had to deal with Noah like this," he murmured, his voice a soothing balm against the sting of Noah's words. "You wouldn't believe me if I told you he used to be the life of the party. Contagious as the plague, everyone's best friend."

I let out a shaky breath, my tears still falling as I clung to him.

Cooper kissed the top of my head, then rested his cheek there instead. "He's had it rough. Honestly, the guy's been through hell. But that doesn't excuse the way he's treating you, especially without explaining himself."

There was no judgment in Cooper's hold, no complicated feelings weighing down the moment. Just pure kindness. He was my rock when everything else felt like it was falling apart.

"Thank you," I whispered as he finally released me.

Cooper stepped back, but only enough to lift his hand and gently wipe the remaining tears from my face with the back of his knuckles. His touch was soft, reassuring, and just what I needed.

"Have you met Trish yet?" He caught me off guard with the change in topic.

"Yeah," I replied, sniffing slightly. It seemed like an odd question, but I wasn't about to question it.

He cupped my cheek, his palm warm against my skin. "She'll tell anyone a story if they'll sit still long enough to listen. Just don't let her know I warned you," he added with a faint smirk.

Then, his expression turned more serious, and he leaned forward to press a soft kiss to my forehead.

"When two people are as right for each other as you and Noah," he said quietly, "it's a damn shame when the past gets in the way. Right now, the way he's acting, he doesn't deserve you. But deep down, he's a good guy. Trust me on that."

CHAPTER 18

Bailey

When I walked into the café, Trish was wiping down tables. She looked up and grinned. "Hello, Bailey. Lovely to see you again."

I returned her smile, feeling the warmth of her welcome. "After the dish Cal whipped up the other day, did you think I'd stay away for long?"

Trish laughed. "Yeah, well, he's quite the cook. So, what can I get for you today?"

It was well past lunchtime, and although I hadn't eaten all day, my eyes landed on a sinful-looking chocolate cake in the glass cabinet. I couldn't resist.

"Can I get a latte and a slice of that delicious looking chocolate cake, please?"

"Oh, it's delicious, all right," Trish said as she moved to prepare my order. "That cake's been flying out the door ever since Cal came back. Baking isn't my specialty, and I think everyone around here heaved a sigh of relief when he left the mines and returned to Bennett Springs. This place has started thriving again."

I smiled, leaning against the counter. "Speaking of business, I don't know if Jack's mentioned much about mine?"

Trish nodded. "Oh, yes. He updates me on Cooper's progress all the time. It's like a dream come true for him, seeing you bring some of Maggie's ideas to life."

"I want to include the town businesses as much as I can," I said, feeling a spark of excitement about my plan. "I thought I'd create a wall collage with business cards and menus so the guests can browse. If they're in town for a few days, they might enjoy some local shopping."

"What a wonderful idea." Trish beamed. "Jack always said you were a sweet heart. He was an excellent judge of character."

Her praise warmed me. Jack's opinion mattered

more to me than I liked to admit.

Trish leaned closer, her expression turning conspiratorial. "He's keen on setting you up with Noah, just so you know. Noah's a beautiful boy, but he carries too much guilt on his shoulders."

I nodded, thinking of Noah's aloofness. "I've noticed he doesn't go easy on himself."

"Well, it started when he was just fifteen," Trish said, her voice softening. "Stacey had her fall then. Poor Noah's been blaming himself ever since."

I frowned, confused. "Why would he blame himself for Stacey's accident?" I hoped she didn't think I was prying too much.

Trish sighed and looked down, her eyes misting. "They were close, even with nine years between them. When the boys were in upper high school, they went off to boarding school. Stacey missed Noah the most. Dan was older, more serious. But Noah—he was her buddy. She was so excited to see him after a term away. When he came through the door, she ran to greet him, called out his name, and tripped." Trish paused, swiping at a tear. "She fell down the stairs and didn't make it to the hospital."

The sorrow in her voice pierced my heart.

Trish pulled herself together, giving me a sad smile. "Sorry, love. You're right. There was no reason for him to feel guilty. But he came up with every *what if* in the book. It was a devastating time, as I'm sure you can imagine."

I nodded, speechless. Poor Noah. Losing Stacey must have torn his family apart.

"I'll bring your order over in a few minutes," Trish said, excusing herself as a couple walked in and took a seat nearby.

When Trish set down my coffee and a large slice of cake, I smiled up at her. "Thank you."

"Don't leave without meeting Cal," she added. "He'll be back soon."

"Of course. I'd like that," I replied, already considering how I might involve the café in catering for my retreat.

I took a bite of the cake, and my appetite returned with a vengeance. Cal's baking was incredible, far better than mine. If I wasn't careful, my guests might sneak into town for meals instead of staying on-site.

I was savoring the last bite when a younger, slightly fairer version of Noah slid into the chair opposite me.

"You must be Cal," I said, covering my mouth with my hand. I offered the other hand for him to shake, but instead, he turned it and kissed the back of it with a cheeky grin.

"Great to meet you," he said, his smile infectious.

"Likewise. If you keep cooking like this, I'm going to be rolling out the door soon. This cake is amazing."

Cal leaned back in his chair, still holding my hand. "I hear you're a pretty good cook yourself."

I laughed. "Jack exaggerates, but he's very sweet."

"Yeah, he's great," Cal said, his tone shifting. "Unlike that jerk of a cousin of mine. I assume you've met Noah? I'd steer clear of him if I were you. He's got all kinds of diseases—you never know what you might catch."

His words made my blood boil. I yanked my hand back, glaring at him. "Good thing women can form their own opinions these days, isn't it?"

Cal's grin widened. "Yep, she's a keeper, mate," he called out, looking over my shoulder.

I turned to see Noah standing there, his expression unreadable.

"Hi," I said, unsure how to navigate this moment.

"Hi," Noah replied, his tone curt.

"Thanks for that, mate," Noah said to Cal, his sarcasm biting. "I'm guessing this is your strategy? Tear down the competition so you look like the best option?"

Cal leaned forward, reclaiming my hand. "If my good looks don't do the trick, my cooking seals the deal."

Noah laughed.

It was a pleasant change to see Noah relaxed and carefree. It didn't happen often enough, from what I'd seen.

"Go back to work, or hit on another woman. I need to talk to this one." Noah shoved his hands into the pockets of his jeans, his unease as obvious as if he'd announced it.

"Okay, I can take a hint." Cal squeezed my hand one last time before letting go. "See you soon, gorgeous."

I couldn't help but smile. Cal was young, cocky, and utterly shameless. I tried to imagine Noah being like that at his age but came up empty. Somehow, I doubted it.

"Do you mind?" Noah gestured to the chair Cal had vacated, his voice tight.

"Of course not." I wished he wouldn't be so formal. Fun Noah was so much easier to deal with. "What's up?"

He pulled his hands from his pockets and sat down, his expression somewhere between determined and unsure. "We had fun last night, didn't we?"

I waited for him to elaborate, but when he didn't, I sighed. "What part of it was fun for you? Because from where I'm sitting, the constant push-pull is exhausting." I bit my tongue before saying anything harsher. I'd seen glimpses of the man Noah could be, but the effort it took to get there felt like too much. Sure, he'd been through a lot, but unless he took a double dose of relaxants, I couldn't see myself going out of my way to spend more time with him.

"Look, Bailey." He leaned forward, taking my hand in his. The gesture felt sincere, unlike Cal's earlier theatrics. "Since you arrived, I've been uptight. Jack never mentioned the financial problems he was having, and it all came as a shock. Then you rocked up, and we were expecting Bailey to be a guy. Instead, this sexy little thing slid out of a truck most of us could only dream about owning."

I raised an eyebrow, but he pushed on. "The excuses could go on for hours, but what they all boil down to is me behaving like a jerk. And I'm sorry."

It seemed like every time we talked, he ended up apologizing. There was no simple solution, except maybe avoiding each other altogether. "I don't expect to get along with or even like everyone I meet, Noah. You don't need to keep apologizing to me. But I do think we should reconsider how much time we spend together if it's going to keep ending like this."

His hand tightened on mine as his gaze locked onto me. "I was actually hoping you'd agree to spend more time with me. Maybe go out. See where this goes." His voice softened. "But we don't have to."

A flush crept up his neck, and I could've kicked myself for speaking too soon. I groaned. "This is such a mess."

To my surprise, Noah laughed. The sound was warm and genuine, catching me off guard. "Okay, fine. When were you thinking?"

"How about tomorrow night?"

"Before I agree, I need to lay a few truths on the table. Whether you like them or not." I straightened my shoulders, meeting his gaze. "I'm ridiculously wealthy. And while money doesn't buy happiness, it does make life easier most of the time. I enjoy spending money on my friends, not because I'm trying to buy their friendship but because their happiness makes me happy. If the rich thing is an issue for you, this won't work."

His expression didn't change. "Is that all?"

"No." I leaned in, keeping my voice low. "I don't

want you to keep stopping at first base. Do you know how frustrating that is?"

Noah tipped his head back and laughed, full-bodied and unapologetic. "Do you know what's frustrating? That you're telling me this in the middle of my cousin's café where there's absolutely nothing I can do about it."

I tilted my head, pretending to consider his words. Should I let him set the pace or make an offer of my own? After a moment's thought, I decided against it. "I should get going. I have a lot of work to do this afternoon."

"I'm just picking up dinner for Jack," Noah said, rubbing his thumb over the back of my hand in soft strokes. "Trish cooks him a feast once a week, ever since Maggie passed."

The tenderness in his touch sent an unexpected warmth through me. "Shall we?" He gestured to suggest we leave.

I nodded, and we walked to the counter together.

I paid for my order and turned to Trish with a smile. "Thanks. Delicious as always. I'll see you next time." Then I turned to Noah, throwing him a playful wink. "See you soon." And with that, I left.

As soon as I walked into the kitchen, the red light on the answering machine caught my eye, blinking like a little beacon of hope. Was it ridiculous to get excited about a message? Maybe, but I didn't care. I pressed the play button, holding my breath.

"Hi, Bailey. I'm interested in the retreat you're hosting in a few weeks and would like to book for me and a friend. My name's Sarah, and I look forward to hearing from you soon."

She rattled off a phone number, but without a pen in hand, I missed it.

I squealed, the sound breaking the quiet of the kitchen. My first inquiry. It was the best message I could have hoped for.

Before I could celebrate further, Noah burst through the door without knocking. "Are you all right?" he looked concerned as he rushed toward me.

"More than all right." I pointed to the answering machine, practically bouncing on my toes. "I got a message, about the retreat."

His lips quirked into a grin. "That's great news." Then, with a playful edge, he added, "I'm not stalking you. You never answered me about going out tomorrow night."

"Oh, right. Sorry." I walked to the fridge and pulled out a beer. "You want one?"

"Sure, thanks." He shrugged, taking the bottle from me, his fingers brushing mine briefly.

"Do you want to sit?" I gestured toward the couch. My nerves were still buzzing from the message, and honestly, Noah was a good distraction.

"Yeah, okay."

I joined him on the larger of the two couches, trying to find a topic that wouldn't dampen my excitement. "So, how's Jack?" I leant back against the cushions. His grandfather was always a safe subject.

"Good," Noah said, his face softening. "He loves it when Trish makes a fuss over him. She's a top lady."

"She really is. And Cal—he's a character," I said with a chuckle. "I was thinking about asking them if they'd cater the last meal for the retreat. I'd pay them, of course. It'd be a nice way to promote local businesses."

"That's a great idea," Noah said, taking a swig of his beer.

"Oh, and by the way, I will go out with you tomorrow night."

His smile spread wide. "An even better idea."

The way he smiled—relaxed, genuine—made my insides clench. That yearning for him never seemed to fade. Before I could second-guess myself, I leaned forward and kissed him.

His free hand came up to cup the back of my neck, pulling me closer as he responded to my kiss with a hunger that matched my own. When he leaned forward to set his beer on the table, I did the same, freeing my hands.

I straddled him as he leaned back into the couch, his hands sliding over my hips, anchoring me to him. His lips left mine to trail along my jaw and down my neck, sending shivers through me. I gripped the hem of his T-shirt, tugging it upward. He got the hint, lifting his arms so I could pull it over his head.

In turn, his fingers found the clasp of my bra, undoing it with ease. His hands replaced the fabric, cupping me firmly as his mouth moved to taste my skin. I gasped, arching into his touch.

Then came a knock at the door.

We froze, his lips still on my collarbone.

"Do you want me to get it?" His voice was low and rough.

"If you don't mind," I whispered, sinking back into the couch and pulling a cushion in front of me. Whoever was at the door could take the hint when they saw Noah shirtless.

"Oh, Noah," a familiar voice said as the door opened. "I didn't realize you were here. I called in to have a coffee with Bailey."

Tracy.

"Mom, you have lousy timing, you know that?" Noah groaned, stepping aside to let her in.

Peeking over the back of the couch, I caught the look of shock on her face as she registered Noah's lack of a shirt. It quickly turned to delight.

"Oh, I'm sorry," she said, clearly not sorry at all. "I'll go see my dad and let you get back to it."

"Mom." Noah gasped.

Tracy left, and Noah turned back to me, running a hand through his hair. "I'm sorry about that."

I grinned. "So, are you going to get back to it, or is the mood gone?"

He looked a little awkward, his hands tucked into his jeans pockets. "I'm not sure. Now that we've had time to think instead of just getting carried away, it changes things. I don't want to rush you."

"I don't feel rushed," I said, sitting up straighter. "How about you stop overthinking and come here?"

He hesitated for only a second before sitting next to me. Not giving him a chance to retreat, I climbed onto his lap again, cupping his face as I kissed him.

This time, there was no interruption.

The heat between us had been building for weeks, like kindling waiting for a spark. And now, in the quiet of the room with nothing but the sound of our ragged breaths, it finally caught fire.

Noah's touch was demanding, insistent, like he'd been starving for me, and I was just as desperate for him. His hands were everywhere, tracing paths along my skin that made me shiver and arch against him, silently pleading for more. His mouth moved over me, tasting and teasing, leaving a trail of fire in its wake.

"Bailey," he murmured, my name a growl that sent a jolt of need straight through me.

I tangled my fingers in his hair, pulling him closer as his lips claimed mine. His stubble grazed my neck when he moved lower, the roughness only heightening the sensations as I tilted my head back, giving him access.

I couldn't get enough. The feel of him, the way his body pressed against mine, solid and strong—it was everything I hadn't let myself admit I wanted.

He looked up at me then, his eyes dark with desire and something deeper, something that made my chest tighten. "You're beautiful like this," he said, his voice rough and low. "I could watch you for hours."

I didn't doubt it. The way he watched me, like he

wanted to memorize every reaction, every soft sound I made—it was almost too much.

Almost.

He guided me down, his touch a mix of tenderness and urgency, and when he kissed me again, it was slower, deeper, like he wanted to savor every second. I gasped as his hands roamed lower, and he smiled against my lips, clearly pleased with my reaction.

"Noah..." My voice came out in a breathless whisper, his name carrying every ounce of longing I felt.

"Feel me inside you, baby," his lips brushing my ear, as he picked up the rhythm. Hard and fast, but not enough to hurt me. The way he moved, the way he touched me, made me feel like I was the only thing in the world that mattered.

He brought me to the edge and over it, again and again, each time holding me close, his eyes never leaving mine. It was intimate in a way I hadn't expected, a way that left me completely undone.

"You feel incredible," he murmured, his voice thick with need. His words, his touch, the way he looked at me—it was overwhelming, and I gave myself over to it, to him.

Time blurred. Each time he pulled me back to

him, his hunger for me was insatiable, and I couldn't resist the pull of him. His hands, his mouth, the warmth of his body against mine—it all ignited parts of me I hadn't realized were starving for contact.

By the time we collapsed together, tangled on the rug like we'd always belonged there, I'd lost track of how many times he'd taken me, how many times we'd given in to the need that had simmered between us for so long.

He wrapped his arms around me, his breathing still uneven as he pressed a kiss to my forehead. "You okay?"

I laughed softly, exhausted but sated in a way I'd never been before. "Better than okay."

He smiled, his eyes softening as he brushed a strand of hair from my face. "Good."

And as I lay there in his arms, our bodies still tangled together, I realized that this—this warmth, this connection—was exactly where I was meant to be.

CHAPTER 19

Bailey

The outdoor furniture arrived late in the afternoon. I let out a relieved sigh as the guys unloaded and carried it to the back entertaining area. Some potted color would have been nice, but I wasn't much of a gardener. Besides, there wasn't time. I'd have to organize some arrangements from the local florist—if there was one.

Between those and the fairy lights, the area was going to look stunning.

"It's looking great, sweetheart." Jack's voice

pulled me out of my thoughts, and I turned to see him grinning.

"Thanks. With Sophie's hen's night on the weekend, I was a little concerned I'd have to offer her guests a cushion to sit on."

"Change the theme. It's acceptable in other parts of the world. Why not here? Besides, country girls are used to sitting on the floor."

"Yes, but not all of them are country girls, from what I'm told." I shot him a sidelong glance. Meeting Charlotte wasn't high on my priority list, but it would be a lie to say I wasn't curious about her.

"We don't put her in the category of a guest." Jack knew exactly who I was talking about without me saying her name, and his disapproval was clear. "Don't let her get to you. And believe me, you'll be her target. Charlotte is threatened by anyone who might steal her spotlight."

I could already imagine Noah would still be skirting in her glow. I got the distinct impression Charlotte still saw him as one of her possessions, and any woman who dared stand in her way would face the consequences. It was a good thing I wasn't easily intimidated.

"Hey you, what's with the frown?" Noah's voice

rumbled from behind me as he tucked his arm around me, drawing me into his side.

The familiarity of his touch couldn't have come at a better time. And when he kissed me, just a soft peck on my lips, I couldn't help but tilt my face toward him and smile. "Just hoping I'm ready for this weekend. The only events I've organized have been large, stuffy corporate affairs—not these intimate, friendly ones. I want to get it right for Sophie."

Noah brushed a strand of hair from my face, his touch lingering. "You'll do great. Now, about tonight, do you still want to go out?"

The question made me uneasy. Was he ditching me on our first date? "Only if you're up to it."

"You aren't coming to the movie in the park, then?" Jack piped up.

"To be honest, I forgot it was on." Noah looked over at Jack, offering an apologetic smile.

"What's that?"

"Every year, the school hosts a picnic and movie night in the park as a fundraiser for their end-of-year graduation. Most of the town goes. It's become a bit of a tradition over the years," Jack explained.

I peeked up at Noah, trying to read his expression. "Sounds lovely. What a nice tradition." I wanted to say I'd love to go, but I wasn't sure how Noah would feel about such a public event.

"Would you prefer to do that?"

I shrugged. "I'll leave it up to you. It suits me, but I want you to be comfortable."

"It's for the kids, so I hate to be the one to break tradition. Do you need a lift, Jack?"

"Thanks, but your mum said she'd pick me up on the way." Jack seemed pleased with Noah's decision. "Anyway, I'll leave you to it. I'm going to head in for a shower and a rest before she gets here."

Jack seemed to tire more easily these days, but I put it down to the recent virus still lingering in his system.

Once Jack was inside, Noah swept me into his arms, pressing a kiss to my lips that stirred something deeper inside me. "I hope you're not disappointed about tonight. I'll make it up to you," he promised.

"I'm looking forward to it. The only reason I didn't jump at the idea was because I know everyone will be there, and I didn't know how you'd feel about us being seen together."

"Why wouldn't I want to be seen with you?" His brow furrowed slightly as he kissed my forehead.

"Town gossip—I don't know."

Noah lowered his lips to mine again, and I melted into the kiss, my heart racing. He kissed me back with equal intensity, pulling me closer.

As much as I wanted to savor the moment, there was still so much to do. Reluctantly, I pulled away. "If we're going to a picnic, I'd better start cooking."

"I'll take care of everything. All you need to do is get your gorgeous self into something a little more comfortable and be ready by six."

"I don't mind helping." Aside from returning Sarah's phone call and online shopping for more art supplies and equipment for the retreat, I hadn't done much else. The idea of a picnic with him seemed like the perfect way to escape the weight of everything on my mind.

"I know you don't, but I already had something prepared for tonight anyway, so it's all done."

I grinned. He'd planned a picnic for us. The closest I'd come to a picnic as an adult was eating a sandwich in the park during my lunch break the day I found out my ex was cheating on me with my father's personal assistant. I couldn't help but think this one would be a far better experience.

"Do you want to come in?" I had work to do, but he was a far more appealing distraction.

"Do you actually think I'll leave if we go inside

and close that door?" Noah raised an eyebrow. "I'm having enough trouble from out here."

"And who said that was a bad thing?" I whispered, leaning in to kiss him on the neck.

"Okay, I'm going now. You're dangerous, you know that?" His voice had taken on a low, teasing edge.

I pulled back, feigning disbelief.

Noah laughed and shook his head. "Don't give me that innocent look. I'll see you soon."

As he left, I made my way upstairs to search my wardrobe for the perfect outfit. It was a date, after all, but a picnic in the park didn't leave much room for dressing up. Plus, Noah's comment about dressing for comfort had stuck with me.

Jeans weren't exactly the most comfortable for a picnic, though. I pulled out a tank-style jumpsuit from my drawer, wondering if with flat shoes and my hair left down, it might pass as casual enough. The fabric didn't crumple, and the fitted pants would stop me from feeling cold, as nights in the park could often be.

I figured that by getting ready early, I could write up a list of things I still needed to do before Saturday.

"Hey, you look too good to take out," Noah's

voice greeted me as I came back downstairs. His compliments were coming easily these days. The change in him over the past few days had surprised me, but I wasn't complaining.

"Likewise."

"Shall we leave?" Noah shoved his hands into his pockets. I noticed he did this whenever he was nervous.

I nodded, falling into step beside him. Noah opened the passenger door of his truck for me, and I slid in. The inside of the truck was immaculate, a far cry from the usual clutter I associated with most guys. Boys and their toys, right? I wondered if this neat, orderly, well-maintained truck was an example of how he liked his life to be. I could relate to that. I appreciated the comfort of things being well-kept.

The car park was packed, so we had a bit of a walk ahead of us. But Noah was well-prepared, carrying the picnic basket—thanks to Trish—and a bag containing a blanket, two cushions, and a picnic rug.

"I have fold-out chairs if you'd prefer," Noah offered, but I declined. The thought of cuddling up with him on a picnic rug sounded far more appealing.

Noah carried the basket, but when I reached for the bag, he protested.

"Noah, it's not heavy, please," I said, slinging it over my shoulder. "See, easy."

"Independent little thing, aren't you?" He grinned and slid his free hand into mine.

So, he planned to announce we'd arrived together. The realization surprised me, but I couldn't say I was disappointed.

"So, did you respond to your answering machine message?"

"Yes. This morning. Sarah sounds lovely, and she booked for her friend, too. And, I had an online booking come through after you left last night," I said, feeling pleased with the progress I was making.

"Good job." Noah glanced down at me and smiled. "How many do you need to make a go of it?"

"I could run with three if I had to, but I think sharing the experience with a group of at least eight would be better. I think when I have the full eighteen, the women will group off, anyway."

"That's a good thing, I'm guessing. I mean, with so many different personalities, not everyone's going to get along."

"You're right. And uptight city chicks can be hard

work." I grinned, hoping Noah would see the humor in my comment and not take offense.

"Yeah. Like this black-haired bombshell that rocked into town a few months ago. One night with her, and I'm exhausted."

"Not too exhausted, I hope." I kept my voice low, my intention clear as I peered up at him through my lashes.

"Behave yourself, baby, at least for a few hours." Noah's voice carried a husky edge that made my pulse skip. For a moment, I longed to tell him to skip the movie altogether and take me home, but I resisted. The night was just starting, and I wasn't about to spoil it.

"Why? What happens in a few hours?" I arched an eyebrow. I could tell from the flush in his cheeks he was embarrassed, which only made me laugh. He looked good when he was flustered.

I decided to change the subject. "Will I know many people coming tonight?"

"Probably everyone you've met in town so far. Not much happens around here, so the community events tend to have a decent turnout. Besides, if it's for the kids, who can resist?" He smiled, though his eyes were elsewhere, scanning the crowd.

"You like them, don't you?" I asked, unable to hide the curiosity in my voice.

"Who?" Noah frowned and glanced around, as if the question had taken him off guard.

"Kids," I clarified.

"Oh yeah. Most of them are great." He didn't elaborate further, but the glint in his eye told me everything. I imagined Noah would like to have children of his own one day, and the fact that his ex-wife had a baby would be another experience that had been stolen from him. It stung more than I cared to admit.

"Oh Bailey, I'm so glad you came." Tracy's voice cut through my thoughts, her genuine pleasure in seeing me always welcome. "Are you sitting with us?" She directed the question at Noah, who looked at her with a small smile.

"Don't look at me, you're taking me out, remember? I'll sit where I'm told."

I was happy to share him with his family. It had been a lonely few months, and there was something so refreshing about being out in a crowd, surrounded by people who knew each other.

Noah shrugged, his easygoing demeanor back in place. "Here's as good as anywhere." He placed the picnic basket down and reached for the strap of the bag slung over my shoulder. He pulled the blanket from the bag and spread it out in front of the chairs his mother had set up for her, Mike, and Jack. Dan and Emily were getting themselves settled next to them.

"Hey, Noah and Bailey." Dan called out, waving as he approached.

He was the first of many to stop and greet us. Noah introduced me to the people I hadn't met yet, and I couldn't help but notice the curious glances exchanged between couples when they realized who I was—the one who bought the farm from Jack. It was strange, like I was suddenly a part of something bigger than myself.

"Do you want a beer?" Noah took two bottles from the cooler bag inside the picnic hamper.

"Thanks," I said, accepting one from him.

"Are you hungry?" His eyes scanning the crowd as people began pulling food from their coolers and picnic hampers.

"Starving." I hadn't eaten since lunch, and my stomach had been rumbling since before he picked me up.

He'd gone all out for this picnic. There was enough food to feed us for three meals—seasoned chicken, three fresh salads, herb and olive rolls, and chocolate cake for dessert.

"Are you sure you've got enough food?" Rick teased as he crouched down to chat with us.

"Want some?" Noah held out the chicken, and Rick eagerly grabbed a piece.

He bit into it and closed his eyes, savoring the flavor. "Trish?" he groaned, his tone full of appreciation.

Noah nodded, a knowing grin on his face.

"Bastard," Rick said with a laugh, and Ali swatted him on the shoulder as she joined us.

"She's terrible for a wife's ego, Noah. You need to tell her to stop feeding the men in town. Honestly, I'm surprised she's remained single for so long." Ali pretended to scold him, but her tone was light. "Hey, Bailey. Good to see you're starting a tradition already. You'll be here every year now."

Fitting in somewhere was all I'd ever wanted. Tonight, it felt like I had finally found a place where I belonged.

After they left to finish their food before the movie started, I glanced around, feeling a little more at ease. "If this is a fundraiser, where do they collect the money?"

"I bought us tickets after I left your house this afternoon," Noah explained, "and they have raffles and auctions and stuff before and after the movie starts."

"Oh, how much do I owe you?" I reached for my wallet, though I had the nagging feeling I was about to offend him.

"Seriously? It's a school fundraiser. Believe me, it didn't blow my budget." He raised an eyebrow, his expression a mix of amusement and something else that I couldn't quite place.

I regretted asking. "I don't like to just expect you to pay, that's all. It's called manners." I shrugged. "So, what's up for auction? You?"

Noah raised his eyebrows at me, a sly smile tugging at his lips.

"Oh well, what do I get if I purchase you?" I teased, feeling a warmth spread through me.

"I'm teasing," he said, shaking his head. "Farmers usually offer livestock or produce. Occasionally, you can pick up a bargain, like the Dexter bull they have on offer."

"Are you going to buy it?" My curiosity piqued.

Noah shook his head. "When I get a farm of my own, that's what I'll breed. They're easier to manage because of their size, and they're not so harsh on the fences."

I nodded, impressed. "Sounds like a solid plan."

The night stretched out before us, filled with good food, laughter, and the kind of comfort that came from being with people who cared. For the first time in a long while, I felt like I was exactly where I was meant to be.

I nodded, considering Noah's suggestion. "But, if he's such a good deal, why not put him on my place? It's plenty big enough. You could build your stock up, and when you buy your property, you wouldn't have to start everything from scratch."

Noah didn't respond immediately, and I could feel the wheels turning in his mind. "Let's just see the sort of dollars they're asking first."

I nodded in agreement, although I couldn't say I'd ever had to worry about following a strict budget. But I could imagine how disheartening it would be to constantly have to calculate every penny.

"Do you want dessert now? Or should we have it when we get back to your place?"

"Noah Taylor, are you inviting yourself in on a first date? That's very forward of you," I teased, letting a playful edge slip into my voice.

"Oh, you better believe it." His smirk was enough to make my heart race.

I tipped my head back and laughed. "Baby, please

behave yourself," I teased, but my tone was light, and I could see the spark of amusement in his eyes. He grinned, and I could feel my heart flutter just a little bit more.

After we cleared away the food and plates, Noah pulled the cushions and blanket from the bag. He glanced at me, his expression suddenly serious. "Did you bring a jacket?"

I had meant to, but it was still in the chair back at my place. "I forgot," I admitted with a sheepish grin.

Noah spread the blanket out and arranged the cushions at the end furthest from the screen. The evening air was cooling down, but I didn't mind. Being with him made me feel warmer than any jacket could.

A group of children approached, calling out to Noah. "Hey, Uncle Noah and Bailey, do you want to buy a raffle ticket?"

I wouldn't have recognized Ben if it weren't for him addressing Noah as *Uncle*. I smiled at the sight of him. "Sure do. How much are they?" I reached into my bag to grab my purse.

"Fifty cents each, or five for two dollars," Ben announced proudly.

I pulled out a ten-dollar bill. "I'll let you do the math," I said, handing him the money. Ben didn't

COUNTRY CHARM

hesitate—he counted out twenty-five tickets and handed them over, all while moving on to the next potential buyers before Noah could dig his wallet out of the picnic basket.

"I'll share with you," I offered, tossing the tickets between us.

"Great," Noah said, with a grin. "But I get the cow if it's a raffle prize."

I raised an eyebrow. "Is it a good one?"

"One of the top breeding lines around," he said, and before I could ask more, the movie started, and our conversation was cut off.

I had to admit, though, as the lights dimmed and the first few frames of the movie flickered on, I was eager for the distraction. The way Noah looked at me, though, made it hard to focus. He had that playful yet uncertain look in his eyes, like a teenage boy trying to make a move but fearful of rejection.

"Are you going to lie down with me?" His voice soft and hesitant.

I smiled and nodded, feeling a flutter in my chest as he lay back and wrapped his arms around me, pulling me close so my head rested on his chest. The sound of his steady heartbeat was a comfort, and I couldn't help but feel like I was exactly where I needed to be. I caught a glimpse of Tracy watching us, and I smiled back at her.

The movie was entertaining enough—nothing too complicated, perfect for both kids and adults. But honestly, it was the atmosphere that had me hooked. The people, the warmth, the sense of community—it made me feel like I was a part of the town, despite being the newcomer so many of the locals resented for *taking* Jack's farm.

A couple of times during the movie, Noah shifted, and I offered to reposition myself, but he just tightened his embrace, pulling me in closer and brushing my lips with his. I felt that familiar flutter deep inside, the kind that never got old.

I snuggled into him, wrapping my arm around his waist. It was a good thing the movie was easy to follow because my mind kept drifting from the plot and towards him.

Slipping my hand up under his shirt, I felt the warmth of his skin beneath my fingertips. I glanced at his face to gauge his reaction, and the slight smirk that teased the corners of his mouth told me everything I needed to know.

There were too many people around for me to do anything too daring—his family was sitting right behind us—but the occasional touch, the pressure of my fingers against his skin, was enough to make me feel like I was living in the moment. He kissed the top of my head once, and I melted a little. His thumb traced the skin of my arm, sending shivers down my spine.

I slid my arm a little higher, and Noah's hand shifted from my arm to my breast, resting there for a moment. I tilted my head so I could look up at him, and when our eyes met, there was no denying the heat between us. Even though we hadn't known each other in this way for long, I could tell his mind wasn't on the movie either.

When the credits finally started to roll, it felt like a relief. The area darkened, and I stretched, sliding my hand over his stomach and lightly running my fingers down his side. Noah responded by teasing my nipple through the fabric of my shirt, and I sucked in a sharp breath, my body responding instinctively.

He kissed the top of my head again before sitting up, pulling me with him. I felt his muscles tense beneath my touch, his body hard as concrete, and I couldn't help but let my fingers linger for a moment longer before I pulled away, letting the blanket shift lower.

"Did you enjoy that?" His voice low.

"Some parts more than others," I admitted with a smirk, glancing up at him. "Now, are we going to find this cow or what?"

Noah chuckled, shaking his head. "You have a one-track mind, you know that?"

"You have no idea." I grinned, but I guessed he did now.

The floodlights were turned on, illuminating the picnic area. A stage had been set up with a microphone and podium off to one side. Families were tidying up their areas or chatting among themselves while others got up to mingle.

Noah stood and reached out a hand to help me to my feet. "Come on, I'll educate you on livestock."

"Oh good," I teased, letting my sarcasm flow. "How can I refuse such an offer?"

Noah raised an eyebrow, clearly amused. "Are you being sarcastic?"

"Actually, no. I'm genuinely interested."

"Good," he said with a grin. "I'll convert you into a country girl yet."

"Huh," I said, rolling my eyes. "I am a country girl."

Taking my hand, Noah led me along the row of auction items. There were hampers filled with jam and wine, chickens, sheep, and even a cow. My eyes fell on an alpaca, and I couldn't help but smile.

Noah laughed. "What are you going to do with an alpaca?"

"Feed it, pat it, or just look at it if it's scared of me," I said with a grin.

"You're adorable, you know that?" he said, his voice soft, but there was no denying the affection in his words.

"Well, what else would I do with it?" I glanced back at the alpaca.

Noah shrugged, his expression thoughtful. "They're good for keeping foxes away during lambing season. Or, farmers breed them for their fleece."

I wasn't sure I really needed an alpaca, but those big doe eyes tried to convince me otherwise. The soft, fluffy creature seemed to look right through me, almost as if it were begging me to take it home. But I knew better.

We moved on, and soon we reached the bull. The animal was small compared to the others I'd seen, but it was clear that was part of the appeal. The crowd gathered around it, mostly men, talking in hushed tones. Noah's gaze lingered on the bull, his eyes full of longing. I could tell he was serious about wanting it.

"Let's buy the cow," I said, breaking the silence.

Noah shook his head slightly, not meeting my eyes. "As I said before, let's wait and see."

"Okay," I said, though I couldn't help pushing a little. "For argument's sake, what would a Dexter bull like this be worth?"

Noah shrugged. "I couldn't tell you, especially on a night like this. It just comes down to who wants it the most and has enough cash to buy it."

My stomach twisted slightly. "Do you have to have the money on you tonight?" I knew it was probably a silly question, but it was better to ask than to assume. I didn't have more than a few hundred dollars in my purse, and that might not be enough.

Noah reassured me, sensing my concern. "They'll accept an I.O.U. No one's going to rip off a school charity event. Don't worry about it."

We made our way back to where Mike, Tracy, and Jack were standing, talking among themselves.

"Got your eye on that bull, haven't you?" Jack said to Noah as soon as we approached.

Noah's only response was a single nod, his eyes never leaving the animal in the pen.

The auction began shortly after the raffle, which Ali ended up winning. As Noah had said, the price of anything at the auction depended on who wanted it most and how much they were willing to pay. It quickly became a game to see who could outbid their neighbor.

The livestock portion of the auction turned serious, though, especially the bull. But even the chickens weren't safe from a little good-natured competition. Sophie, with a little playful grin, ended up buying five chickens for seventy dollars—a steal, really.

Everyone seemed to be waiting for the bull. The alpaca went for six hundred dollars, and though I would've loved to have it, Noah was right. What would I do with an alpaca?

The bidding began for the bull with a starting price of fifty dollars. I glanced at Noah as the price slowly rose, and I could see the hesitation in his eyes. He didn't want to get involved in a bidding war, but I could tell that he was in it. He stayed quiet, watching the auctioneer. When the bid hit two hundred and fifty, Noah finally raised his hand.

For a while, the bidding was between him and a farmer I didn't know. They went back and forth, each raising the price by twenty dollars. Then the bid reached eight hundred dollars. I saw the way Noah's hand dropped, signaling that he was out.

"Going once at eight hundred and fifty dollars, going twice—"

I noticed the disappointment in Noah's eyes when I looked up at him. The intensity of it hit me unexpectedly. Without thinking, I raised my hand, cutting through the tension.

"One thousand dollars," I called out, my voice clear, maybe a little too loud in the stillness of the room.

Noah's arm went rigid around me as his eyes shot to me, his face a mixture of surprise and worry. "Please don't," he whispered urgently, leaning in close.

The other farmer countered, raising his bid by twenty dollars. Without hesitation, I raised the bid again, this time by a hundred.

The farmer countered with the same twenty-dollar increase. I could tell he was pushing his limit, and I wasn't going to let him win this easily.

I took a deep breath and called out with confidence, "Fifteen hundred."

The room fell silent for a moment. Whispers swirled around us, but there was no immediate counteroffer. I held my breath, hoping I hadn't just made a huge mistake.

"Congratulations, young lady, you're the proud owner of that fine Dexter bull." The auctioneer's voice rang out, and I felt a rush of exhilaration flood my chest. I had done it.

I beamed, my heart pounding in my ears. But as I glanced at Noah, my smile slowly faded. His expression unreadable as if he was in shock. There was a trace of something else in his eyes, though—something I couldn't quite place. It wasn't just the surprise. It was something deeper, and it made me feel suddenly unsure of myself.

I waited for him to say something, but he just stood there, his gaze fixed on the bull, and I couldn't help but wonder if I'd done the right thing.

CHAPTER 20

Bailey

"You're angry at me, aren't you?" I confronted him as soon as we closed the car doors.

Noah didn't look at me right away, keeping his eyes on the road. After a long pause, he muttered, "I asked you not to do it, and you totally ignored me."

I wasn't backing down, though. "But you wanted that bull so much. You should've been the one to have it."

"No, I shouldn't," he snapped, his voice tight. "I couldn't afford it. Besides, the guy you were bidding against is my ex-father-in-law."

I frowned. "I don't care who he was. What makes you think he deserves it more than you?"

"Because he was paying for it with his own money," Noah shot back, his voice laced with frustration. "Do you have any idea what everyone will say about us now? Or, rather, what they'll say about me?"

I tried to brush it off. "It's no big deal. It's just a cow, for goodness' sake."

Noah's hand gripped the steering wheel tightly. "It's the fifteen hundred dollars that'll make the gossip columns. And the title *gold digger* will be written in bold on top."

"Are you a gold digger?" I teased, trying to lighten the mood, but his mood was far from playful. "Do you want me for my money, or is it my body?"

"At the moment, I don't want either," he replied, his words cold and cutting.

His comment stung more than I expected. I stared out the window, my thoughts swirling in a messy cloud of confusion. Noah was angry, and I knew it, but hearing him say that felt like a slap in the face. I hadn't thought buying the bull would upset him this much. If I had, I never would've let it spoil our evening.

Noah drove too fast toward my house, and I

couldn't shake the uneasy feeling in my chest. When he pulled up outside the gate, he didn't even put the car in park, keeping the engine running.

"I thought you were coming in for dessert?" I tried to sound casual, though I was anything but.

The look on Noah's face told me everything I needed to know. He wasn't coming in. I felt a knot tighten in my stomach. But to my surprise, he turned off the engine and got out of the car. He retrieved the cake from the basket and handed it to me without a word. "Enjoy," he said flatly.

"Noah, please don't leave like this," I pleaded, desperate for him to stay, to talk this out.

"Like what?" He turned back to face me, his eyes dark with frustration. "You made me look like a fool tonight, Bailey. I let you talk me into buying the bloody thing, to get excited over a dream, and for what? So that jerk could take it from me? Or so you could flaunt your riches to everyone in town?" His words cut deep, and I felt my chest tighten.

"I thought he lived in the city?" I was trying to make sense of it all.

"He does," Noah replied, his voice bitter. "But he'd rather slaughter the cow than see me have what I want."

COUNTRY CHARM

I took a step closer to him, my heart pounding. "All the more reason for him not to have it."

"That wasn't your call to make, at least not on my behalf," Noah shot back, his frustration rising. He took a deep breath, clearly trying to calm himself, but his eyes were still full of anger. "Bailey, I said I wanted to try and make this work. I said I wanted to spend time with you, get to know you, but—" He didn't need to finish. The punch to my stomach was enough. His words stung so much harder than I expected. Was he really going to play the *too much money* card again?

Tears blurred my vision as I blinked rapidly, trying to stop them. "What am I supposed to do with the cow?" I said, my voice trembling.

"That's your problem, you bought it," he muttered, his voice tight with frustration.

"Fine. I'll breed Dexter's myself. Just another dream I can rob you of," I snapped, my voice rising with anger. I could feel the heat building inside me, the frustration pouring out in a wave of bitter words. "Damn it, Noah, you said the money wouldn't be an issue from this point on." I didn't care that I was ranting now. I had to get this out. "Was that until you got what you wanted—by sleeping with me? Or was I the only one stupid enough not to see through the charade? You didn't want to appear alone at the wedding while your ex-wife spun bullshit about being happy in her relationship with a child that should've been yours."

I knew I was stepping into dangerous territory, but I didn't care. Even rational thoughts couldn't stop me now. "I bought the fucking cow because I thought it'd make you happy, and you punish me for it. What about the rest of the time we spent together? Did yesterday afternoon mean nothing to you?"

The tears I'd been fighting spilled over, streaking down my cheeks. I hated myself for sounding so pathetic, for letting him see how weak and desperate I felt.

I shoved the cake back into his hand, the box pressing against his chest. Without a word, I turned and stalked away. As I reached the top step, I tripped, losing my balance. My forearms slapped hard against the decking, the sting jolting through me. I didn't dare look back at Noah. I couldn't bear to see the disappointment in his eyes again.

I picked myself up quickly, trying to ignore the ache in my arms, and went inside. With my back pressed against the door, I waited until I heard the car start, the sound of his engine fading into the night before I allowed the tears to fall freely.

The next morning came too soon. I hadn't slept much, the humiliation of being dumped over a cow weighing on me. It was worse than discovering my only long-term relationship had been nothing more than a career climb for him.

After feeding Freya, I borrowed a ladder from Jack and started stringing up fairy lights around the edge of the patio. I wound them in crisscrosses up and down the poles, trying to focus on something other than last night's mess.

But the events of the previous night kept running through my mind. The humiliation when people would inevitably ask what went wrong, and how I'd never be able to escape the gossip. Especially after our first date.

"Hey." Noah's voice startled me, and I lost my balance on the ladder. Panicked, I grabbed hold of the beam to steady myself, but in the process, I dropped the strand of fairy lights I was holding. Tiny bulbs shattered on the ground with a sharp crack. I groaned, feeling the weight of everything pressing down on me once more.

"Sorry, I startled you. I just wanted to see if you were okay after last night." Noah dragged his hands through his hair, his voice laden with regret. "I was embarrassed, and I behaved like a jerk again. I'm sorry."

"What do you want from me, Noah?"

"I want us to be friends."

Bailey's head jerked up. Was he serious? Offering friendship after we'd slept together just two days ago?

"Leave me alone, please." I had no fight left in me, nor did I want any. He was unreasonable and so far past damaged. I didn't need his crap in my life. I had enough of my own to deal with.

"But—"

"How dare you come around here now and say anything? You got what you wanted out of me, and I got a cow. If you want to come over to see Jack, by all means, but we are not friends, and no, I am not okay with any of this." I stepped down from the ladder, my movements stiff with frustration. I had a cow to pick up, and I wasn't going to stand here and keep talking in circles with him. But first, I crossed over, knocked on the glass door of the flat, and stuck my head inside. "Hey, Jack. I'm going to pay for my cow, and I was wondering where's best for me to put him?"

"What did Noah suggest?" Jack frowned, obviously curious about the shift in the dynamic. Noah had been calling most of the shots, and Jack just went along with it.

"He didn't."

"Well, he always planned for them to go in the paddock closest to the stable. It's a nice size for at least a dozen."

"Thanks, Jack." I closed the door behind me, not bothering to acknowledge Noah. I walked past him and into the house.

I approached the stone farmhouse at the address I'd been given the night before at the auction. It looked deserted, but considering it was after nine, everyone was probably out already.

I rapped on the front door, and as I waited, I glanced around at the half wine barrels ablaze with bright yellow, pink, and orange flowers. It must be something they learned growing up. Bailey Cooper, plant killer. I couldn't even keep a lucky bamboo alive. With the number of plants I'd killed under my care, it wasn't any wonder I had so many failed relationships in my life. It was a good thing I stopped buying them when I did, or else I'd be alone for a long time.

The door creaked open, and an elderly lady stood on the other side.

"Hello, my name's Bailey Collins. I was wondering if Max is home?"

"I thought Bailey would be a man. Max said you were coming, and to point you toward the barn. If you follow the driveway around to the left, you won't miss it."

"Thank you, and have a nice day." I appreciated the honest nature of the locals. Usually, I'd get a surprised look or a smirk, but most didn't point out the gender mix-up.

The land was magnificent. Rolling green hills dotted with clumps of jarrah trees and natural moss rock features. Paddocks lined the driveway, all with cattle in them.

The barn was something else. At least three times the size of mine and packed with machinery. It was like nothing I'd ever seen before.

Max greeted me with a grin. His sun-worn skin creased around his features. "Bailey, lovely to see you again." He was a mountain of a man. His hand engulfed mine in a firm handshake.

"And you. This place is amazing. I love it."

"My piece of paradise. I'm a lucky man." Max gazed over the land, admiring what he clearly never tired of.

I appreciated the simplicity of what obviously

brought more happiness than I'd ever known. Maybe that was something that came with maturity. I sure hoped so.

"So you bought yourself a bull?"

"Well, sort of. I wanted Noah to have it, but—" I stopped myself. There was no need to go into the details.

"He's a proud man. I've offered to give him stock before, to get him started. He's had a rough trot. But he's determined to do it on his own. I respect that."

I didn't know why I felt the urge to cry, but I did. I cleared my throat and thought about what Max had said. Noah was so angry with me now, I figured it didn't matter if I went over the top with my apologies. "So, the starter deal you offered him? How much would that cost me, and is it still available?"

Max looked at me as if I'd gone mad. "You're playing with fire, Bailey." He scuffed the toe of his boot over the gravel. "The prime stock he'd be needing doesn't come cheap."

"I appreciate that, but I think he's worth the risk, and I'm betting you agree."

"I'm sure we can come to an arrangement."

By the time I drove away, I was the proud owner of not one, but five Dexter cows and the prized bull. Max was loading up the truck and planned to deliver them in the next few hours. In the meantime, I had groceries to buy and another strand of fairy lights to source.

Getting to know the locals and being accepted was exactly what I'd hoped for, but it did make grocery shopping take much longer. By the time I stopped to talk with everyone who cornered me, an hour had passed, and I still had to go through the checkout.

Tracy stood in line in front of me.

"Oh, Bailey love, it was wonderful to see you and Noah together, at last." Her grin was as wide as the Cheshire cat.

"Um, yes, about that—I messed up by buying him the bull. Seems my money's a problem. He doesn't want everyone in town thinking that's why we're together, so now we're not." I shrugged, hoping the busybody gossip at the checkout overheard. Maybe I could do some good for Noah with her ever-flapping mouth.

"I thought he seemed a little uptight when he got home last night. I'm so sorry." A frown and genuine look of disappointment replaced her smile. "I thought he wanted the bull."

"He did, but not for me to buy it for him. I

embarrassed him, and I should've thought my actions through a little better."

"So, what's happening now?"

"With us or the bull?" "Both." Tracy was practically salivating for all the gossip. "We're finished. He's angry, and by lunchtime, he'll be furious at me." I felt the regret settle in my chest. Maybe I shouldn't have alienated him further. "Oh, Bailey, what did you do?" "I bought some prime female friends for Dexter." I tried to force a smile, but I knew it wasn't convincing. Tracy burst into laughter. "Farmer Bailey, it suits you. And yes, I'd say you're in for one hell of a fight." Her voice had an almost gleeful edge to it as she continued bagging her items. "Well, I'll see you tomorrow night. Let me know if you need any help. Emily mentioned she's coming over with Cassie and Ali, but I'm happy to pitch in." "Thanks, Tracy. We should be okay, but I'll let you know."

By the time I made it home, I managed to get my groceries inside and put away the cold stuff before Max arrived with the truck. I greeted him outside, but then ended up catching a ride to the paddock where I planned to put the cows.

Freya pranced around the yard, her glossy black coat catching the light. "Your horse?" Max raised an eyebrow. I nodded. "Magnificent creature. Is she a Friesian?" "Yep."

I caught Max shaking his head as I glanced up, but his smirk stayed firmly in place. I almost asked him what was going through his mind, but thought better of it. Instead, I climbed down from the truck's cab when he stopped.

Jack and Noah came out of the stable, and my stomach dropped.

"Max," Jack greeted him with a nod, while Noah offered a handshake, his face unreadable. "Jack, Noah. It's been a while since I stepped on this land. How are things?" Max's voice had that relaxed charm that came with years of knowing people. "No doubt you've heard the whispers spreading through town. We've got this sweet young thing—or more to the point, she's got me, but I see you're already acquainted." Jack's voice carried a playful tone, but there was tension in his eyes. "That I am," Max chuckled. "She's got spunk, that's for sure." He shot me a quick grin. "Would you mind helping me with these cows? Not interrupting anything, am I?" "Not at all," Jack replied, clearly glad to avoid whatever uncomfortable conversation was brewing. But Noah didn't move, his eyes pinned to me with an intensity that felt suffocating.

"What have you done, Bailey?" Noah's voice was quiet, but I could see the rage simmering beneath the surface, barely contained. "I bought Dexter some friends, because spending money is what I do best." I aimed to provoke him, but the words felt harsh coming out. "You really know how to drive the knife in, don't you?" Noah's words cut deep, and before I could react, he stormed past me. His anger twisted into something else—hurt, disappointment. It stung more than I wanted to admit.

Jack tried to keep the conversation light, but the atmosphere was thick with tension. Noah barely said anything, and I knew he was fighting to keep his emotions in check.

"Well, I'd better get back to it," Max said, breaking the silence. "Bailey, it's been a pleasure. Don't be a stranger, you're welcome to visit anytime."

"Likewise." I appreciated Max's easygoing nature. He reminded me of the grandfather I never knew.

Jack made himself scarce as soon as Max closed the truck's door. I couldn't blame him; he was trying to avoid the inevitable storm brewing between me and Noah.

"Noah, before you say anything, hear me out." I squinted against the sun's glare, shifting so I could look at him. "You were already so angry with me. I figured it'd be better to get everything out in the open, and then maybe we can move past this."

"You're unbelievable," Noah muttered, his voice dripping with hurt. "You talk about not getting in the way of anyone else's dreams. But standing in that paddock right now are six of mine. And from this day forward, every time I come here, they'll be another reminder of my failure." The fire in his eyes dimmed, replaced by something deeper—defeat.

I closed the distance between us, unsure whether to hug him or just let him be. Noah lifted his gaze, meeting my eyes for the first time in what felt like forever.

I reached out, my hand trembling slightly as I touched his cheek. "I want your dreams to flourish. These cows, they're just steppingstones to get you where you need to be. Like the barn you built—it helped me get closer to mine." I wasn't foolish enough to think that the barn was intended for me, but it sure made my dreams a whole lot easier to realize.

Noah didn't speak, a frown knitting his brow. I stood on my tiptoes, leaning forward, brushing my lips against his for the briefest moment. "Please, let me help you," I whispered, hoping he could hear the sincerity in my voice.

He closed his eyes, turning his head away as though he needed space to think. I knew it wasn't going to be easy for him. The pride he held so tightly would make everything harder, but at some point, he was going to have to let it go. Otherwise, it would keep him trapped, drowning in his own hurt.

"You're generous, Bailey," Noah finally said, his voice soft, almost regretful. "And I appreciate what you're trying to do, but—"

"You already told me you don't want to be with me. I heard you loud and clear. I'll deal with that, but please, don't be stubborn. These are my gift to you. The livestock sales paperwork will need your signature, and after that, you can do what you like with them."

Noah's eyes were fixed on the six cows grazing in the paddock, but I couldn't tell if he was even seeing them. I could feel the weight of the silence pressing down on us both, suffocating in its heaviness.

"To you, this may seem like a big deal, but in my world, it's no big deal." There was no point denying it. "I understand why being a part of my lifestyle doesn't interest you. Sometimes, I wish I didn't have to be a part of it either."

It hurt to think that money meant more to him than I did, and not in the way most others would have reacted, but I could understand it in some way. This world, my world, wasn't simple. But knowing I'd hurt him, it made something inside me ache—something deep and raw that I wasn't sure how to fix.

"I like you, Noah," I said quietly, the words tasting heavier than I thought they would. "Too much to just be your friend, but if that's all you're offering, I'll take it."

I saw the way his jaw tightened, but he didn't respond. He didn't say anything. And I knew, deep down, that it was already too late for words to change anything. He let me say what I needed to, and that was all.

When the silence stretched too thin, and I couldn't bear it any longer, I stepped around him. My heart hammered in my chest, but I didn't wait for him to say anything more. I walked back toward the house, the tears I'd been fighting for our entire conversation finally slipping down my cheeks.

I'd messed up. I knew it. But sometimes, things slipped past the point of being salvaged, and I could feel it in my bones—that this was one of those moments.

CHAPTER 21

Bailey

The phone rang, and I was in the middle of filling vol-au-vent cases with creamy salmon mornay. My hands were a mess. "Ali, would you mind getting that for me, please?"

She nodded, disappearing toward the phone. I kept working, carefully filling the pastry cases, trying to ignore the nagging thought that the phone call could be important.

A few moments later, Ali's voice interrupted. "Bailey, you might want to take this."

I sighed, placing the bowl of mixture on the bench and washing my hands quickly before drying them off. "Hello, Bailey speaking."

I waited until I hung up to let the excitement burst out of me. Another booking for the upcoming retreat.

Ali grinned, eyes sparkling. "How many is that?"

"Four definite, and I've had two more online inquiries. I know it's small, but I haven't put it out there much because I wasn't sure Cooper would manage to get the barn finished on time."

"That's wonderful, and you've still got two weeks to go."

"Until what?" Cassie's voice caught the tail end of our conversation as she entered.

"The first retreat. Is there stuff in the car you want me to get out?" Ali moved around aimlessly. It wasn't like her to be so distracted.

"Thanks, there are more flowers if you don't mind. Bailey, where are these going?" she added as she started to leave.

"Perhaps on the coffee table for now. They'll wilt outside in the heat." The white and apricot floral arrangements were beautiful—soft and delicate to match Sophie's color scheme.

"Hey, Em," Cassie greeted Emily as she entered the lounge room.

Ali returned with more flowers, but her eyes were red and swollen. She wasn't just holding the flowers anymore—she was wiping away tears.

"What happened?" I rushed over and gently took the flowers from her hands.

Ali sniffed and shook her head. "I'm fine, just being silly and sentimental."

She continued into the lounge room, and I followed.

Cassie was talking about the schedule for the night, and I forced myself to focus on her words. "So the entertainment will arrive at nine o'clock, which gives us plenty of time to eat. Afterward, we can have dessert and coffee."

"Oh, Can, you can take full responsibility if she spits it over having a stripper," Emily teased, looking at me.

"No way, we're in this together." I glanced at Ali, who nodded in agreement.

"What's up, Ali? You don't look so good," Cassie said, worry creeping into her voice.

Her face was definitely pale, and I could see she was struggling. "I think I'm going to be—" Before she could finish, she darted off toward the downstairs powder room.

"I think someone might be suffering from morning sickness," Emily said, the words out of her mouth before I had a chance to fully comprehend.

"She's pregnant?" Cassie's voice cracked with disbelief, and I couldn't understand why she sounded so shocked. Emily was the only one of us with kids, after all.

"Well, it was bound to happen, eventually," Emily said with a grin, clearly unbothered by the situation.

Ali came back looking a little better, but saying she was glowing would have been a lie. "It's really quite disgusting, having morning sickness, isn't it?" she said, looking at Emily for reassurance.

Emily nodded sympathetically and then rushed over to give her a hug.

Cassie squealed, her excitement impossible to hide. "Babies are so exciting."

Emily let out a dry laugh. "And when it lingers throughout the day and night, you never think you'll feel normal again. You do, though. And then the heartburn or some other dreadful symptom kicks in."

I listened to their conversation, not saying much. I'd never given much thought to having children myself, but living in this large house, where everything was quiet and still, made it impossible to ignore. My maternal clock was ticking. Two would be the minimum, I thought, but even that seemed like a far-off dream. It really sucked not having siblings. Even the arguments over the years would have been better than being alone.

But now wasn't the time to dwell on it. I had far too much to do. Charlotte was due to arrive in a few hours, and I needed time to get ready.

Sophie arrived at six o'clock, a half-hour before the others were due.

"I would like to propose a toast to my soon-to-be sister," Cassie announced, her voice full of excitement. "We love you and wish you and my brother lifelong happiness and bliss." She clinked glasses with Sophie. When Sophie saw Ali's glass filled with juice, she squealed. "You're having a baby."

After hugs and happy tears, they all went to get ready, except for Sophie, who stayed behind to wait for the guests to arrive.

Seeing as it was my own home, I decided it wouldn't hurt to dress a little less conventionally for country living. Besides, Noah didn't want me, country girl or not, so what did I have to lose? I dragged the second-skin leather pants up my legs, the smooth material hugging my curves. Stretching out on the bed, I zipped them into place. The slinky silver tank top fit snugly across my bust and hung—rather than clung—over the waistband of the pants. It created a sleek silhouette. I left my black hair loose, in shiny waves, and put just enough makeup on to highlight my features. A spritz of my favorite perfume, and I slipped my feet into strappy black stilettos. Ready to go, I was downstairs just before the guests arrived.

"How you manage to look like that in fifteen minutes is beyond me," Sophie said, shaking her head in disbelief. "Thank you for tonight. It looks beautiful."

I grinned, feeling proud of how everything was coming together. "I'm glad you like it."

Stepping outside to check everything one last time before the guests arrived, I caught sight of Noah walking out of the granny flat. He released a low whistle as he scanned me from top to toe, his gaze appreciative. He changed course and headed straight toward me. "Wow."

I smiled. He looked pretty good himself, but I

couldn't bring myself to comment. It felt… complicated.

"You've done a great job. This place looks amazing—and so do you." He stopped right in front of me, and without warning, reached up to cup my cheek in his hand. Our gazes locked for a moment, an unspoken connection humming in the air between us. Then, as if realizing what he was doing, he quickly withdrew his hand and took a step back. "Sorry, I—sorry."

"Don't keep apologizing, please." I didn't know why he always felt the need. He wasn't the one who had to be sorry.

"I told you already you're irresistible. I don't think I need to say it again."

"You seem to be managing well enough," I teased, my voice playful. I wasn't going to make this easy on him.

"What?"

"To resist," I said, pouting and jutting my chin out. If he wanted to play games, I was ready.

"You think it's easy for me to resist you? The more I try, the more mess I seem to make." His voice dropped an octave, his lips curling slightly.

"Oh, baby, you haven't been trying hard enough. My bet is we could make a lot more mess, if that's the way you like it," I shot back, giving him a teasing glint in my eyes.

Noah frowned. "Have you been drinking?"

I grinned and stepped closer, my hand raking through his hair. I leaned toward him, my lips brushing lightly across his. My body pressed against his, and I raised my knee to meet his groin. "Enjoy your night, Noah."

I could feel his desire growing, the heat of it pressing against my knee as I pulled away and turned to leave.

"Ahh, no you don't." He grabbed my wrist, pulling me back into his arms. "Two can play this game, Bailey." His body fit to mine like a glove as he lowered his mouth to mine. He kissed me fiercely, plunging his tongue into my mouth. It wasn't just a kiss—it was an overwhelming surge of heat and hunger. His hands gripped my ass through the leather, pulling me even closer.

"Hah hum," came the voice from behind us, cutting through the moment. "I think the rules state all cocks must leave the henhouse." Only Cassie could interrupt a moment like this and get away with it.

Noah loosened his embrace and glanced up.

"Give me thirty more seconds and I'm out of here." He shot Cassie a grin no girl could resist.

"Fine, but I'll be counting," she called over her shoulder as she went back inside, counting out loud.

"What was that for?" I demanded, a mix of confusion and amusement in my voice as I tried to regain my composure.

"Stall tactics," Noah said, still grinning.

"No, why did you kiss me like that?" The question slipped out before I could stop it.

"To remind you what it feels like to have me wanting you," he replied, covering my mouth with his again, his body pressing mine back into his. The kiss was urgent, full of unspoken promises.

"Okay, times up—bloody hell, Noah, get a room," Cassie's voice rang out again, forcing us apart.

Noah stepped back, releasing me. I gripped the chair beside me, trying to steady myself.

"Never forget it," Noah murmured, his voice low and serious. "Now, you enjoy your night."

I nodded, my heart still racing from the kiss, my body still tingling. What was happening between us?

At exactly six-thirty, the guests began to arrive. I set up champagne cocktails and poured glasses of white and red wine, making sure everything was just right. Beer and mixed vodka drinks were placed in large ice buckets on stands outside, while jugs of juice and cool drinks were set on tables, both inside and out.

Cassie was busy collecting car keys from those who planned to drink, and I had set up rows of mattresses in the bedrooms upstairs. There was plenty of room, and everyone seemed excited about staying the night. That was until Charlotte arrived.

Tracy stood close to me, almost like a protective shield, and Ali's mum, Judy, didn't leave Tracy's side. Ali had thought of everything, including the place settings for the tables, making sure to keep the older generation together. For me, that meant enduring a night with Noah's ex-wife—the woman who had once stolen his heart, chewed it up, and spat it out. Part of me was grateful for that, because if she hadn't, maybe Noah would still be spoken for. But with the damage she'd caused, perhaps he'd always be spoken for.

Charlotte was pleasant enough looking, but wore far too much makeup. Her fuller figure was obviously the aftermath of childbirth, a look some women end up with, but whatever it was that had captivated Noah, I couldn't figure it out. Her bitter, catty comments—supposedly meant to be funny—

were anything but, and she didn't have a kind word to say about anyone.

The conversation moved to the fundraiser from the other night when Ali asked Sophie if they'd raised enough money to cover the graduation costs.

Sophie beamed, a bright, proud smile on her face. "Yes, it's going to be a good one this year, especially after the success of the auction."

Charlotte saw this as just another opportunity to take a swipe at Noah.

"Daddy told me all about the bidding on the bull," she said with a twisted delight. "He said he really wanted it, and there was no way he was going to lose it to Noah, so he pushed him to his last dollar." Charlotte relished telling the story, her eyes flicking to the table of Noah's closest female friends for their reaction. When no one joined her in celebrating Noah's loss, she shifted tactics. "But then Daddy said some rich woman—who looked a lot like the bull—ended up paying a fortune for it. A cow for a cow." She chuckled, and the others waited for me to react, like they knew something was coming. But I held my ground.

"Probably lonely and wanting to get started with her breeding program," Charlotte added with a sly grin as she took another mouthful of her vodka mix.

Cassie was the first to fire back. "Speaking from experience, are you?"

I couldn't help but watch as the others exchanged knowing glances. I'd been waiting for Cassie to speak up, and it didn't take long.

Charlotte's face twisted with irritation. "So tell me," she slurred. "Since you're probably the only girls in town of an eligible age, who's sleeping with my husband?"

I wanted to say something cutting but didn't give her the satisfaction of a response. Cassie, though, didn't miss a beat.

"Oh Charlotte, I didn't realize you and Matt got married. Congratulations." Emily gushed, feigned sweetness and innocence didn't seem didn't seem out of place coming from her.

That got Charlotte's hackles up. "Okay, so I meant my ex-husband," she snapped.

Whitney, the first to speak up, didn't miss a beat. "Oh, believe me, Charlotte, I'm working on it."

Charlotte completely ignored her and turned to me. "What about you?"

I glared at her, trying to hold back my growing anger, but I wasn't about to give her the satisfaction of a confession. "What about me?"

She rolled her eyes like she was bored. "I take that as a no."

"I wouldn't be so quick to place bets on that one, Charlotte," Cassie retorted with a scoff. "Don't you see the resemblance, a cow for a cow—or was it a rich woman buying a gift for Noah?" She picked up her glass of wine and stood, walking inside without another word.

"You bought the bull?" Charlotte's voice was thick with venom.

I arched an eyebrow, feeling the slight smirk tugging at the corners of my mouth. She wasn't going to get an answer from me. I'd intimidated many a powerful businessman under my father's watch, but with Charlotte, I had personal reasons to despise her. There was no way I was going to engage.

A loud blast of tacky stripper music suddenly cut through the tension. Sophie groaned, and everyone's attention shifted away from Charlotte, but I still felt her glare burning into me from across the room.

Cassie had arranged for everyone to gather around a chair she'd positioned for Sophie to sit in. When Tracy stood next to me and wrapped her arm protectively around my waist, Charlotte's glare turned sulky.

"Ali said she's targeting you already," Tracy whispered in my ear. "Ignore her, she's evil."

"I'm fine, really—at least now that my blood pressure has lowered from boiling point."

Tracy laughed softly, resting her head against mine. "You're beautiful."

Sophie, bright red in the face, sat in the center of the crowd as the man who was about to get naked, paraded around in front of her. When he turned to the crowd, trying to entice them to get involved, he struck out until he reached Whitney. I didn't know who looked more ridiculous—the way they pawed at each other was gross.

I was glad he didn't linger too long before crossing back to Sophie. That was until he danced up to me, gripped my hand, and pulled me to his chest. I didn't react, instead tilting my head to whisper in his ear. "We're paying you to dance with the bride, touch me again and I'll stand on your foot with my stiletto."

He released my hand immediately, stepping back and bowing.

Making a scene wasn't my style, nor was dealing with a stripper.

He danced for an hour, but I retreated to the

kitchen, where I was busy preparing dessert when he finally changed and was ready to leave.

"Hey, can I get you a drink?" I smiled at him now that he was clothed and no longer sliming all over me.

He smiled back, his demeanor much more polite now. "Thanks, I'd appreciate it."

"What would you like?"

"Beer would be great, if that's okay."

I grabbed two bottles from the fridge and handed him one. "Has anyone paid you yet?"

He nodded, tipping his head back to drink. "Cassie did. Thanks. And about before, thanks for not spiking me with those lethal looking things." He nodded toward my heels.

"Yeah, no worries. I don't have a problem with what you do, I just don't enjoy being on display."

"If you don't mind me saying so, looking as you do, you don't really have a choice."

I smiled, a bit amused. "Well, thank you."

He nodded, raising his bottle. "Thanks for the beer."

"Don't mention it." I smiled back and said goodbye, then carried the cake outside to add to the other desserts.

When I turned around, Charlotte was standing directly in front of me, her eyes glistening with unshed tears. She put on a faint, pitiful smile. "Noah will always love me, you know. You'll never own him the way I did."

I met her gaze, calm and collected, my voice steady as I responded, "Thank you for pointing that out, Charlotte, but I have no interest in owning him." My smile was sweet, and stepping around her, I walked away without another glance.

I didn't feel a shred of sympathy for Charlotte. She had her chance with Noah—and she had shattered him. Now it was my turn to try and piece him back together, to give him a chance at something real. It wouldn't be easy, but I was willing—if he would just let me in.

After the stripper left, Whitney was nowhere to be found. Ali told us she'd seen her in the passenger seat of his car when he drove past the house.

"I should have placed money on it," Cassie laughed, her voice laced with amusement.

Emily shook her head, a look of distaste on her face. "You still have his number, don't you, Cas? In case anything happens to her."

"Honestly, Emily, you know Whitney. There's no way he'll kidnap her," Cassie roared with laughter at her own joke.

"I think she was worried he might smother her with a pillow," Ali added, her voice dripping with sarcasm.

"You guys are cruel," Emily interjected, though it was clear her attempts to defend Whitney were only making things worse. "Whit's just desperate."

"So desperate, all the guys in town hide when she comes their way. Poor Noah's been dodging her for years," Cassie quipped, and I couldn't help but chuckle.

At the mention of his name, Charlotte's gaze darkened, and she stormed over to us. "What's this about Noah?"

I couldn't resist the urge to tease. "Was someone talking to you, Charlotte? No, I don't think so." Cassie was on a roll tonight, and the alcohol only fueled her lack of tolerance for the drama.

Charlotte stood there, hands on her hips, her eyes narrowing as she spoke. "Why is everyone so secretive about him? We established earlier that he's obviously still in love with me, seeing no one else in town is getting any from him."

I glanced down for a moment, and a vision of me and Noah, lying naked on the mat Charlotte was standing on, flashed into my mind. I couldn't help but laugh, the ridiculousness of the whole situation overwhelming me. The harder Charlotte tried to demand answers, the harder I laughed.

She was a joke. I just wished someone would take her home already.

It was such a relief when Rick's mother announced she was leaving, and Charlotte finally gathered her things and said her goodbyes. The air seemed to clear once she was gone.

As soon as she left, Ali leaned in, curiosity sparkling in her eyes. "So, Bailey, what was so funny?"

I looked at Tracy, who had already sat beside me, silently pleading with her to pick up on the hint.

"Oh my God," Cassie gasped, eyes wide with realization. "She was right—you *have* slept with Noah."

I was about to protest when Tracy chimed in. "Well, of course she has." She patted my leg, laughing at her own audacity.

"Tracy," Emily said, her voice filled with disbelief.

"What? It's true," Tracy said nonchalantly. "I came over the other day for a coffee and caught them." She turned to me, a mischievous grin on her face. "I waited at Dad's for two hours. Finally, I gave up and went home."

The group erupted into laughter, the sound so

loud I thought it might wake the entire neighborhood.

"Oh, Tracy," Cassie said, wiping tears from her eyes, "Why couldn't you have told us that story at the beginning of the night? Everyone else would've loved to hear it."

And just like that, I was suddenly the center of attention again—though this time, it wasn't for anything I'd planned, and I wasn't about to stop it. Let them have their fun. At least for now, Charlotte wasn't around to make things worse.

CHAPTER 22

Bailey

The night only got messier. The more alcohol they drank, the more the closet stories came out, and the chaos seemed to multiply with every glass. Emily, Sophie, Ali, Cassie, Judy, Trish, and Tracy were the last ones standing. When things turned sentimental, and a few tears were shed, Ali—being the only sober one—finally suggested it was time to call it a night.

With the food already packed into containers and shoved back in the fridge, I didn't have much to clean. I stumbled upstairs, half-walking, half-swaying, hoping the night would end peacefully. The sun would be rising soon, anyway. My head hit the pillow, and almost immediately, the room started to spin. I didn't fight it. The swirling sensation wrapped around me like a blanket, pulling me under until I finally drifted to sleep.

I woke up still feeling the aftereffects of too much alcohol. I squinted at the clock—it was past eight. My first priority was the shower. I hoped it would make me feel better, maybe wake me up a bit. At first, the hot water soothed my tired muscles, but as the room heated up, the discomfort kicked in. My stomach churned, and I felt nauseous.

I managed to pull on denim shorts and a black singlet, leaving my hair loose. I was too hungover to deal with tying it up. My head throbbed with every step I took as I went downstairs.

Ali was the only one up when I reached the bottom. She was sitting on the couch, flipping through one of the home decorating magazines I kept on the coffee table.

"Good morning," I said, though I wasn't sure *good* was the right word considering how much my head ached.

"Hey, how are you feeling?" Ali sounded just as rough as I felt.

I groaned, holding my head in my hands. "I think

I'm still drunk," I giggled, even though it hurt to move. The smallest motion made my head throb painfully.

Ali raised an eyebrow, clearly not in much better shape herself despite not drinking. "Do you remember much about last night?"

I frowned, trying to recall the details of the night before. "Did I do something really bad?"

Ali laughed. "No, but Tracy told everyone she caught you and Noah... well, you know... in the act."

My face went white, and I could feel the blood draining from it. "Oh no, she didn't." I was mortified. "Why would she do that?"

Ali shrugged, still laughing a little. "Well, when Charlotte said no one could've slept with Noah because he was still in love with her, you started laughing, and you couldn't stop. It was pretty amusing. Charlotte was furious."

I couldn't believe it. "I need coffee," I muttered. "Want one?"

Ali looked at me, clearly considering, before nodding. "Can I make myself a cup of tea, though? If that's okay?"

"Oh, of course, the baby," I grinned, trying to lighten the mood. "Is it as exciting as I imagine it would be?"

"More," Ali laughed, but despite looking under the weather, I could see the sheer joy radiating from her. "You'd like to have children?"

I didn't want to sound too eager, so I just nodded. I wasn't sure what I wanted, but I had to admit, the idea was appealing.

Ali followed me into the kitchen as I started the coffee maker.

"Do you have plans today?" she broke the silence.

"Not with the way my head is pounding," I replied, my voice thick. "If we're feeling lousy, can you imagine how the guys must feel?"

Ali thought for a moment. "Maybe we could go for a swim in the dam and then come back and eat? There's so much leftover food, and it'll just go to waste otherwise."

"Great idea," I said. "But probably best not to call them too early, though."

The smell of fresh coffee eventually dragged the others from their beds. No one was feeling particularly perky, so we all gathered outside, wearing sunglasses to shield our eyes from the bright morning light. The only visible sign of the chaos the night before was an empty box of paracetamol sitting in the otherwise pristine party zone.

"Well, I guess I should get going," Trish

announced after a few minutes. She'd hired staff for the early shift but was due in for lunchtime.

"Me too," said Tracy, picking up her mug and the empty paracetamol box to take inside with her. "Thank you for a wonderful night, ladies. I thoroughly enjoyed myself."

Ali and I exchanged a look, but didn't comment.

The younger girls stayed, though, and Emily was relieved her mum wasn't dropping the kids home until after dinnertime, giving her the day to hang out.

"We're up, so I think the guys should be too. What do you say we give them a call?" Emily suggested, trying to rally the group.

"Yeah, but I say we each call their cell and the home phone number, too. That'll wake them up for sure." Ali's energy was infectious, and she wasn't feeling the aftereffects of last night like the rest of us.

I realized the only number I had for Noah was Cooper's, so Cassie dialed Noah's.

"On the count of three," she said, and we all prepared ourselves.

To say they weren't impressed with being woken up so early was an understatement. The others received nothing but grumpy responses, but Cooper

—being Cooper—greeted me with his usual cheerful voice. "Hey-hey, beautiful girl."

I rolled my eyes and smiled. He was so much easier to be around than Noah. Why did I have to fall for the most complicated guy in town?

The thought of spending the day with Noah made me nervous. What would we be? Friends? Lovers? Enemies? I could barely keep up.

I suggested spending the day at my place, trying to gauge his reaction.

"Does this mean you love me, and not Noah?" Cooper teased. I could hear him hold the phone away from his mouth as he called out, "Hey mate, looks like she loves me."

I couldn't quite make out Noah's response over the noise. Cooper's voice cut through, and I barely caught his words. "Sorry, Bailey. I don't know how to tell you this, but Noah said, *Get fucked, man*. But hey, I'd love to come spend the day with you."

I tried not to laugh, though the pain in my head was excessive, like someone had taken a hammer to my skull. My brain was still swimming from last night.

Cassie stood up, completely matter-of-fact. "So, are we going home to get bathers, or are we skinny-dipping?"

For a moment, I thought she was serious, but then she added, "I might have enough spare if you want to borrow some."

I racked my brain for where I might've left my spare set of bathers, but before I could speak, Cassie grinned and added, "I was joking." She grabbed her car keys, clearly ready to go. "Who wants a lift?"

"I asked Rick to bring mine, and Sophie's given Ben his orders. What about you, Em?" I asked, turning to Emily.

She nodded, clearly relieved.

"Yep, the lonely heart is the only one having to fetch her own," Cassie added, sounding half-amused, half-resigned.

"Hey, I would be too if I weren't at home," I said. "But honestly, you're welcome to a pair of mine."

"I'm flattered, really, but there is no way I'm squeezing into one of your tiny little numbers. I'm like a foot taller and wider than you. I think I'd feel more comfortable in my own, but thanks anyway." Cassie shrugged, and with that, she was off. The rest of us lingered for a moment.

"Anyone want another drink?" I was trying to distract myself. "I can cook some croissants or eggs for breakfast if you're hungry."

Sophie and Emily opted for juice, the same as me.

"Can I just make a slice of toast, please?" Ali blushed, her voice a little sheepish. "I'm feeling a bit off."

"I'll get it. What do you want on it?"

"Just butter, if you don't mind. I find plain is easier to manage."

I set the toast to cook and grabbed a tray for the glasses, juice, and Ali's food once it was ready. Carrying the tray outside, I set it down, and everyone helped themselves.

"I'll be back in about ten minutes," I said, feeling guilty. "I have to feed Freya. Please help yourself to whatever you feel like, and if you want a shower, there are fresh towels in the linen cupboard."

It wasn't fair for Freya to go hungry because I had been irresponsible the night before. Besides, what was with Tracy's story about Noah and me? She'd told everyone we were sleeping together. He'd flip if he knew.

I couldn't shake the feeling of unease. When I hurt my leg and couldn't walk, there was never a time I didn't stand to groom Freya, even for a few minutes. But with my head still pounding and the others due to arrive soon, I decided to skip brushing her today.

As I turned the corner, I could hear laughter in the distance.

"Ahh, there's my girl." Cooper greeted me, sweeping me into a hug and planting a loud kiss on my cheek.

I glanced over at Noah. He was watching me, draining the contents of his glass, and then heading inside without a word.

"Does anyone want a tea or coffee?" As much as I longed to sit and do nothing until my head stopped throbbing, I was back to being host.

"Six for coffee, and Ali wants tea," I added, already moving to the kitchen.

Noah was leaning against the bench, waiting for me.

"So, how are you feeling this morning?" His voice was neutral, but there was something off about his posture. He didn't even smile.

"Seedy. And you?"

"Same," he muttered, his arms crossed as he watched me.

The tension between us was thick. We were back to being awkward.

"Do you want coffee?" I was trying to ease the silence.

"I'd prefer you," he replied, the words coming out a little too casual.

I blinked, unsure how to respond.

"Why'd you call Cooper this morning and not me?" His tone had a slight edge to it, the jealousy simmering just below the surface.

Even simple math felt like a chore with my head still thumping. Seven people were outside, and Noah and I made nine. I took two mugs from the drawer, filled the kettle for Ali's tea, and let the words hang in the air before answering. "I don't have your number in my phone."

"But you have Cooper's."

I stopped what I was doing, my pulse quickening, and walked over to stand in front of him. "Do me a favor?"

"Of course," he said, but I could hear the suspicion in his voice.

"Stop with the jealousy where Cooper's concerned. If I wanted him, I'd tell you." I cupped his cheek gently. "I have Cooper's number because he's working for me." I didn't try to kiss him, knowing better than to push it when he was in one of his moods. It was safer to let him make the first move.

"Oh, and can you carry some of these drinks

outside for me, please?" I added, hoping to shift the focus.

Noah didn't respond immediately, but he nodded and grabbed the tray I prepared. I continued making the drinks, starting with Ali's tea. I knew exactly how she liked it, so I asked Noah to take it to her and set up the sugar bowl and teaspoons on the tray outside so everyone could help themselves.

By the time Noah returned, I had two coffees finished. The little coffee machine wasn't fast by any stretch of the imagination, but I kept them coming. Just when I thought I was done, Cassie walked in and added one more to the list.

When Noah came back, he walked up behind me, slipping his arms around my waist and kissing my neck. My stomach clenched at the sudden contact, and I leaned back into him, feeling his warmth against me.

I finished up the last coffee, setting it on the counter. "Orders up," I breathed, trying to push down the tension that seemed to hang in the air.

But Noah wasn't done. He slipped his hands up under my shirt, pressing his body against mine more firmly. I turned my head, and before I knew it, his lips were on mine, claiming me with a kiss that stole my breath.

"Oh, for fuck's sake, you two," a voice cut through the moment. "Why do I always have to be the one to catch you at it?"

I stiffened, my heart sinking. But Noah just laughed, a devilish grin spreading across his face. "Cas, go outside, will you?"

"Already going, you bossy bastard," she shot back, and I heard her telling the others we were *doing it* in the kitchen.

"Don't exaggerate, Cas, and shh, they'll hear you," Ali called out, though I could still hear the teasing tone.

I cringed, mortified, but Noah laughed again. I couldn't move until he released me.

"I'd offer you a rain check," I said, my voice low, "but those seem to be a common occurrence for us."

"Or," Noah whispered in my ear, "we could head upstairs and let them fend for themselves a bit."

Something told me they'd notice if we slipped away. I smoothed my top as Noah stepped back, and there was no denying it—his lips were as bruised and swollen as mine felt. I picked up my coffee cup and sipped it, trying to shake the tension that hung in the air.

"Do you want me to take yours outside?" I was hoping to avoid an awkward silence.

"That'd be great, thanks. I'll be just a minute."

I didn't want to go out alone, especially not after what Cassie had just teased. But the longer I waited, the worse it would look. I slid my sunglasses in place, steeling myself for what was about to come, and walked out to face the accusations.

"Glad you decided to join us. Where's your partner in crime, taking care of the evidence?" Cassie teased, a mischievous grin on her face.

"Give it a rest, Cassie." Cooper came to my defense, his voice warm and protective.

"Sorry, Cooper, I forgot you've got the hots for her too." Cassie's laugh rang out like a challenge.

"Cas, zip it," Ben said, his voice calm but firm. When he spoke, everyone listened.

The silence that followed was almost lovely—if not a little awkward. A few moments later, Noah joined us, and the others tried not to laugh, but failed miserably.

"Oh my God, does anyone remember Tracy telling everyone she caught them doing the deed the other day?" Sophie burst out laughing, and suddenly all eyes were on me and Noah.

"She said what?" Noah growled.

A knot formed in my stomach.

"I was pretty drunk, but I thought that's what she said," Sophie added, still snickering.

I sighed. "Who wants to go swimming?" I tried to distract them, but no one seemed to be paying attention.

"Ali?" Sophie was looking for backup, and of course, Ali was the only sober person she could count on.

"Really, Soph? How about we go swimming?" Ali said, eyeing me as she spoke.

"Out with it, Ali, what'd my mother say?" Noah's voice was low but insistent.

Ali looked at me, her expression serious. "He won't let it go until you tell him. You may as well just spill."

Trying to keep a straight face, Ali retold Tracy's version of the story. Even Noah chuckled. I was mortified, but what could I do now that everyone knew? I wondered if Tracy even remembered what she'd said.

"Okay, enough talk about my sex life. Who wants to go swimming?" Noah's voice broke through the tension, and the others quickly scattered.

"Someone keep him down here while she gets changed. We don't need any more babies cropping up," Rick teased.

I had a feeling it was going to be a while before I lived this one down.

I passed the keys of my truck to Noah. "Do you want to drive? You know this place better than I do."

"I want your car, Bailey," Rick announced as he climbed into the back. I laughed and took the passenger seat. Sophie climbed in with Ali. Cassie would've fit, but she opted for the tray with the boys instead.

The sun glinted off the water, blinding me. Even with sunglasses on, I squinted against the glare. Cooper was the first to dive in, and Ben followed right after. Sophie took her time removing her clothes to reveal a hot-pink bikini.

"Hurry up with those clothes, Bailey, because you'll be going in with or without them," Noah teased, pulling his t-shirt over his head in one swift movement.

I would've preferred to just sit back and enjoy the view for a while, but I had a feeling Noah wasn't joking. I slipped my shorts off, my top halfway covering my face, and Noah scooped me up over his shoulder. He didn't give me a chance to react before he was running straight for the water. I managed to drop my top away from the edge so it wouldn't get wet.

The water felt like ice when it hit the back of my legs. I reached up instinctively to hold my sunglasses in place, knowing that if they fell off, I'd never see them again in the murky depths of the dam.

I imagined Jack had been the one responsible for lining the dam walls with coffee rock and building the wooden deck anchored in the middle. When I mentioned it to Noah, he laughed.

"Nah, this is the work of the awesome foursome. We built it, intending to sleep out here one night."

"You slept out here?" I couldn't imagine it would have been safe.

"Nah, our parents wouldn't let us. They said we'd probably drown. We weren't too happy about it, I can tell you."

There were so many memories for him here. It broke my heart to rob them from him.

I stretched out on the warm wood, the sun beating down on my wet skin. This lifestyle—the one Noah was so accustomed to—was so different from anything I'd ever known. It beat everything I had experienced before. Noah sat beside me, the side of his leg pressed against mine.

After a few minutes of silence, I opened my eyes. Noah was gazing out over the water, lost in thought.

We were alone on the pontoon, but I could hear the others laughing back at the shore.

"What are you thinking?" I noticed how closed off he still seemed. He always held something back from me.

"I used to bring my little sister here. She said it was her favorite place in the world," Noah said quietly, his voice distant. He fell silent again, and I didn't push him. Instead, I placed my hand gently on his back.

Leaning back on his elbow, Noah turned his body toward mine. He traced circles around my belly button with his fingertip, sending little shivers through me.

"Can I stay with you tonight, Bailey?" His voice was low, barely above a whisper, as though trying to keep the others from hearing.

I lifted my hand to touch his cheek, smiling softly. "I'd like that."

Noah closed the distance between us, bringing his lips to mine in the most tender of kisses. I drew my knees up, rolling into him, my arms wrapping around his neck as I kissed him back.

Noah shifted his body, partially covering mine. His hand slid up my thigh, and I felt the heat of his touch. He ran his fingers along the edge of my bathing bottoms before snagging the elastic with his thumb and slipping his hand inside. Wet and wanting, I moved my legs, silently opening myself to him, all while trying to remain unnoticed by the others, who were still back at the shore.

Noah pushed me onto my back, blanketing me with his body, deepening the kiss. "I want you so bad," he whispered, his mouth still pressed to mine, muffling the words I longed to hear.

"I—"

"For Christ's sake, you two. Get a room." Cassie called from the shore, interrupting us.

Despite being snowed under with the final touches on the barn for the retreat the following week, I couldn't help but get distracted by last-minute wedding details.

I'd booked an appointment with Ali the day before, hoping for a chance to talk to her about the type of dress I should wear. With Charlotte in town, there was no way I wanted to get it wrong.

"Is everything on track for the retreat next week?" Ali's excitement matched my own. Even Emily had offered to help out during the day while the kids were at school.

"Yes. I finished painting the bedroom area last night. The windows are open, airing it out. Cooper has the carpet guys coming in first thing Monday morning. Other than that, it's just as Cooper said—ready with days to spare."

"Good job. Now you can sit back, relax, and enjoy the wedding."

"Huh, that's what you think. Charlotte will be a nightmare when she sees me and Noah together. I just hope she doesn't make a scene."

"She won't. Matt will be there, remember?"

I nodded but still felt a knot in my stomach. The idea of Charlotte making a scene was all too real.

"Now, this is a stupid question, but you have something amazing to wear, don't you?" Ali asked, already fussing. I knew why.

"I was going to ask you for advice. Do you think I should go sexy and conservative, or maybe a bit more daring?"

"What were you thinking?"

I gave it some thought. "I feel more comfortable in the classy, sleek type of look rather than something too suggestive."

"Not suggestive—he's had enough of that in this lifetime. Stick with classy."

That was helpful, but I still wasn't any closer to

figuring it out when I got home. So, I called Tracy for another opinion.

"Of course, love. Come on over."

Twenty minutes later, I arrived with dress boxes and a pair of heels to try with all four dresses. Tracy didn't waste any time.

"Now, don't tell me which one you like best. I'll tell you what I think. Mike should be in soon, too." She bustled me into the study to change.

The first dress was black, sleek, and long to the ankles. The neckline was a little low, as was the back. Stunning, but a bit risqué, in my opinion.

The second one was plain in petrol green—again, sleek and full-length, but this one was strapless. The most uncomfortable of them all, but I'd put up with it if I had to.

The third was my favorite. The midnight blue figure-hugging dress was boat-necked, cut across the collarbone. From the front, it was conservative—like a librarian. When I turned around, it was completely backless.

Mike walked into the kitchen and whistled. "You look stunning, love." He reached into the fridge, grabbed a beer, and offered one to me.

"Thanks," I said, smiling. "I have one more to try on."

I disappeared into the study again, and when I emerged, Noah was standing in the kitchen, his presence commanding my attention.

The last dress was the red one. By far the most daring, and my least favorite.

"Are you planning to wear that to the wedding?" Noah's eyes swept over me more than once, his gaze intense.

"Shh, Noah, I'm trying to decide." Tracy, ever the voice of reason, looked deep in thought. "The third one."

I sighed in relief. "Oh good, that's my pick too."

"No, this one," I said, motioning to the red dress. "I feel like I'm dressed for a nightclub or street walking in this one."

Noah nodded in agreement.

"Well, there's no need to agree," I laughed, picking up the beer Mike had opened for me and taking a swig.

"Now that's a classy look," Noah grinned, then ducked out of the room.

CHAPTER 23

Bailey

I didn't normally feel the need to outdo or compete with other women, but I had a feeling Charlotte was pining for Noah's attention, and I had no intention of sharing.

After curling my hair, I swept it to the side in a loose braid, letting pieces escape, giving my look a sexy, wild edge. My strappy stilettos were classic, with thin ankle straps adorned with two strands of diamantes, like little anklets on either side.

As soon as I walked down the red carpet aisle, linking arms with Jack, I caught Noah staring. Abandoning his post as a groomsman, he came over to say hello.

"You look beautiful," he said, his gaze soft and warm. As he lowered his head to kiss me, the music began, and he pulled back, his expression changing. "Gotta go."

Jack edged between the rows of seats closest to where we were standing, and I couldn't help but watch as Noah turned back to his position.

Jodie and Thomas were the first to walk down the aisle. Thomas wore a suit matching Noah's, and Jodie's golden curls bobbed around her face, a vision of Emily. Her ivory dress was every little girl's dream—a satin bodice with layers of tulle for the skirt, and around her waist, an apricot bow that matched the rose petals she threw from her basket.

The bridesmaids, Emily, Cassie, and Ali, looked beautiful in matching apricot dresses.

The crowd stood for the bride. Being on the shorter side, I didn't have the best view, but as Sophie passed, I caught a glimpse. Dressed in ivory, her straight style was similar to that of the bridesmaids, only more elaborate with delicate lace overlay that formed a small train behind her. She looked stunning. Her hair was pinned up, and a thin veil covered her face.

I glanced up, wanting to see Ben's reaction. He beamed as she walked toward him.

My eyes flicked to Noah, and as if he sensed my gaze, his eyes met mine. He winked before quickly turning back to face the front as required.

The ceremony was one of the most intimate I'd ever attended. The celebrant spoke of Ben and Sophie as a couple, sharing quotes they had each spoken during her time knowing them.

When the formal part was over, Noah joined me to congratulate the newlyweds.

"I don't know how I'm going to keep my hands off you tonight," he murmured, his hand resting on my lower back, his touch warm against my skin. "This dress should be outlawed."

"Oh, you don't like it?" I teased, glancing up at him.

"Of course, but I'd prefer to be peeling you out of it."

I leaned in closer to him. "I'll hold you to that."

Noah grinned and kissed me tenderly on the lips. There was no denying we were involved. When he lifted his head, he gazed into my eyes, his voice low. "Good thing everyone's caught up in the bride and groom, or else we would've just hit the top of the gossip list."

We congratulated Ben and Sophie before moving aside for others. Jack was standing with Max, so we walked over to join them.

"How are your Dexter's faring?" Max's eyes flicked between Noah and me.

"Noah?" I raised an eyebrow.

He'd finally accepted the Dexter cattle as his own.

A smile spread across Max's face as he clapped Noah on the back. "About bloody time you got in the game, mate. What's your plan?" Bailey listened as the men talked farming. She liked hearing Noah's plans, but was taken aback when he mentioned a small farm on the outskirts of town that he was considering making an offer on.

I wanted to tell him not to be a fool—that he could share my land—but I held back. This wasn't the time or place for that discussion. Besides, I summed it up perfectly—*my* land. If I felt it, then it was bound to be an issue for him.

Noah left to take photos with the rest of the bridal party, and Jack didn't leave my side.

"If there are people you want to catch up with, please don't feel you have to babysit me," I said as we wandered over to grab a glass of beer.

"No one I'd rather be with than you. Besides, I

have no interest in leaving you for the vulture to feed on."

I almost choked on the mouthful of beer I had just taken. "The what?" I managed to gasp, coughing from the liquid.

"That Charlotte has been watching you like a vulture watches its prey, waiting to take it by surprise. Well, I'm not going to give her the opportunity."

His concern for me was touching. "Thank you, but believe me, I've had tougher opponents for breakfast. What did he ever see in her though? She's awful—a real sniveler."

Jack choked on his beer. I patted him on the back as he coughed. "That's what Maggie used to call her. Oh, she would've loved you." Jack's eyes brimmed with tears, partly from the beer threatening to go the wrong way.

Tucking my arm through his, I suggested, "Why don't you show me around the magnificent grounds of Ben's family farm?"

A marquee had been set up alongside a large lake. The soft ripples of the water sparkled under the setting sun.

"Is that a natural landform, or manmade?" My curiosity piqued.

"Natural. Spring-fed and good enough to drink if you had to," he replied with a grin. Having lived in the town for so long, Jack was practically a walking tour guide.

Ben's family owned the largest winery in the area and regularly took home top prizes for their finer drops. The rows of grapevines behind us, sprawling across the hillside, created the most romantic of backdrops, with the sun slowly sinking lower in the sky, casting a warm, golden glow.

I stood with Jack, admiring the view, when I suddenly felt fingers trail up my back and settle at the base of my neck. A shiver ran down my spine, and I knew without even turning around who it was.

"Did you miss me?" Noah whispered, his voice low and familiar, sending an electric charge through me.

"I might head over and see Trish. Thanks for the walk, Bailey," Jack said, giving me a small nod.

Before I could respond, Noah draped his arm around me, pulling me close. "Are you having a nice time?" His voice was warm, his touch even warmer.

"Yes. Jack's a sweetheart, acting as my bodyguard," I said with a light laugh, not entirely joking.

Noah's fingers lightly traced up and down my arm, sending goosebumps across my skin. "I'm sorry she's here, but you know she means absolutely nothing to me, don't you?"

I turned to face him, and Noah instinctively wrapped his arms around my waist, pulling me closer. I could feel the steady beat of his heart against mine.

"You mean so much to me, and—I just wanted you to know that." His words were sincere, a quiet confession that made my pulse quicken.

I stood on my toes, closing the space between us, and kissed him gently on the lips. "I'm glad to hear it, Noah, because I've fallen for you big time."

He brushed his fingertips over my shoulder and up the side of my neck. "Good," he whispered, his lips grazing mine once more, softer this time. "Now, we must get back to the party."

The evening was meant to be casual, with no assigned seats—it was a cocktail-style affair. I was relieved. With all my friends in the bridal party, it would've been a completely different experience, but right now, this one felt perfect. I was enjoying every moment of it.

When the bridal waltz began, Noah started the dance with Emily, but the moment he saw his chance, he abandoned her and pulled me onto the floor.

My father had made sure I was a competent ballroom dancer, as many events we attended required me to be. I had no trouble keeping up with Noah as he effortlessly swept me around the dance floor, his hands firm and confident at my waist.

As the song ended and another began, Charlotte tapped me on the shoulder. "May I cut in?" Her smile was tight, her eyes hard with jealousy. The bitterness in her tone was unmistakable.

"No, you can't," Noah growled, his arm tightening around me, not giving me a chance to speak for myself. Without another word, he whisked me away in a waltz that had my head spinning, my feet barely touching the ground.

I would've loved to see Charlotte's reaction. Serves her right for how she'd treated him.

When the song ended, Noah led me off the dance floor and along a quiet path that took us to a bench beside the lake. The moonlight reflected on the water, its glow almost as beautiful as the sunset. It was serene, private, and exactly what I needed.

"I'm sorry. I had to get out of there for a while," Noah murmured as we sat down, his voice tinged with frustration.

I nodded, understanding completely. When

Charlotte had tapped me on the shoulder, I wanted to throttle her for even suggesting I hand Noah over.

"Why are you looking at buying a farm?" I attempted to change the subject. It seemed like a good distraction from the tension in the air.

Noah seemed unprepared for my question, his laugh escaping before he could control it. "What do you want me to do? Live at my parents' for the rest of my life and run your land?"

I shook my head. "I know it's probably a bit soon to know where this is going, but I thought you might one day move in with me, and we could share the farm, as it should be."

He fell quiet for a moment, his jaw tightening. "Let's not talk about it tonight, Bailey. I don't want to argue."

"I didn't plan on arguing," I said softly. "I just want us to be together, that's all."

Instead of answering, Noah leaned in and kissed me, his mouth pressing urgently against mine. The kiss left me breathless, and when he finally pulled away, I leaned into him, not against the cold bench, knowing the wood would be uncomfortable against my bare skin.

A chill ran through me, and I shivered. The

breeze from the lake felt like ice shards piercing through the thin fabric of my dress.

"Come on, we should get back. I have a speech to make," Noah said, standing up. He shrugged off his jacket and draped it over my shoulders, instantly warming me. With his arm securely around my waist, we rejoined the party. The simple gesture—him covering me with his jacket—was enough to announce that he'd staked his claim. Jack was the only one privileged enough to drag me away for a dance.

∼

Noah

Charlotte, always opportunistic, saw her chance. She descended on us with a sharp smile. "Bit out of your league, isn't she, Noah?"

"Obviously not, Charlotte," I didn't hide the chill from my tone. "So why don't you scamper back to whatever hole you crawled out of and stay there."

"Oh, Noah, don't be like that. We had fun together, and believe it or not, I miss you. It pisses me off to see her with her perfectly manicured hands all over you." Charlotte's voice was dripping with feigned sweetness, but there was an edge to it that I couldn't ignore.

"This is not the time or the place for your games," I cut her off.

"I'm happy to take it back to your place if you'd prefer," Charlotte taunted, not backing down.

My stare was fixed on Bailey as she and Jack walked back toward me. The weight of her gaze on me, steady and possessive.

"Go away," I muttered, but didn't waste my breath on slinging insults. My attention was elsewhere, and I had no intention of glancing back at Charlotte as she faded into the background.

"What'd she want?" Jack snarled, his voice low and filled with a hint of irritation.

"Just offering herself up for the taking. Nothing unusual." I shrugged, nonchalant, then took Bailey's hand and brought it to my lips, kissing it softly. "Isn't she breathtaking?" I said to Jack.

"From the moment she stepped out of the truck on that first day," Jack replied with a knowing smile.

I grinned. "I'm just glad he's too old for you, or I'd have some hearty competition."

"You'd better believe it." Jack laughed, giving me a

friendly clap on the shoulder before heading off toward his table.

"You want to sit for a while?" Those shoes she was wearing had to be uncomfortable to stand in for so long.

She nodded, clearly grateful for the chance to rest her feet.

Ali, ever the ball of energy, collapsed into the chair beside us. "I'm shattered." She rested her head on Bailey's shoulder and wrapped her arm around her. "Are you having a good time?" Her voice warm with curiosity.

"The best," Bailey replied. "This place is amazing, and everything has been beautiful." Except for Charlotte. But Noah had taken care of her pretty quickly.

"Including you. This dress is amazing, isn't it Noah?" Ali said with a grin.

"Sure is." I returned her smile and shook my head. Ali was right up there with Jack, shaking her poms and singing a cheer about the status of our relationship.

"It's good to see you happy. I'm guessing you're too loved up to be packed and ready for next week?"

"Huh, you better believe it." A tradition started when we were thirteen years old, our annual boys' trip didn't take much planning. Camped out under the stars, a few snacks and our motorbikes—*what was there to pack?*

"Oh, and if you think you'll ever take priority over one of the awesome foursomes' traditions, think again. Ben made Sophie change the wedding date because of that weekend," Ali warned Bailey.

Bailey laughed as if Ali was joking, but I could totally believe it was true.

"So, are you going to kick off the retreat with a barn dance?" Ali seemed as excited about the retreats as Bailey.

"That was the initial plan," she said. "But, with everything that's been going on, and how fine we're cutting it to have the barn ready, I didn't want to push my luck."

"There's always next time," Ali suggested. "Besides, it gives us something to look forward to. Life can get pretty monotonous around here without community events—probably why we have so many kids. The school tends to bring everyone together."

Kids were something I hoped for in the future, but not a topic I wanted to get into tonight. Even an inkling I was thinking along those lines and the town grapevine would be planning our wedding next. It was early days, but I didn't even know if Bailey was up for having a family of her own.

"Well, that's my rest over. I must go and perform my bridesmaid duties. They'll be leaving soon." Ali gave Bailey a quick squeeze before she stood up and headed back toward the festivities.

∼

Bailey

Noah draped his arm across my shoulders, pulling me close. "Are we staying at yours tonight?" he spoke close to my ear.

"Sounds good to me, unless you want to try out that pontoon," I teased with a grin. It sounded like fun, but probably better when Noah was sober.

"That's a must when the weather gets hotter," he replied with a laugh, clearly indulging me.

Before the night came to an end, Ben and Sophie took the mic to thank everyone for sharing their day with them. It was the usual heartfelt speech, full of gratitude and love. Then, it was time to cut the wedding cake. I couldn't help but feel a pang of regret, knowing someone had gone to so much trouble to create such a beautiful work of art, only to see it cut into. But they didn't seem bothered at all. Ben, in fact, went so far as to smudge cake on Sophie's face, and the look of shock followed by a roar of laughter was the perfect reaction from her.

If I wasn't standing here with Noah's arm around me, I would've gone home feeling lonelier than ever before. But tonight, I wasn't alone. I was with him.

Falling asleep with Noah wrapped around me was something I wanted to experience at the end of every day. The innocence and simplicity of it was, in some ways, more intimate than sex. For me, the security of being with him was enough—anything more was a bonus. Waking up that way was even better.

Leaving him to sleep, I wandered downstairs to cook him pancakes for breakfast. I was still smiling, thinking about the way he'd held me close all night, like he was afraid I might slip away.

Noah wandered into the kitchen not long after I made the first cup of coffee and cooked a quarter of the batter. I'd chopped strawberries, then mixed them in a bowl with fresh blueberries and mulberries. I set the fruit on the table alongside maple syrup and an assortment of jams.

"I was wondering where you'd disappeared to. Leaving me all alone up there." His voice was sleepy, but it had that teasing edge that always made my stomach flutter. He was still warm from bed as he folded me into his arms, pressing his chest against my back.

"I thought you might be hungry. Do you like pancakes?" I continued stirring the batter.

"Sure do." Noah kissed me on the neck, his lips lingering there for a moment, sending a shiver down my spine. Then he let me get back to cooking.

"Coffee?" I offered, glancing over my shoulder at him.

"I can make it if you show me how to use that thing."

"Yeah, sure, it's easy." I talked him through the process, the familiarity of it all grounding me in the comfort of his presence.

When he was finished, he took a mouthful and sighed. "Mmm, you're right, it's not you, it's the machine."

I swatted his shoulder playfully. "Watch it."

He grinned and watched as I piled more

pancakes onto the already large stack. "Who's going to eat all those?"

"You. Now hop to it, get them while they're hot," I teased, nudging him toward the table.

He raised his eyebrows, the familiar mischievous glint in his eyes. "You know, I could have made a fool of myself with a really corny comeback after that comment."

I laughed, shaking my head. "I'm pleased you're learning to restrain yourself, now start eating."

Noah didn't stay for long after breakfast. There was always something that had to be done on the farm, and since he wasn't hungover, he didn't have an excuse not to work. I could tell he didn't mind it, though. The farm was his life, and I loved how passionate he was about it.

After cleaning the kitchen, I took my computer to the table to check my emails. It had become a daily ritual since I sent one to my mother, who still hadn't responded. Each day, I couldn't help but feel a little disheartened. It was possible the address was wrong—I'd copied it from my father's diary many years ago, and my mother had never contacted me from it before.

There were the usual marketing emails from my online purchases, especially now with Christmas specials starting. Then two last-minute email bookings for the retreat came through—one from an inner-city address, and the other local. I found the local one odd, but with the way Jack marketed my retreat to everyone he met, I shouldn't have been surprised.

A door slamming upstairs startled me. I didn't bother investigating. It had been almost a week since the last sign of activity from that room, but then again, Cooper had set up a lamp to a timer for me so I wouldn't have to remember to turn it on before bed. He was considerate like that.

The last time I'd heard noises was the night of the picnic in the park after Noah and I argued. I hoped this wasn't a warning of what was to come. Some would call it coincidence. I wasn't convinced.

The knock at the front door made me jump for the second time that day. I sighed and went to answer, wishing I'd just ignored it—like I had the door slamming upstairs.

"Charlotte. What can I do for you?" I couldn't keep the edge out of my voice. I didn't have time to listen to more of her garbage today.

"I was wondering if I could come in for a minute." Her voice was as smooth as ever, but there was something about her demeanor that made me think she wasn't as confident as she was trying to appear.

I couldn't imagine what we could possibly have to talk about, but I was curious to see where this was heading.

"You've really made this place lovely," she said, looking around with a forced smile. I guessed she wasn't as sure of herself here as she tried to make out.

"Would you like a coffee or some juice?" I offered a small-town gesture of hospitality. Maybe it would calm her down a bit. We were in the country now, after all, and I didn't want to be rude—though I really wasn't in the mood for whatever game she was playing.

"Um, a coffee would be lovely, thank you." Charlotte's voice was soft, but there was something in it that made me bristle.

I didn't look at her as I made the coffee and carried it to the table, setting it down in front of her without a word.

"I can see why Noah's in love with you." She took a sip of her coffee, her eyes studying me with an intensity I didn't care for.

"If you came here to discuss me and Noah, think

again. Our relationship—every aspect of it—is off-limits," I warned, my tone sharp.

"Fair enough," she said with a sigh. "I was jealous. I have no right to be, so I'm sorry." Charlotte took another mouthful of her coffee. "Mmm, this is good."

I sat back in my seat, watching her carefully. Charlotte wasn't here for small talk, I could feel it. She was stalling, trying to find the right words. Was she hoping to see Noah, or was she looking for some sign that he'd stayed the night?

"What do you want, Charlotte?" I couldn't keep the impatience out of my voice, but I kept my tone as even as I could. I had work to do.

She reached into her bag and pulled out an envelope, sliding it across the table to me. "I was hoping you would give this to Noah for me. He won't have anything to do with me, and it's important."

I stared at the envelope for a moment, disbelief creeping into my chest. I couldn't believe I'd almost fallen for her conniving manipulation tactics. "What makes you think I'll give it to him?"

"Because you're a woman, and it's eating you up to know what's inside that envelope." Charlotte leaned forward, a smugness in her voice. "Just because you get around in all your fancy shit doesn't mean you're any better than I am. You can't give him what he wants any more than I could."

I shook my head, my patience wearing thin. "I told you before, Noah and I are off-limits. As for your envelope, I suggest you pick it up and take it with you." I leaned forward, my voice low and controlled, but with the cold edge I was known for. "You don't want to mess with me, Charlotte. The amount it would cost to have your father investigated for shonky dealings and thrown in jail would be like petty cash to me. I'll still be one of the richest women in the country once I'm finished. Do you understand me?"

She nodded, looking suddenly small under my gaze.

"Now pick up your cheap stationery and put it back in that tacky thing you call a purse, and get out of my house." I stood up, my voice hard. "And if you dare come near Noah again, I'm going to be like a rash on your ass that never clears. Do you understand?"

Before Charlotte could respond, a chuckle from the lounge room caught my attention. I turned to see Noah standing in the hallway, his arms crossed, a smirk on his face.

I flashed Charlotte the most angelic smile I could

muster as Noah walked over and stood beside me, placing his hand on my shoulder.

I stood up, and Noah slipped his arm around my waist, pulling me close. "Charlotte was just leaving, weren't you?"

Charlotte stood, her face flushed. She reached into her bag and pulled out the envelope, her expression unreadable. "Maggie's ring. I didn't feel right keeping it." She handed him the envelope and headed for the door, her heels clicking loudly on the floor.

"Charlotte."

She stopped and turned, a smug smile still lingering on her lips.

"You're wrong, Bailey is everything I've ever wanted." Noah's voice rang clear, and his words had the desired effect. The smile quickly disappeared from Charlotte's face as she slammed the door behind her.

"Charming," I said, raising an eyebrow and glancing up at Noah, still holding me close.

"As were you," he teased, looking at me with amusement. "A rash all over her ass? Really?"

I flushed, realizing what I'd said. "I guess you just witnessed hardcore businesswoman Bailey," I muttered, looking down at the floor. "Who uses her financial situation to intimidate your ex-wife."

Noah chuckled. "I guess so." He paused, then added with a grin, "When were you going to tell me you were one of the richest women in the country? Or was that an exaggeration, like the rash?"

I couldn't help but smile. "I told you I could afford the cows."

CHAPTER 24

Bailey

"Oh, can you believe it?" I linked my arm through Ali's, fighting the urge to jump up and down in excitement. "They're actually here."

The retreaters pulled up outside the barn at half-past two, just as planned.

"How many are there?" Ali's voice was laced with curiosity.

"If they all show up, including the one who called yesterday, only seven," I answered, trying to sound more confident than I felt.

"That's okay considering you didn't really advertise," she pointed out.

"I know. It'll give me a chance to iron out any rough spots before we get a full house. Plus, Emily and Tracy are going to spend the days here too. It'll be fine." I tried to convince myself more than anyone else.

The café was the meeting point for my guests, where afternoon tea or coffee and cake were included as part of their retreat package. Trish had volunteered Cal's services to act as their escort. Traveling in convoy to the farm meant no one would get lost, and they'd get a taste of what we were offering right away.

It worked for both of us. I paid him cash, and his charming manner and good looks would make a wonderful first impression. The retreat was supposed to be a whole new experience, and that's exactly what I planned to give them.

I felt as though hundreds of bubbles were forming in my stomach, and with every passing second, one would pop. Though excited, I was petrified that something would go wrong, or worse, that the ladies would be fed up after a day or two and want to go home.

Ali squeezed my hand, grounding me. "It's going to be amazing. You'll see."

I'd never experienced nerves going into a job before. Now definitely wasn't the time to start doubting myself. Once the art activities began, I'd be too busy to worry about what could go wrong.

"Well, this is it." I released a deep breath as the women parked their cars in an orderly row.

Cal was the first to approach, giving me a huge hug and a kiss on the cheek. "I hear we're going to be cousins soon."

"I don't know who told you that, but tell them to keep it down, or they'll frighten Noah off," I replied with a laugh.

Cal winked at me, his grin never faltering. "I'm more charming, anyway."

I laughed again as he moved on to greet Ali with the same friendly warmth. "How's my favorite mama?"

"Cal, that is so wrong," Ali teased. "You make me sound like an old lady. I thought you said you were charming."

I watched as the ladies started to get out of their cars, pulling their bags from the trunks. From what I could see, they ranged in age, and one woman in particular caught my eye. She was younger than the rest, with long blonde hair and, even from a distance, I got the sense she was out of her comfort zone by being here. I smiled at her, and she returned the gesture before quickly glancing at Cal.

When the women were gathered in front of me, I took in their faces and tried to gauge the atmosphere. One woman stood at the back, her attention fixed on her feet, never once looking up.

"Welcome to Maggie's Place." I called out, my voice bright and welcoming. "Just to confuse you, I'm not Maggie. My name's Bailey, and this is Ali. We're so happy to have you here as our guests. Let's go inside so you can put your bags down before we start on introductions."

I gestured for them to follow as I led them inside the barn.

The gasps were exactly what I had hoped for. From the outside, the rustic look of the barn wouldn't appeal to everyone's taste, but inside was like an artist's and crafter's heaven. Shelves of bits and bobs lined the room, each one labeled and displayed in jars and decorated boxes. The business card collage I had worked so hard on took pride of place on the wall next to the door leading to the meditation room. The white kitchen, shiny and new, with an easy to use coffee machine, a freshly baked cake on a covered stand, and a bowl of fruit for the ladies to help themselves.

"The sleeping area is upstairs, but we can venture up later," I said, making sure they were following along. "If you pop your bags down, we'll head into the meditation room. Oh, and the bathroom is just through there on your right." I pointed to the door next to the meditation room.

I pushed open the door to Ali's room, and the soothing scent of warming sandalwood and citrus filled the air. A massage table and stool were set up at one end, with products and fresh white towels neatly folded on the shelves. A white shutter screen was folded back but could be used for additional privacy during treatments. Ali had set the mood perfectly with tea lights lit in lanterns around the room, and large earthy-colored cushions were scattered in a circle on the floor. A comfortable sofa was positioned against the wall for anyone who struggled to sit on the floor.

"Please, come in and make yourselves comfortable," I said, gesturing for them to enter. I took a seat next to Ali on the floor, and the others followed. A few of them removed their shoes before stepping into the room.

"I can't begin to tell you how excited I am to have

you here," I said, trying to calm my nerves. "As I mentioned outside, I'm Bailey. I trust you all met Cal, your escort. He's an amazing chef and cooks at the café you visited in town." I paused, taking a deep breath to slow my racing heart and steady my voice. "He'll be cooking lunch for you on Friday, so he'll be back." I tried not to glance at the blonde woman, who had been stealing glances at him earlier. "I'd also like to introduce you to your gorgeous beauty therapist, Ali. She has a salon in the town center, but this is the room she'll work from when she's here. Included in your retreat is a pamper package, but if you'd like anything extra, feel free to talk to Ali about it."

"Now, Cal has to get back to the kitchen—so, bye Cal," I waved, and he offered a dazzling smile.

"Pleasure to meet you, ladies," he said, tipping his head, and with a wink, he left.

I would definitely have to pay him extra for his charm. As soon as he was out of the room, the women giggled like giddy teenagers.

"Okay, now I think it would be nice to go around the circle and introduce ourselves," I suggested, trying to ease the tension. "Feel free to share whatever you like. We'll break the ice and go first, if you like."

A few of them nodded, and I took a deep breath before starting. "I'm Bailey, and I moved to Bennett Springs to establish my dream business. But since arriving, I've made some beautiful friends, met a spunky man, and, somehow, accumulated more animals than I ever thought I would." I gestured toward Ali, who smiled and nodded at me, then turned her attention to the group.

"Hi, I'm Ali," she said, her voice warm. "I'm looking forward to getting to know you all. I'm expecting a baby, which is consuming most of my excitement at the moment."

The mention of her pregnancy had the room buzzing with *ohh's* and *ahh's*. Ali's joy was contagious, and I couldn't help but share in the excitement.

As the introductions went around, I noticed a similar pattern—businesswomen, overworked, and living in a world where their jobs seemed to be all-consuming, leaving little space for anything else. It felt too familiar. That used to be my story too, before I broke free.

Sarah, my first booking, was a mother of six who was looking to find herself again now that her youngest child was about to turn eighteen.

Then, it was the turn of the woman who hadn't

lifted her eyes from the floor since she arrived. She intrigued me—her posture seemed familiar, and I suspected she was local, though I couldn't be sure.

When she finally looked up, I gasped, my hand reaching across to grip Ali's. "Hello, my name's Rhianna," she said, her voice soft yet steady. "I've just moved back to Australia from Ireland." She met my gaze for a brief moment before lowering her eyes again.

I blinked, trying to clear the tears that suddenly filled my eyes. The emotion swelled in me, and I was grateful when the next woman, the pretty blonde, started speaking, offering me something else to focus on.

"Hi, I'm Brittney—Brit for short," she said, her voice shaky but warm. "This retreat was a gift from my mother. I have a little boy who's been very sick, but now that he's in remission, Mom thought it'd be good for me to have a rest. I'm so happy to be here."

A tear escaped, sliding down my cheek. I didn't try to hide it. I had expected there would be more tears in the coming days. "I'm happy you're here too," I said, my voice thick with emotion. "And I'm so glad to hear your son is doing better." I knew remission didn't mean he was cured, but I prayed that it would be the case.

"Upstairs on your bed, you'll find a goodies bag," I continued, my voice a little softer than I'd intended. "Inside, you'll find a folder full of the different projects we'll be covering over the next few days. So if you'd like to get settled, we'll meet back down in the art room when you're ready." My excitement was slipping, and I hoped they wouldn't notice. But, truthfully, I felt a little overwhelmed.

Ali stood up and took charge with her usual calm demeanor. "If you'll follow me, I'll show you where to go."

I squeezed her hand, then let go as I stood. I didn't follow them immediately, choosing instead to stay behind.

The room cleared as the ladies filtered out behind Ali, all except for Rhianna, who kept her eyes fixed on the floor, unwilling to look up until we were alone.

"A bit of warning would've been appreciated, especially when you plan to gatecrash my dreams," I said, trying to keep my voice low, though the anger bubbling inside me was almost too much to contain.

"I'm sorry," Rhianna replied quietly. "I wanted to see you, and I thought this would be a way of spending time together."

"That's bullshit, Mom, and you know it," I shot

back, my voice sharper than I intended. "At least start by telling me the truth after all these years. You booked in knowing you'd have others to hide behind, afraid I'd reject you like you did me. I sent you that email to reach out to you—not as a way to rack up business."

I could feel the venom in my words, and I hated myself for it. But at that moment, I couldn't stop.

"I was scared," she whispered, her voice trembling. "I've been holding on and dreaming of this moment for years. I'm sorry. I know it's the coward's way, but I couldn't stand the thought of losing you again."

"We have nothing to lose," I said, shaking my head in disbelief. "You took care of that the day you left." My voice cracked slightly as the weight of those words sank in. This wasn't the reunion I had expected.

"If you'll join the others and get yourself settled, I've got guests to tend to," I added, trying to regain some semblance of control. There were no big hugs, no tears of joy like I had imagined. Instead, all I felt was regret. Regret for sending that email in the first place. Maybe the coward gene ran in the family, because that's exactly why I'd chosen to make contact the way I did.

When the room emptied, I took my cell from the back pocket of my shorts. Noah had given me his number after the morning wake-up call incident, but this was the first time I'd dialed it.

"Hey, babe, I've been thinking about you. How's it going over there?" I said, trying to keep my voice steady.

"My mother's here," I heard myself say. The words felt too heavy, like too many conflicting emotions tangled up inside of me.

"I beg yours?" Noah's voice was a mix of confusion and concern.

"You heard right. She thought booking a retreat would be a good way for us to bond." My voice shook a little as I spoke the words I never thought I'd say.

Just as I expected, Ali stepped into the room, mouthing, *They're ready.*

I nodded in response, but my mind was still on Noah, on my mother, on everything.

"I don't know what to say. I think I'm in shock," Noah's voice came back, quieter now, like he was still trying to process.

"I'll be home late tonight, but can I call you back?" I said, the exhaustion starting to creep into my words.

"Sure thing, and hey—I miss you," Noah replied, before cutting off the call.

I let out a soft breath, the weight of the conversation lingering. He was all I needed to boost my mood, even if just a little.

I slipped the phone back into my pocket, taking a moment to center myself before facing the room again.

"Is she who I think she is?" Ali wrinkled her nose as if something smelt off.

"Ah huh." I didn't elaborate. I didn't need to. I could already feel the tears threatening, and I wasn't ready to break down again.

Ali linked her arm through mine, guiding me over to where the others were gathered, eager to get started.

She stayed with me through the first activity, knowing it was too late for her to head back to the salon. Bailey could tell she was sticking around for moral support. The room was buzzing with energy as the others began, but Ali stayed close, offering small reassurances every now and then.

"We have a few days, so a lot of the projects I've put together will take time," I said, trying to steer the group's attention. "When you do these layering techniques, it's good to have more than one thing on the go. I can assure you, watching paint dry is about as much fun as it sounds."

A few of the ladies admitted, somewhat reluctantly, that they didn't feel they had a creative bone in their body. I couldn't help but smile, hoping by the end of our time together, they'd prove themselves wrong.

It was a relief to focus on something else, anything else, other than my mother sitting at the far end of the table. Her presence was a quiet weight I could feel even from a distance. But despite everything, I couldn't help but admire the way she worked. I had inherited my artistic flair from her, after all—so many traits I'd gotten from her. But my father? He had been my most influential teacher. I could still see his hands guiding mine, even though he'd been gone for a few years.

With everyone absorbed in their work, I seized the chance to escape to the kitchen. I had dinner to prepare, and the lasagna was layered and ready to go in the oven. As the oven heated up, I prepped a salad in a large bowl, covered it, and set it in the fridge. The main meal was rich enough, so I decided to keep things light for dessert—fruit salad and ice cream would do the trick.

"Would you like a hand with anything?"

I didn't need to turn around to know it was my mother's voice.

"No, thank you. It's all done," I replied, sliding two trays of lasagna into the oven—the smaller one for Noah and Jack to share. When I turned back, I smiled. "I hope you don't mind, I used your recipe." I nodded toward the lasagna, trying to keep things light, even if the weight of everything else pressed in.

"Of course not. I don't remember the last time I made it," Rhianna said, a soft smile on her face.

"Can I ask you something?" I wasn't sure if it was the right moment, but I'd been waiting for this for so long. I could feel the question sitting in my chest, heavy and urgent.

"Anything," she replied.

"Can I hug you?" I whispered. Tears threatened to spill, but I didn't care. The shock had passed, and despite everything, I was just glad she was here.

Without another word, Rhianna rushed forward, pulling me into her arms. She stroked my hair the way she used to when I was a little girl, the familiarity of her touch both soothing and heartbreaking at the same time.

We stayed like that for a moment, until I reluctantly pulled back. "I should get back," I said, feeling the weight of time pressing on me.

Rhianna nodded, her hands still resting on my shoulders. "I just need a minute."

I understood that feeling all too well, but I didn't truly get it until I collapsed into bed that night. The exhaustion from the day, the emotional whirlwind, all caught up with me at once. I sent Noah a quick text promising to call him in the morning, knowing he'd understand.

CHAPTER 25

Bailey

I ventured to the stable early, eager to spend some quiet time with Freya before I joined the ladies at ten o'clock for the next art lesson. We had things to catch up on from the day before, and by the time we showered and had breakfast, I doubted anyone would be ready much before then. It was supposed to be relaxing. We all knew how to run on a schedule, but that's not what I wanted for us here. I needed space for everything to just breathe.

"Ah, I see your priorities, Freya, and then me. At least I assume I'd be next." Noah's voice came from behind me, and I turned to find him leaning against the wall of the tack room, a teasing smile on his lips.

"I didn't see your car." I stroked Freya's neck one last time, then stopped brushing, leaving her to enjoy her meal in peace.

Noah pushed off the wall, his shoulder brushing against it as he moved into my path. "I missed you last night." His hand reached up to brush stray strands of hair that had escaped my ponytail, tucking them behind my ear with a soft, almost affectionate gesture.

"Sorry, it was a crazy day, and I was shattered afterward. I wouldn't have been much fun, anyway." I tried to keep my voice light, but I couldn't deny how much I had missed him too.

"I figured you'd be tired. But as for missing you, I wasn't referring to anything more than just curling up in bed with you."

"You could've snuck in." I grinned, leaning toward him, pressing my lips to his in a quick, quiet kiss. "Someone once told me that country folk don't lock their doors."

Noah chuckled, the sound low and warm in my ears. "Tonight, I promise." His arms wrapped around me, and I let myself sink into the comfort of his embrace, resting my head against his chest. "How'd it go with your mom?"

"She hasn't changed, really. I'm kinda glad she's here. It was just such a shock." I didn't realize how much I needed to say that until the words left my lips. The tension in my shoulders started to loosen a little.

"I suppose you have a heap of questions you want to ask her."

"Yes, but they'll have to wait. I was still hoping to have that barn dance." I was cutting it close. The research was done, but I still needed to pull everything together. "I'm running out of time, Noah."

"Bailey, just leave the dance, save it for next time. There's been so much going on in town. Why not organize a Christmas party instead? Give us something to look forward to." He smiled at me, and I couldn't help but see the kindness in his eyes.

"Do you think anyone will mind?" I pulled back slightly, searching his face for answers.

"It was said as a passing comment, nothing was set in stone. You need to give people more than a couple of days' notice anyway. If anyone mentions it, you can give them the new date." He shrugged, as if it were no big deal.

It made sense, and suddenly, a weight lifted from

my chest. I felt a little more grounded, a little less overwhelmed.

"Did Ali mention anything about our annual boys' night?" Noah wrapped his arms a little tighter around me. "Every year, the last weekend in November, we go bush for an overnight trip—to ride motorbikes, skinny dip in the quarry dam, and bond. You know, it's a bloke thing."

"And a chick thing would be to sneak out there and spy on you."

I laughed again, the sound bright and light.

"Perhaps you could start a tradition of your own." Noah grinned, pulling me closer, holding me tightly.

Reluctantly, I drew away. "I'm sorry, I still have to have a shower and get ready before I head over to the barn." I hated leaving his arms, but there was too much to do.

Noah lowered his head, brushing his lips over mine in a tender kiss. "Sounds good to me. Mind if I join you?"

"I'd like that." The words came easily, and I meant them more than I realized.

By the time I turned up at the barn, I felt more relaxed, thanks to Noah. The stress from the morning seemed a little less overwhelming, and I was finally ready to face the day.

"Why do you look so pleased with yourself?" Ali raised her eyebrows as I walked in. "It wouldn't have anything to do with a hot-looking guy I ran into at Jack's, who smelled a lot like your shampoo, would it?"

"I don't know what you're talking about." I continued preparing the morning tea, trying to hide my grin as Ali went about fixing herself a hot drink.

"He mentioned the Christmas party idea, and I think it's a great idea. It's been so busy these last couple of weeks." Ali's voice was light, but I could tell she agreed with Noah's suggestion.

I nodded, feeling a sense of relief. "And with their cute tradition, we don't want them too tired for it."

"We should start one of our own." Ali grinned at me. "You know, have a girls' night. I'm sure Emily could do with one."

"One what?" As though on cue, Emily walked through the door, and Ali flashed her a mischievous look.

"A girls' night. Rick and Noah are heading off on their overnight trip, and I think we should organize something."

"Great idea. What are we doing?" Emily chimed in, enthusiasm in her voice.

"We could stay here. The ladies leave in the

morning. It could be fun." I shrugged, throwing out the idea without thinking much about it.

"Excellent." Ali clapped her hands together. "Now let's get to work. I have my first appointment in ten minutes."

As the buzz of activity picked up around me, I couldn't help but feel like everything might just turn out okay after all.

The morning passed quickly.

"Is it possible to have a chat, when you're not too busy." Mom waited until I'd finished demonstrating a layering technique for Sarah.

I looked up and smiled. "Of course. Do you want to sit in the meditation room for a few minutes?"

I wanted to speak with her too, but as the others weren't aware of our relationship, I didn't like to approach her in front of them. It felt too personal, too complicated for public consumption.

I closed the door behind us and joined my mother on the couch. Ali was on a break, sitting with Tracy and Emily in the other room. The peaceful quiet in here felt like a rare oasis.

"I wanted you to know that I'm renting a place in town at the moment. You probably have plenty of questions, and I promise I'll answer all of them. I'd really love for us to get back what we had." Her voice was tentative, but there was a glimmer of hope in it, and I couldn't help but feel the pull of that hope despite everything.

I didn't answer her straight away. I needed a moment to process. "I think too many years have passed, and I've been hurt for a long time for us to go backward. But perhaps we could start afresh. I'm not that little girl anymore."

She nodded, her eyes softening as she studied me. "I can see that. Although I see her shining through more brightly than I did back then. You're more beautiful than ever, Bailey. And I look forward to spending time with you."

The compliment should have made me feel lighter, but all I could think about was the years we had lost. "Why did you leave, Mom?"

Her gaze shifted, but she didn't look away. "The reason never changed. Your grandfather was sick. He died three months ago."

"I get that, but that's not what kept you from contacting me. Why did you never respond?" I kept my voice steady, but inside, a thousand emotions churned, each one making it harder to stay composed.

"I don't want to upset you, Bailey." Her voice wavered, and I could see the hesitation in her eyes, like she was bracing herself for my reaction.

"You said you'd be honest with me." I couldn't hold back now. I needed the truth, no matter how painful.

"Okay, fair enough." She paused, swallowing hard, and I watched her brace herself. "Your father had me sign a contract." She looked at me carefully, as though waiting for my reaction, but I kept my face neutral. "He made a deal to continue paying for my father's care and medication if I vanished from your life." Tears slid down her cheeks, and my stomach clenched. "He wasn't the best husband, but he loved you, and I knew you'd be well cared for. My dad was a good man, and he provided well for me. I couldn't bear to see him suffer, so I signed the contract. I'm sorry."

I held my hand up to indicate I'd heard enough. My mind was spinning. I didn't know what was worse—thinking my mother had left me, or knowing that both of my parents had betrayed me. "You're right. You've upset me. I don't want to hear anymore."

Tracy, ever perceptive, must have picked up on my mood because, after we left the meditation room, she came over and stood beside me. "Is my boy causing you grief again?"

I forced a smile, trying to push the emotions down. "Oh no, Tracy, he's been wonderful." But my eyes were swimming with tears, and I could feel them threatening to spill over.

"You're in love with him, aren't you?" Tracy caught me off guard, and I blinked in surprise.

"What?" I couldn't hide my confusion.

"Just a feeling I get." Tracy grinned, her eyes sparkling with mischief. "Mixed with wishful thinking."

I laughed, a breathy sound that felt surprisingly light. "Fair enough. And if you must know, yes, I've fallen for your son in a big way. Don't tell him, though. I haven't mentioned it to him yet."

Tracy's laughter rang out, giddy and relieved. "Your secret is safe with me." She slung one arm around my shoulders and kissed me on the cheek. "My mom would've been so proud of you, with what you've done to the place. You've brought her dream alive. Does Noah know what you've named it?"

I hesitated, unsure whether I should tell her the truth. "No, I wanted to have a big wooden sign made to hang outside, but I ran out of time. I meant to ask Jack if he knew anyone who was good with wood."

Tracy frowned, her brow furrowing in concern. "You're serious? What about Noah? I'm sure he'd be honored. Why don't you give him a call?"

I gave her a quick hug, grateful for her suggestion. "I might just do that. Thanks, Tracy."

I crossed to the kitchen to get some privacy, hoping to collect my thoughts before calling Noah.

"Hey, beautiful girl, I'm just driving past your barn right now."

The sound of Noah's voice made my heart skip. "Oh good, stop out front, will you?"

"Sure thing, baby." The connection cut off, but I could hear his truck approaching, the low rumble of the engine getting closer.

I stepped outside just as he was leaning against the cab, arms folded across his chest, looking effortlessly handsome. I slowed my pace, taking a moment to admire him as I approached. "I still want to paint you. Just as you are, so I can hang you in my bedroom."

He raised an eyebrow, his lips curling into a grin. "I don't want to look at myself on the wall of your room."

"Okay, the study then." I teased, leaning forward and kissing him quickly.

Noah shook his head with a smile. "You're crazy.

Is that why you asked me to stop, as part of your art lesson?"

"No, your mom suggested something, and I wanted to ask you before I sourced someone else." I paused, taking a breath. "I need a sign with the retreat name carved into wood to hang outside the barn."

"Not a problem. What's it called?"

I hesitated for a moment. "Please don't get mad, I asked Jack first—"

"Just spit it out," he said, laughing at me. His cheeky grin made my heart flutter, and I couldn't help but feel the heat rise in my chest.

"Maggie's Place."

His smile faded, and he scuffed his boot over the gravel, clearly processing the name. "You called it Maggie's Place?"

I nodded, unsure what to expect next.

"That's what she wanted to name it." The words came out softly, a confession in the air between us.

Noah didn't speak for a moment, and when he did, his voice was quiet, almost reverent. "Oh, I'm sorry, I didn't know. It just came to me one night, and it felt right, I—sorry."

He reached up, gently touching my cheek, and I felt a wave of warmth spread through me. "Don't be sorry," he said, his voice full of emotion. "It makes me happy she's still a part of this place."

I nodded, my heart settling in my chest. I hoped, with everything I had, that we would all be a part of this place for a long time to come.

Four days hardly seemed long enough for all the art projects I had planned for them. Not to mention the extra pamper sessions Ali was booked for. The only one who didn't seem to go back for more was Brittney.

It became our early morning ritual—making a hot drink together, chatting about art, and sharing plans for the day. I was going to miss spending time with Ali when it was over. We'd all gotten into a nice groove, and the days felt like they were slipping through my fingers.

"Hey, has Brittney mentioned having any more treatments?" I couldn't help myself. I felt sorry for her. She looked so young, yet she'd been through so much. It didn't seem fair.

Ali shook her head, a slight frown tugging at her lips. "She took a brochure, but I don't think she has a lot of spare cash."

I felt a pang in my chest. "Do you have time today if I bought her another treatment?"

Ali glanced at the clock on the wall. "Yep, I have a

ten o'clock, and I don't have to be back in town until two. It's a good thing the wedding was last week. I crammed so many appointments in, there's no one left in town to buff, wax, or massage."

I laughed, shaking my head in disbelief. How Ali kept going despite her morning sickness was beyond me. I would've been a wreck. "Can you just call her in as you would the others and give her whatever she wants? I'll fix you up once you're finished."

"I'm happy to pitch in for her," Ali offered, but I shook my head quickly.

"Thanks, but no. You've done so much extra already. I've got this."

Cal would be arriving soon. He was preparing some food at the café, but anything that needed to be done last-minute would be cooked on-site. I was looking forward to eating a meal I hadn't cooked myself. As much as I loved cooking, it was nice to have someone else take care of it for once.

I was going to miss the bustle of activity when they left in the morning. But at least I was pleased the girls would be staying the night with me. I'd never had much company in this old barn, and it was strangely comforting to have so many people around.

I took a seat beside Brittney at the table. She was

working on a bright blue and red wall hanging for her son.

"That looks fabulous. What's your son's name?"

"Mason." She smiled as she spoke, her voice soft but filled with warmth. "Red and blue are his favorite colors."

I could see the sadness in her eyes, the kind that came from carrying the weight of too much. I imagined it was the stress of having a child suffering from cancer. That kind of grief was hard to hide.

"How old is he?"

"Five. He'd love it out here. He's crazy about animals and tractors. Reckons he wants to be a farmer when he grows up." Brittney laughed, and her bright blue eyes glistened with unshed tears, the kind that threatened to spill over but never did.

"Well, he's more than welcome to come and stay during the school holidays. The barn will be free, or I have lots of spare rooms you're welcome to crash in."

Brittney flushed a bright shade of pink, and I instantly regretted offering. "That's very kind of you, but I'm not sure we could afford two trips in the same year." She didn't sound resentful or bitter. It was as though she'd long accepted the financial strain as part of her life.

"I don't expect you to pay me," I said, my voice soft but firm. "The barn will be vacant, so you'd be welcome to use it. Since moving here, I've learned that country hospitality is a way of life I'm happy to adopt. We pitch in and help our neighbors and friends—just because, with no expectations."

Brittney nodded slowly, her gaze softening. "I've always wanted to live in a town like this, but after Mason got sick, and his dad left me, it wasn't practical—"

Ali interrupted with a gentle pat on Brittney's shoulder before she could say more, her smile warm and reassuring.

I frowned, sensing the discomfort in the air, but Ali's touch had silenced any further mention of it.

"I didn't book—" Brittney began.

"Country hospitality, remember," I said, squeezing her hand as I stood up. "Cal will be here soon. I better wash the dishes or he might refuse to cook for us, and that'd be miserable."

Rhianna followed me into the kitchen, picking up a tea towel and starting to dry a cup without saying a word.

"You don't have to do the dishes while you're here as my guest."

"That's okay, I need to move a bit, anyway," she replied.

I suspected my mother wanted to spend time with me, and I had to admit, ever since my confession about the contract, I'd been avoiding time alone with her. She had always been a force in my life, but that conversation had stirred up more than I was ready to face.

"Look, Mom, I wanted to talk to you about something, and I hope you agree. Whatever happened in the past, I'd prefer to leave it there. I don't want my memory of Dad to be tarnished any more than it already is. I'd just like to move forward and leave all the negativity behind, because it won't change our relationship in the future. We have time to make amends, but he doesn't have that opportunity."

She paused, watching me closely, her expression unreadable. I could see the hurt flicker across her face before she masked it with a small nod. I knew she wanted to say something, but she also knew it wouldn't be the right time.

Before she could respond, there was a knock on the kitchen door.

"Hey, Bailey, sorry to interrupt."

"Not at all. Come in. We were just cleaning up for you."

"You're a doll. I can see why my cousin loves you so much."

I rolled my eyes at Cal's teasing, as though he really knew how Noah felt about me. Sometimes, I didn't even think Noah knew. Besides, it was still early days, and Noah had always been unpredictable. I could never quite tell what he was thinking, and that made things both exciting and frustrating at the same time.

We finished up with the dishes, and after offering to help, we left Cal to start working.

Brittney emerged after an hour-long massage treatment, looking as though she could curl up in the corner and fall asleep right then and there. She shuffled over to me and wrapped me in a tight hug, her voice soft and full of gratitude.

"Thank you for being so kind to me."

I hugged her back, feeling the warmth of her appreciation. "It's my pleasure. I left some morning tea on a plate in the kitchen for you. Help yourself to coffee, too." I raised my voice so Cal could hear me from where I stood. "Don't mind him; he's a messy cook, but you should be safe enough to go in there."

From the kitchen, Cal stuck his head around the corner. "She's just jealous."

I laughed, rolling my eyes. "Actually, I am. This guy is a magician with food."

Cal winked at me, and I left Brittney to fend for herself. I'd seen the way she and Cal looked at each other, and I couldn't help but hope that time alone together would do them both some good. It was a shame she was leaving so soon, but then again, there were complications in her life that made things more difficult.

As predicted, lunch was divine. Cal fussed over us, and the guests hung on his every word. I could see how women might find him attractive, but honestly, it was hard not to compare him to Noah. They were so alike in so many ways, and I found myself feeling a little nostalgic for the things I wasn't sure I could have with Noah.

Even Brittney was all smiles for Cal, though she wasn't as openly flirtatious as the others. Maybe it was because she was the youngest one of us and, as much as she tried to hide it, she was still probably the most eligible match.

That evening, I gave the ladies the option of a meditation session or continuing to work on their projects. Art won, as it always did, so I cracked open a few bottles of wine for us to enjoy after dinner.

They'd be leaving in the morning, and I was

going to miss them—Brittney most of all—but I made her promise to think about my offer. I suspected that Cal might be enough of an enticement to bring her back to town.

"I can't thank you enough for making my first retreat such a success," I said, my heart full of appreciation. "I loved sharing this with you all and hope you enjoyed the experience."

We sat around on cushions on the floor of the meditation room, the air filled with the quiet hum of satisfaction. Ali had taken time out to come and say goodbye. She had been such an integral part of their stay, and I knew it wouldn't have been the same without her there.

"I second that," Ali chimed in, her voice thick with emotion. "Getting to know you all enriched my week, and I cherish the new friendships I've formed." She choked up a little, blaming it on pregnancy hormones, but we all understood.

"I hope you take some of what you've learned and remember to take time out to be creative when you're back in the real world," I said, my voice steady. "You all have what it takes to build your dreams. It's just a matter of unleashing them."

We lingered in the room, savoring our goodbyes, each of us holding on to the connections we'd made.

After the last person left, I stood alone in the barn, the silence settling around me like a soft blanket. The pure satisfaction of what we'd achieved over the past few days set in. I couldn't have done it without everyone who pitched in, and I was more grateful than ever for the wonderful friends I'd made.

The most exciting part of all was that this was only the beginning.

CHAPTER 26

Bailey

"Have fun, and don't do anything too stupid," Ali called out as the boys piled into two trucks, each loaded with camping gear and motorbikes.

"Yes, Mom," Cooper squeaked, his voice cracking like a teenage boy going through puberty.

"Smartass," Ali muttered under her breath, rolling her eyes.

I couldn't help but laugh. Ali was very much the mom of the group, at least when Emily wasn't around to take over the role. I loved the easy dynamic we shared, the lighthearted teasing that always made the atmosphere feel like home.

"Bailey, Noah loves you," Cooper continued, his voice high-pitched as he followed up with obnoxious kissing noises.

I shook my head, smiling despite myself. Honestly, I was exhausted after the events of the last few weeks and looking forward to a quiet night with the girls.

"We're such a boring bunch," Cassie complained, flopping back onto the couch with exaggerated drama. "Drinking tea and eating cake like a group of ancient old women waiting for the men to return."

I chuckled. "Come on, Cas, even you have to admit this is the best cake you've ever tasted. Cal is going to make some woman very happy one day."

Sophie shoved a large spoonful of chocolate cake into her mouth and gave me a thumbs-up. "Totally. He's got some serious skills."

"Either that, or he'll make some poor woman very fat," Emily added, her eyes twinkling with mischief.

I sighed with a grin, shaking my head. "He's such a cutie. I just love him." My words came out a little more enthusiastic than I intended, but I couldn't help it. Cal's charm was undeniable.

"That's just because he looks so much like Noah," Ali said, rolling her eyes. "You've got it bad."

I felt my cheeks warm slightly. "Well, I can't help it, can I? I mean, the resemblance is hard to ignore."

Cassie snorted. "Well, I'm just glad Noah's not here for me to walk in on you two, again. I mean, you're both hot-looking peeps, but that doesn't mean I want to see you steaming up the place." The disgust oozing from her voice made me laugh despite myself.

"Oh, Cas, if only you could see your face." I tried to keep my expression serious but failed miserably. "I'm sorry. I'll try to behave in the future, but you have to admit, he is pretty irresistible."

Cassie groaned, covering her face with a pillow. "You're both a mess. I swear, the minute you two are alone, the steam starts rising."

Emily, always the one to ask the most unexpected questions, looked at me with a wide grin. "So, do you think you'll get married and have lots of babies?"

Only Emily would think of something as fluffy as that. I choked on my tea, unsure whether to laugh or groan. "Jack and Tracy would be over the moon. I'm telling you, if you don't marry Noah, they'll kick him out of the family and adopt you instead."

The room erupted with laughter at Emily's

dramatic take on things. She spoke as if it were a scandal about to break out.

"Well, then," I said with a teasing smile, "we're lucky it's early days, aren't we?"

The others cracked up, and the tension in my chest loosened just a little. Despite all the recent chaos in my life, these moments with the girls, with the easy banter and their constant support, reminded me that there was still room to not take life too serious.

∽

Noah

"Who's up for a midnight swim?" Rick called out, trying to rouse the group from the mellow scene we'd set.

Always competitive, Ben immediately took it up a notch. "I'll beat you there." Before Rick even had a chance to react, Ben was already at his bike, kick-starting it.

I wasn't far behind, and Cooper was hot on my heels.

It always amazed me how Cooper and Ben could

remain such good friends despite being so damn competitive. They were always pushing each other, testing their limits, and yet, no matter how heated things got, they always had each other's backs.

Cooper's foot slipped off the kick-start, giving me the advantage I needed. I revved my engine and tore off, leaving him in a cloud of dust. Ben's bike was still ahead, the dim light his only beacon.

I knew I'd need speed to catch him. He was flying down the tracks, faster than I'd expected for a night ride. It'd been years since we'd ridden these trails, but Ben had always been the fearless one—the one who pushed boundaries. Rick, on the other hand, had always been more casual, more likely to sit back and watch us go head to head than to join in himself.

Over the years, though, Rick had changed the most. He was more uptight than before, especially after the whole Charlotte situation. I couldn't fault him—he was responsible for what she and his brother did.

As I rounded a bend, something caught my attention. Spotlights, flashing in the distance.

"Shit," I muttered, slamming harder on the throttle. Ben had to see those lights by now, even though I couldn't see his bike anymore. If he came around that corner at the speed he was going, there was no telling what would happen.

I hit the turn just moments after Ben. And then, the world seemed to slow. The sound of metal colliding with metal shattered the night. My eyes locked onto the scene before me—Ben's bike was ripped from the track and disappeared under the front end of a four-wheel drive. In the next instant, Ben was flung through the air like a rag doll, his body hurtling up the bonnet, smashing against the windscreen before being tossed over the roof.

I didn't have time to react. My focus was entirely on Ben, and that's when my bike hit a mound of rubble. I was thrown forward over the handlebars, landing hard on the gravel track. Pain shot through my body, but I barely registered it. The four-wheel drive came to a screeching halt, its bull bar now inches from my head. I scrambled to my feet, ignoring the sharp burn in my leg.

"Ben." I called out, panic rising in my chest. My eyes darted around, desperately searching. "Ben, answer me." My voice cracked, desperation mixing with dread. "For fuck's sake, can someone get a light over here?"

I hadn't even heard the other motorbikes pull up, but soon enough, Cooper and Rick were beside me.

A beam of light swept over the ground where I'd been searching, and then it stopped on a crumpled figure lying in the bushes. Ben. His leg was bent at an impossible angle, the only part of him still on the track.

Cooper and Rick reached him first. The pain in my leg intensified as I moved closer, and I couldn't suppress the cry that escaped my lips. But nothing mattered more than Ben right now.

Cooper was kneeling over him, and Rick was yelling, his voice full of urgency, "Call an ambulance. Someone, get help."

I glanced over my shoulder, frustration flaring. "Fuckin' move it," I snapped. Whether I was yelling at the guys to hurry up or cursing at my own body for not keeping up, I didn't know.

I dropped to my knees beside Ben. "Ben, come on, mate, answer me." I checked for a pulse. Nothing. My heart sank. My hands were shaking as I scooped my fingers into Ben's mouth to clear his airway, trying not to think about the broken teeth and the blood mixing with dirt.

Rick turned away, and I heard him vomiting in the distance, but I didn't have the luxury of paying attention to that. Ben was the only thing that mattered.

The pit in my stomach deepened with every passing second. I knew the sinking feeling wasn't a good sign—Ben wasn't in a good way. But I had to try. I couldn't just sit back and do nothing. If I didn't try, I'd never forgive myself.

The pain in my leg was almost unbearable, but I forced myself to focus on Ben. I turned to Cooper, voice strained. "I need you to help me turn him onto his back." I moved to where Ben's head was awkwardly positioned, the angle all wrong. "On three, we'll turn him, okay?"

Cooper's face was pale in the spotlight's glow, but he nodded. His expression was tight, but he understood the urgency. Bracing Ben's head between my arms and gripping his shoulders, I counted, "Three, two, one."

Together, we managed to shift him, and I immediately began chest compressions. Each push was a fight against the fatigue threatening to drag me under. As I pumped Ben's chest, I stole a glance at Cooper. His face was pasty, like a ghost in the night. The light from the spotlight made him look almost unreal. "Check on how long the ambulance is gonna be," I muttered through gritted teeth.

Cooper hesitated, clearly reluctant to leave, but I could see the same doubt in his eyes that I felt. I wasn't sure how much longer I could keep this up. The sweat was stinging my eyes, and my arms felt like lead.

Rick, who had been trying to steady himself, finally returned to my side. "Need me to take over for a while?" he asked, his voice calm but tight with worry.

I shook my head, the refusal automatic. "Not yet. Where the hell are the bloody ambos when you need them?" I was starting to get frustrated. It was dark, the tracks were rough, and the wait was unbearable. If the ambulance was local, they'd know the area, but even that didn't seem to help.

I was exhausted. My entire body was screaming for a break, but I couldn't stop. Not now. Not with Ben's life in my hands.

It felt like an eternity before I finally heard the sirens in the distance, and even then, it was hard to let go. I kept working on Ben, each compression more forceful than the last, refusing to let up even when I was on the verge of collapse.

When the ambulance finally arrived, it took a few moments of pleading to convince them to let me keep going. They hesitated, no doubt seeing the state I was in, but I wasn't about to stop now.

It wasn't until one of the paramedics tried to

check on my leg that I snapped. "Just help him," I growled, my voice rough. "I'm fine, for Christ's sake." It was a lie, but I wasn't about to admit how much pain I was in. I was still responsive, which was more than I could say for Ben.

"Please, help him," I begged, my voice breaking with urgency. My mind raced. Why didn't they feel the same urgency? Why couldn't they understand how close Ben was to slipping away? Every second felt like a lifetime.

"We'll follow you there," a police officer reassured the ambulance crew, his tone firm as if trying to push them into action. The ambulance officer was reluctant to leave, but I could see that something had clicked for them. They weren't going to waste any more time.

∽

Bailey

The sound of my phone ringing jerked me awake. Groggy and disoriented, I fumbled in the dark for the switch of the bedside lamp. When I remembered I was in the barn, I rolled over and reached out to the other side, finally finding the switch just as the ringing stopped.

I froze when my ringtone pierced the silence. "Hello," I whispered, careful not to wake the others if they had managed to sleep through the noise.

"Bailey, there's been an accident. Can you all come to the hospital?" The voice on the other end was frantic, and still half-asleep, I couldn't figure out who it was. "Who is this?"

"Rick. Sorry, I tried calling Ali first—I thought you were all together."

"We are. It's fine. We'll be there." As soon as I ended the call and threw the blankets off, I was fully awake. How the others hadn't heard the commotion was beyond me. My heart began pounding in my chest as Rick's words sank in. There was an accident. I needed to get to the hospital.

"Wake up," I said, my voice more urgent than I meant it to be.

"No, sleep," Cassie groaned, rolling over.

There wasn't time to wake up slowly. What if Noah was hurt? What if that's why Rick called me after trying Ali? I hadn't even thought to ask who was at the hospital. But a phone call at four in the morning wasn't good news.

"Rick called. There's been an accident, and he

wants us at the hospital." I blurted it out before I could second-guess myself. It worked. It got their attention.

Sophie was out of bed in seconds, followed by Ali. Cassie sat up, her eyes squinting against the dim light. "Are they having you on?"

"Not by the sound of Rick's voice," I said, the tension tightening my chest. "And if they are, I'll bury them alive. But I'm not taking any chances. He sounded frantic. I didn't even recognize his voice." I was starting to feel just as frantic, pulling on my jeans and running my hands through my tangled hair.

The others quickly followed my lead.

"Did Rick say anything other than to come to the hospital?" Ali's voice was soft, and I imagined the relief she felt at not being the one injured—relief mixed with guilt, knowing that someone else was in trouble.

"No, and I didn't think to ask. Sorry, I panicked." I could feel the panic rising in me now, the reality sinking in. I didn't want to think about how bad it could be, or if it was Noah. My eyes pricked with tears, but I quickly looked away. "I'll meet you downstairs."

Not wanting anyone else to end up in the hospital, I went ahead to turn on the lights. Heading to the bathroom, I rinsed my mouth with mouthwash—anything to occupy myself while I waited.

They were taking too long. I paced the room like a caged animal, heart hammering in my chest.

The sound of them coming down the stairs snapped me into action. Grabbing my handbag and keys, I hurried for the door. "I'll drive." I had to do something—waiting for them felt like an eternity. There was no way I could sit in the passenger seat now.

We didn't speak much on the drive to the hospital. Each of us lost in our own thoughts. If they were anything like mine, I knew their minds weren't offering up anything hopeful.

I pulled into a parking bay as close to the emergency department as I could.

"Tracy and Mike have just pulled up," Sophie said before I even turned off the car.

I glanced over my shoulder, catching sight of Tracy climbing out of the car and heading for the front door before Mike had even finished parking.

Ali reached over and gripped my hand. "He'll be okay," she said softly, but even she didn't sound convinced.

As we walked inside the emergency room, Rick

and Cooper rushed over to greet us. Rick took Ali in his arms, his face crumpling as he began to cry. Cooper stood beside him, pale-faced and awkward, his hands shoved into his pockets.

"Where are Ben and Noah?" Sophie demanded, her voice sharp.

"The doctors haven't told us anything," Cooper said, shaking his head.

"Well, what happened?" Cassie's voice was tight, not happy with the lack of information, especially when it came to her brother. Bailey felt a knot tighten in her stomach.

"There was an accident," Cooper finally said, his voice low. "A four-wheel-drive. They were out shooting on the same track we were riding on. It came out of nowhere. Ben and Noah were up front."

Bailey gasped, her breath catching. Had they been hit by the car? Or shot? The question burned in her throat, but she was too afraid to ask.

The color drained from Sophie's face. She looked like she might pass out at any moment. Without another word, she rushed up to the nurses' station. "My husband, Ben Dunstan, was brought in a little while ago. Can I see him, please?"

"I'm sorry, Mrs. Dunstan. A doctor will be with you shortly."

I wished I could do the same for Noah, but what right did I have to ask about his condition? His mother was obviously with him. Still, I found it strange that Mike hadn't joined them.

Not knowing was the worst feeling. I knew I couldn't do anything to help the situation, but standing around and speculating was like torture.

"You said Ben and Noah were out front. Surely, there's more to it than that. Were they okay? Did you speak to them?" A tear slipped down Sophie's cheek, but she didn't bother to wipe it away.

Rick pulled away from Ali, and I noticed the look he exchanged with Cooper, the slight nod Cooper offered in return.

"Soph, why don't we all sit?" Rick gestured to a row of empty seats, and they all moved to sit down. "I don't know any details. All I know is that Ben wasn't in a good way when we were out there. Noah was injured, but he still managed to take control and was trying to help him. After the ambulance showed up, they brought us here, and we haven't been told anything else." Sophie didn't respond. Rick held her hand, speaking so softly that I had to strain over the noise of the television in the corner to hear him.

Ali reached out and took Cassie's hand. I could tell it wasn't easy for her to hear that her brother was in bad shape. I couldn't help but feel a slight sense of relief that Noah had been conscious when they brought him into the hospital.

Mike entered, accompanied by the other boys' parents.

Ben's mother didn't seem to notice them as she walked straight past and approached the same nurse Sophie had spoken to just moments before. After receiving the same speech Sophie had, Ben's mother turned and walked back over to them. Cassie stood and hugged her, looking as though she'd been crying.

"Have they told you anything?" Mrs Dunstan looked from Cassie to Sophie. Both women shook their heads. The parents stood in silence, but their support was palpable.

Having been on my own for so long, it was a change to have so many caring people around me, even if their concern wasn't directly for me. These were my friends, and I just prayed they'd all be okay.

A few minutes passed before the doctor arrived. "If I could ask Ben's family to follow me, please."

Sophie moved immediately, but remained silent. It was Ben's mother who spoke first, firing questions at the doctor. "Is he going to be all right, Doctor? How bad are his injuries?"

The doctor's face remained unreadable. My gut sank. I had a horrible sense he wasn't taking them to see how Ben was holding up. He was taking them to say goodbye.

Tears threatened to betray my thoughts, so I looked down at my lap, trying to blink them away. Cooper, sitting next to me, reached out and grabbed one of my hands. I glanced sideways at him and noticed his eyes were red and glassy. He was trying not to cry too.

I squeezed his hand. How could a night that had started so full of fun turn into such a disaster?

Tracy returned moments after the others had left with the doctor. Her eyes were bloodshot, her face blotchy—it was evident she'd been crying. She slumped into the seat beside Rick.

"Noah's doing okay," she said, her voice shaking. "He's pretty messed up about Ben—" Her voice broke as she said his name.

"How is Ben?" Rick didn't let her finish.

Tracy scanned their faces. "Has the doctor not spoken to you?"

Mike shook his head. "He's in with the family now."

Tracy released a groan, filled with so much anguish, she didn't need to say anything else.

"Oh no, please no," Rick's mother pleaded.

"Would someone just spit it out already?" Cooper's voice was tight with frustration, and his calm was slipping. "For fuck's sake, what's going on?"

Tracy looked at him, her eyes filled with sorrow. "I'm sorry, Cooper. Ben didn't make it."

CHAPTER 27

Bailey

Even though I'd been expecting the worst, it didn't hit home until I heard it said aloud. It wasn't just the women who cried. Rick and Ali clung to each other as tears flowed. Cooper held his head in his hands, and I couldn't just sit there, so I wrapped my arms around him. His tears turned into sobs, and his body shook with a grief I'd never witnessed before.

They'd been best friends all their lives. The boys would be feeling the emptiness of having the fourth wheel stolen from them too soon.

And then there was Sophie, and Ben's family. How were they going to deal with this?

I didn't want to think about it anymore. I just wished it was over, that we could go back to the happy, carefree place we were at less than twelve hours ago.

I was still hugging Cooper when Sophie and Ben's family emerged. Grief was evident not just on their faces, but in their very presence. Sophie looked like she was in a daze—ghostlike.

As soon as they stepped among their friends, the hugging and crying began again.

I couldn't help but think about Noah, dealing with the loss of his friend on his own. I voiced this concern to Cooper, who agreed it would be good if he and Rick went to be with him. As much as I would have liked to be with him too, I knew Noah needed his friends more than he needed me right now.

It was probably the longest night of my life. One I never wanted to relive or experience again. I was relieved when Tracy asked if she could catch a lift back to the farm with me. She knew Jack would want to know. It was going to come as a shock, and Tracy didn't think it was fair to put the responsibility on me.

He was out in front of the house when the two of us arrived together.

"Hey, you two, you're out early," he said, not realizing that Bailey and the girls were supposed to be staying in the barn for the weekend while the boys were away.

"Hi, Dad, can we chat?"

"Sure, your place or mine? Your coffee tastes better." He grinned, his cheerful mood a sharp contrast to the news we were about to deliver. I wished I could spare him the grief, but there was no way around the truth.

"Actually, I could really use a cup of coffee. Do you mind?" Tracy's voice cracked slightly, and her face looked as if she'd aged twenty years overnight.

"Of course not, come in."

Tracy and Jack followed me inside, Jack still talking about the work he'd been doing on the farm. I was grateful for the distraction, not having to think too hard to answer his questions or nod in agreement at the appropriate times.

When I finished making the coffee, I sat at the dining room table with them.

"Okay, now I'll rest my jaw, and you two can explain why you've been crying."

He was observant. I had to hand it to him.

"Well," Tracy began after taking a sip of her coffee. "You know Noah and the boys went away for the weekend—"

Jack's nod was enough to encourage her to continue.

"Early this morning, there was an accident. A four-wheel drive and Ben's motorbike had a head-on collision."

Jack's face froze. His eyes closed tightly.

Tracy continued, her voice trembling. "Noah came off his bike, but thankfully the vehicle managed to pull up just before hitting him. He's broken his leg and is in the hospital, but they're releasing him this morning. Mike's with him now."

Jack opened his eyes, looking at Tracy with an intensity that made my stomach twist. "And Ben?"

Tracy's voice cracked as she began to whimper. "He didn't make it."

Jack's face crumpled, and instantly tears appeared on his cheeks. He dropped his elbows to the table, tilted his head forward, and gripped his hair. His shoulders shook violently as he wept.

Tears wet my cheeks, too. I don't think I'd ever cried so much, not even when my father died.

After a few moments, Tracy stood and wrapped

her arms around Jack's shoulders. She looked over at me, and I could see the raw emotion on her face.

Not wanting to just sit and watch, I walked around to the other side of the table and draped my arms around both of them.

When Jack stopped crying, he reached up and gripped my hand.

"So, do you think Noah will be up for visitors today?" His voice was rough, like he hadn't spoken in hours.

I sat back down, and after a tight squeeze from me, Tracy sat too. "Of course, Dad. He's sore. He was determined to walk, to try to help Ben—but there was nothing anyone could've done to help him. Noah's pretty cut up about it, taking the blame as always."

Jack shook his head. "No, no one could've done anything."

"Bailey, would you mind giving Dad and me a lift home? I know you'll probably want to see Noah yourself."

I nodded. It had been a long night, and even though everyone said Noah was all right, I wasn't going to believe it until I saw him for myself.

We finished our cups of coffee in silence, the weight of everything hanging over us. Tracy suggested I have a shower while she went over to the flat to help Jack sort things out before they left.

I welcomed the steaming hot water as it washed over me, but nothing could clear the grief that had taken root inside me.

Noah was already settled in his bed when I walked in. Jack had insisted that I see him first. He was staring at the ceiling, not even bothering to look at me as I approached. I pulled the chair closer and sat down beside him.

The silence hung between us, heavy and uncomfortable. He didn't say anything, and neither did I. Finally, I reached out to take his hand, but he flinched, pulling it away as if my touch burned.

"What do you want?" His voice was flat, distant.

"I want to be with you." My words felt like they were sinking into quicksand.

"I don't need you here. To be honest, I'd rather you weren't." He didn't even look at me, his gaze fixed on some spot on the ceiling like he could will me away.

"Noah, please don't shut me out. I know how upset you must be." My voice cracked, the ache in my chest spreading.

"How do you know? You don't even have friends." His words were like a slap to my face. They stung, deep, and I didn't know how to respond. "I want you to leave me alone and forget everything about us."

I swallowed hard. "Can't we talk about this some other time?"

"Like when? After someone else I love is dead? What, do you want to be next?" His eyes burned with pain, and I could feel the weight of his grief pressing down on me.

"What are you talking about?" I was struggling to keep up.

"Ben and Stacey are dead because of me. She was scared of the dark, but you knew that already, didn't you? She'd still be alive if I hadn't come home from school. Just like Ben would've been if I'd caught up to him in time, to warn him."

"Noah, it wasn't your fault. Not Stacey, not Ben." The panic began to rise in me. It had taken a while, but our relationship seemed to be going so well lately. I didn't want to lose him now, not like this.

"You know nothing about Stacey. You don't have a right to comment," he snapped, the bitterness in his tone cutting through the space between us.

I drew in a deep breath, trying to steady myself.

"I've read that sometimes, a presence lingers if they have unfinished business. I've noticed a pattern. At first, the noises only happened when you stayed away from the farm, but when everything was good between us, the noises stopped. I think you're her unfinished business. She wants you to be happy."

Noah turned his head slowly to face me, his eyes sharp, filled with more anger than I expected. "You're more desperate than Whitney, using my dead sister against me to keep a relationship going that never really was." His gaze returned to the ceiling, as if he could shut me out with just a glance. "Go away."

My chest ached, but I refused to let him see how much his words hurt. "Regardless of what you say, for a time—even if only short—we were happy. We had the beginning of something wonderful. If you don't care about me, fine. That's your choice. But if you think you're protecting me from being the next on your hit list—as some sort of hero thing—well, that doesn't work for me. If you want me to go, then I'll go, but don't you dare pretend like you're doing it for me."

Noah didn't respond. He just continued to stare at the ceiling, leaving me no choice but to leave.

I stepped into the hallway, leaning against the

wall for a moment, trying to pull myself together. He was lashing out. That's all it was—at least, I hoped that was the reason—but still, it hurt.

"You didn't have to rush, love. Go back in there if you want to," Tracy's voice came from behind me, soft but firm.

I shook my head. "He doesn't want to see me. It'd be better for him to have you in there with him, than for him to get himself so worked up trying to make me leave." Not to mention, I wasn't sure how many more insults I could handle being thrown my way.

"Don't give up on him, Bailey. He needs time to come to terms with this. He's known Ben all his life."

I sighed, feeling the weight of the situation in my bones. "I know. He can take all the time he needs. I'm not going to judge him for how he deals with this. Everyone handles grief differently. I'm sorry he feels responsible, and for all the other heartache he's suffered. You all have. But I can't do anything to help him if he doesn't want me to."

Tracy nodded, her face lined with concern. "He'll come around."

I forced a smile, but it didn't reach my eyes. "I can come back and pick up Jack if he wants to stay longer." I needed to put some distance between myself and Noah. I couldn't keep breaking my heart like this.

"That's okay. I'll bring him home later. With a bit of luck, I'll convince him to hang around until after dinner. I'll go stir crazy with no one to take my mind off everything, and he deals with Noah better than I ever have." Tracy attempted a smile, but all I could see was the deep sadness she was trying to hide.

"If you could let him know I'll sort the dogs out tonight, but if he wants Zeus back for the company, let me know." I gave Tracy a quick hug before I left. The hallway felt too small, too suffocating. I needed to leave, even if I didn't know where I was going yet.

I didn't want to be on my own, so I took my time grooming Freya. After much deliberation, I decided to take her out for a ride. With the wedding and the retreat, I'd neglected her lately, failing to give her the attention she deserved. With the stallion due to arrive in the next few weeks, I'd have to divide my time between the two horses. I figured I might as well take advantage of the time I had alone with her now.

Riding always helped me clear my head. It was my chance to unwind, to shake off the tightly wound feeling inside me—like a rope pulled too taut, ready to snap at any moment. My worry for Noah had been so great lately, it consumed me. There could only be one reason I felt this way, and the worst part was that he wanted nothing to do with me. The emptiness inside was all too familiar, like when my mother left and refused to respond to me.

I was older now, but the pain still felt the same. As much as I cared about Noah, there was only so much reaching out I could do. No one should have to suffer through so many traumas so young. I could only be there for him, but if Noah didn't want me or continued to push me away, there wasn't much more I could do about it.

The sun had begun to set before I realized how long I'd been out. I turned Freya back toward the stables, hoping the dogs hadn't caused mayhem in the house while I'd been gone. They were usually pretty good indoors, but only when they were supervised.

An alarm went off in the distance, pulling my attention. I looked around, suddenly aware of how long I'd lived there without ever thinking to find out just how close my neighbors were.

Nudging Freya into a gallop, I headed toward the stables, wondering if the alarm was coming from my house. I couldn't imagine what would make such a racket. It didn't sound like a car alarm, though.

Besides, my car, which was still unlocked and parked next to the horse yard, sat silently.

I headed toward the stable first, not wanting the noise to spook Freya. The closer I got to the house, the louder the alarm sounded. Freya tossed her head and danced nervously beneath me, but I kept control, focusing on the sound that continued to pierce the air.

Then, I smelled it—smoke. It was faint at first, but it was unmistakable. I pulled Freya to a halt outside the stable, my heart rate picking up. I didn't have time to remove her tack. I quickly tied her off to the wooden railing and rushed toward my car.

Glancing toward the house, I saw it—a cloud of black smoke billowing from the direction of the granny flat.

The alarm kept screeching.

Once in my car, I grabbed my cell phone, dialing Tracy's number. It took a moment for her to answer as I started the engine and sped toward the house.

"Hello?" Her voice was groggy, like she'd been caught off guard.

"Tracy, it's Bailey. Is Jack home?" My words rushed out.

"Oh, Bailey, I couldn't convince him to stay. I

dropped him off about an hour ago. I thought you were out, or I would've called in."

"I'm at the stables, and the alarm's going off. I see smoke. Can you call the fire brigade? I think it's the granny flat."

"Of course, be careful. The fire brigade will be there soon." Her voice was tinged with worry before she hung up.

I threw my phone onto the passenger seat, my hands tightening around the wheel. My focus narrowed to getting to the house as quickly as possible.

CHAPTER 28

Bailey

The granny flat was ablaze. I parked a distance away, my heart pounding as I ran through the thick black smoke.

It was hot. The flames licked the walls, reaching out from the inside. I could see that the glass windows had shattered.

"Jack," I called, my voice barely audible over the roar of the fire. "Jack, where are you?"

I scrambled around the outer edge of the building, checking to make sure he wasn't already outside. I slipped twice on the loose stones, the smoke stinging my lungs, forcing me to cough. If he were still inside, the fire brigade wouldn't get to him in time. The flames danced and soared, sending sparks into the air that ignited spot fires faster than I thought possible.

I noticed the sliding glass door was still intact. The fire hadn't yet reached that part of the flat, and the temperature there wasn't as intense. I didn't think twice, desperation for Jack's safety pushed my fear aside. I slid the door open, using it as a shield in case a burst of oxygen acted like a flamethrower, but thankfully, it didn't.

The smoke inside was thick, almost suffocating. Even though flames lit the room, I couldn't see more than a few steps in front of me. Dropping to the floor, I crawled forward, trying to stay as low as possible to avoid the worst of the heat. My eyes burned, tears streaming down as I struggled to clear the smoke from them.

The floor was covered in embers, some hot enough to burn through my jeans.

"Jack." My voice was swallowed by the roar of the flames around me. I couldn't tell if I was making any progress, but I knew I had to reach him. I crawled through what felt like endless smoke, praying I wasn't too late. When I finally reached the kitchen, I felt around the floor in front of me, terrified that I wouldn't find him. My lungs tightened with every shallow breath.

And then I felt him.

Relief flooded me. I found Jack, but he wasn't moving.

I knew I had to drag him out, but to do so meant standing, and my eyes and throat were already burning from the smoke. The alternative was to curl up with him and be burned alive. I couldn't let that happen.

Pushing through the pain, I grabbed Jack's arms, staying as low as I could and stumbling backward, dragging him with me.

He was heavier than I expected, and I could feel the strain in my arms. I knew this rescue would leave him worse for wear, but it was better than leaving him to die in there.

Just as I reached the door, my foot caught on something, and I tripped. The heat in the lounge room had grown unbearable. The open door was fueling the flames with oxygen, making everything burn faster. I thought I heard sirens in the distance, but my ears had been ringing for so long that I wasn't sure if it was real.

I could feel myself losing it. My breathing was

labored, and my vision blurred. If we didn't get out soon, we wouldn't make it.

With the little strength I had left, I pulled Jack through the doorway. The smoke outside wasn't as thick, and the flames were now licking at the sides of the house. The yard between us was charred, a barren wasteland.

"Isis. Zeus." The words came out in a hoarse whisper. I needed to let the dogs out, but Jack had to be safe first. I gathered him under the arms, pulling him faster, praying I hadn't gotten to him too late.

Finally, clear of the smoke, the flames, and the burning embers, I lowered Jack onto the ground. My hands shook as I checked for a pulse, and when I found one, a small laugh of relief bubbled out of me. I hadn't lost him.

I stayed beside him, my head spinning as I waited for the fire brigade to arrive. The granny flat was gone, reduced to nothing but smoke and ash. If they didn't act fast, my house would follow the same fate.

From where I sat, Jack's head resting in my lap, the granny flat was like an inferno. The heat from the fire was unbearable, and I knew I couldn't leave him until help arrived.

Panic mounted inside of me as I toyed with thoughts of leaving him for a moment to open the front door of the house for the dogs. Not sure what was the best thing to do, I hesitated long enough there wasn't any point. Sirens grew closer. Flashing lights cut through the darkness, and a small glimmer of hope kicked in.

As soon as one firefighter rushed over to us, I stood, gently resting Jack's head on the ground. "He needs an ambulance. He was trapped inside. He's breathing, though. Promise me you won't leave him," I said, my voice thick with emotion. "I need to get Isis."

When the firefighter nodded, I turned and sprinted toward the house.

He called out to me, but I couldn't stop now. I'd already waited long enough. Other vehicles arrived, and I prayed one was an ambulance, but I didn't stop to check.

If I didn't make it in time to save the dogs, I'd never forgive myself.

~

Noah

. . .

I didn't wait for Mom to come to a complete stop before I unclipped my seatbelt and flung it off.

"Just wait till I stop, for goodness sake." She yelled, as I reached to open the door.

She expertly avoided the thick of the congestion, steering clear of the emergency services. An ambulance was parked nearby, and I couldn't shake the feeling that this night wasn't going to end well. I couldn't lose another person I cared about.

With my leg in a plaster cast, getting around wasn't easy. It sure as hell wasn't the fast pace I was used to keeping up.

"Noah, don't go doing anything stupid." Mom called after me. But I didn't have time to waste. I had to know if Jack and Bailey were okay.

I approached the ambulance and froze when I saw my grandfather on a stretcher. "How is he?" I interrupted the paramedics, not caring if they were busy.

"You are?"

"His grandson." I didn't bother to hide my annoyance.

"He took in a lot of smoke. If that young woman hadn't dragged him out, who knows what would've happened."

"Where's Bailey?" I scanned the scene, but with the flashing lights, she shouldn't be too hard to spot.

"Said something about Isis and took off inside before anyone could stop her—"

I didn't wait for him to finish. What the hell was she thinking?

I headed toward the front door as fast as I could. The closer I got to the house, the hotter the air grew. Shielding my face as best I could with crutches, I made my way up the steps. The flames were threatening the back of the house, but it didn't ease the intensity of the inferno I was walking straight into. At this rate, I'd burn to a crisp before I even reached her.

I propped my crutches against the house and tested my weight bearing. Grimacing, I forced myself to keep moving.

"Bailey." I called out to her, but when there was no response, I limped forward and into the smoke-filled kitchen.

The darkness was disorienting. The light from outside should have cast a glow in here, but not even a shadow was visible.

I tucked my tee shirt over my nose and covered my mouth, calling her name again.

Isis barked. The sound was muffled, but it was

enough to draw me deeper into the house, toward the staircase. Surely, she hadn't gone upstairs. Why the hell wasn't anyone else looking for her?

I called out to Isis instead. Maybe Bailey was injured, or the smoke had become too much for her.

The sound was coming from the room I knew Bailey used as a study. The door was closed, and I wondered if she'd done that on purpose to keep the smoke out. I was about to knock but realized how ridiculous that was when the house was burning down around us.

I pushed the door open and slipped inside, closing it behind me. The room was clearer than the rest of the house, and Isis seemed active enough. "Bailey?"

"Noah? What are you doing here?" Her voice came from the other side of the room.

"If you hadn't noticed, your house is burning down." I tried to make light of the situation, but from the sound of it, she was crying.

"Bailey, are you hurt? What's wrong?" I limped over to where she sat under the window. It wasn't until I got closer that I realized the window had been smashed, and that was why the room wasn't as smoky.

"I couldn't lift both of the dogs out." Her crying became a whimper.

"Isis is here. It's okay." I reached out to reassure her, brushing a hand over her arm. "You're wet."

"The glass is sharp."

If I hadn't been feeling anxious before, her words gave me every reason to panic now.

Standing up, I pulled my top over my head and wrapped it around my hand before smashing the remaining glass from the window.

I scooped Isis up and lowered her carefully to where Zeus waited on the other side.

"Come on, we need to get you out of here." I bent down, lifting her as I had the dog.

"My computer."

"Your what?"

"My laptop. It has pictures of my dad."

"Can you stand?"

"I don't know. I'll try. The computer's in the bag where I was sitting."

I could see how desperate she was, and I knew I couldn't leave without helping her. But right now, the fire was closing in. We needed to move fast.

"Okay, but you're first." I wasn't arguing with her about it, so I scooped her up and leaned out of the window to lower her as close to the ground as possible without causing us both to fall.

"Tell me when to let you go."

She moved in my arms as if trying to find her footing. "Okay, I'm good."

I hesitated a moment before releasing her.

∽

Bailey

His face was beaded with sweat, and I could see the strain on his features as the heat outside seemed even worse than the inferno inside. I could barely catch my breath, still feeling the thick smoke in my lungs.

Noah grabbed the computer bag and followed me out the window. I could hear the struggle in his movements, the weight of his cast making everything harder than it should've been. With every step, his leg throbbed, and I could see the effort it took for him to keep moving. Why hadn't the firefighters come looking for us? It was a disgrace that he had to risk his life like this.

Once we were free of the house, I felt a small relief, but it was quickly overshadowed by the fact that I couldn't even see how bad my injuries were. I wanted to check, but I couldn't bring myself to do it. Noah's grip around me was tight, his muscles straining as he cradled me to his chest. His heartbeat was steady, a comforting presence in the chaos surrounding us.

But even that relief didn't last long. As we got farther from the house, I heard the voice of an ambulance officer. "He's got her." The officer rushed over, a stretcher in hand, and immediately took me from Noah's arms.

I moaned as the movement caused pain to flare up, but I couldn't focus on it.

"Careful, she's hurt. Where the fuck was everyone?" Noah's voice was hoarse with frustration, and I could feel his anger radiating off him. I didn't care that he was upset—it was comforting, in a way, to know he cared so much. But I hated that I was the one who had to make him feel this way.

"They had their hands full trying to stop the gas bottles from going up," the paramedic said, trying to offer some explanation.

I was barely aware of being lifted onto the stretcher and wheeled toward the ambulance, Noah trailing close behind. His face was etched with worry, his body stiff with every step he took. Once I was inside the ambulance, the officer and his partner slid the stretcher in, and I saw Noah pause. He was looking at me, but the expression in his eyes made me feel like he wasn't sure if he should stay or go.

"I suggest you put that leg up and get some rest," the officer said, trying to offer a solution.

Noah shook his head, his determination clear as day. He wasn't leaving me, not yet. As the ambulance doors slammed shut, I could feel the weight of the situation settling on me. Noah wasn't even letting the pain in his leg slow him down. He had too much on his mind.

The siren blared, cutting through the night, and the ambulance sped away. The lights flashed, but even their blinding intensity couldn't mask the hollow feeling that settled deep in my chest.

Tracy rushed over and enveloped Noah in a tight hug. "I was so worried about you," she said, her voice shaking as she held him. She hugged him again, like she couldn't get enough of him being there, safe. "They took Jack to the hospital already. They suspect it's his heart. Do you want me to take you home first? I want to get over there and see how he's doing. How's Bailey?"

I could see the worry in her eyes, but it only

made the ache in my chest worse. Noah shook his head, clearly overwhelmed.

He was struggling with so much. First, Ben, and now this. Jack collapsing. Me, all cut up because I tried to be some kind of superhero. I didn't even know how bad my injuries were.

Noah raked his hands through his hair, the frustration and fear clear in every motion. I knew he was thinking it—he couldn't lose me.

"Let's go. I'm coming to the hospital too," he said, his voice low and firm, though I could hear the unspoken plea beneath it.

I didn't argue. I was too exhausted, too numb to fight. I just needed to get through this.

Like a dreaded case of déjà vu, but this time I was experiencing it from the other side. It wasn't the crowd I'd hoped for, the one I'd imagined seeing the night before. No one was waiting for me.

"How's Jack?" The question slipped out before I could stop it, my voice barely more than a rasp. Not knowing was the cruelest form of torture they could've inflicted on me. I understood the need for privacy, but I just needed to know he was still alive. That he was okay.

The doctor glanced at me, his expression softened by the concern in his eyes. "Bailey, you've suffered a severe laceration to your left side. The wound is deep, and you've lost a lot of blood, but lucky for you, there's little over there to cause the trouble that could have been." He gave me a reassuring smile, but it didn't do much to calm my nerves. "I'm going to stitch you up, and we'll set up some fluids to make you feel better, help with the light-headedness."

He scribbled on my chart, his pen scratching against the paper in a rhythmic, almost detached way before he addressed me again. "I'd like to run some tests. We'll be keeping you in overnight."

I tried to nod, but the movement made my whole body ache, so I stopped. "You know, that's probably a good idea. From what I saw, I no longer have a house anyway," I choked out, trying to force the words past the lump in my throat.

"I'm sorry about that. You're insured, I trust?" The doctor's tone was businesslike, but the kindness behind it still cut through the haze of my thoughts.

I nodded, the action small and painful. Everything hurt—every part of me felt like it had been crushed.

"You ingested more smoke than I'm happy with,"

he continued, and I could tell he wasn't saying it lightly. "We'd like to monitor you for at least twenty-four hours."

"Ah-huh." I tried to smile, but it was too much effort, so I closed my eyes instead, letting them rest for a few moments. I went over the events of the day in my mind. The fire, the chaos, Noah, the way I'd tried to save the dogs. Everything felt like a blur.

My eyes snapped open, and a wave of panic surged through me. I tried to sit up, but my body felt like it was made of lead, sluggish and uncooperative.

The doctor was there in an instant, restraining me gently but firmly. "Bailey, calm down. I need you to settle down for me. Bailey, can you hear me?"

I didn't struggle. There was no point. I could feel the weariness creeping in again, but there was something else I had to do first. "I need someone to take the tack off Freya," I said urgently, my voice hoarse. "I was riding her and had to rush to help Jack, but she could get hurt." My chest tightened at the thought of Freya being left unattended.

"She'll be fine. Is there someone I can call for you?" The doctor's voice was patient, and I could hear the gentle reassurance in it, but it didn't ease the ache in my chest.

"Dan Taylor," I rasped. He was the one person I

trusted with Freya's well-being. "Dan will know what to do."

The doctor made a note of it. "Fine, I'll contact Dan. He'll take care of her for you."

I let out a sigh of relief, knowing Dan would do exactly that. Good old Dan. Solid. Reliable. Far more predictable than his brother.

The thought of Noah, however, wore me out even more. The overwhelming flood of emotions—fear, worry, the chaos of everything—pulled me under again. My eyelids grew heavy, and once again, I drifted off into a sleep I didn't want to take, but couldn't avoid.

∽

The two people I cared about most were behind doors I wasn't allowed to enter, and there was absolutely nothing I could do to convince the staff to let me see Jack or Bailey.

"Trust me, they're in excellent hands. Now be good for us and sit down." One of the nurses from the night before insisted, her tone a mix of concern and authority. "And elevate your leg up for goodness sake." She shook her head, but there was a kind undertone to it that made me think she was more worried about me than annoyed.

Charlotte had always said she wanted to be a nurse when we first got together. I could understand now why she never reached that dream. She didn't have the natural compassion required for the job, and there were some things that schooling couldn't teach.

I shook my head, trying to push her from my thoughts. Why did she invade my mind now? It wasn't often I thought about her, and certainly not when I was sitting here, tortured by the helplessness of the situation. I'd been so consumed by my hatred for her, by everything she did behind my back, that I'd poisoned anything positive in my life.

I even stopped doing things that mattered to me, like going to the pub after work with my dad. I didn't ask if my friends knew she was sleeping with Matt, I just presumed they did. I felt betrayed, like the fool of the town. I withdrew into myself, shutting everyone out. But then came Bailey.

She was everything Maggie would've wanted in a granddaughter. Selfless, kind, and fiercely strong. So much like Maggie in every way—the same spunk, the same sassy nature, the same strong yet soft-as-duck-down personality. She was Maggie, through and through. That's why I kept her at arm's length. I never let myself fully admit how much I wanted her. It was the same reason Jack had taken such a shine to her from the beginning.

A tear slipped from my eye, and I wiped it away, angry at myself.

Waiting was torture. They'd had enough time to sort them out.

Sophie wandered over and sat beside me.

"You shouldn't be here," I muttered, but my voice cracked with the weight of everything I was feeling.

"Where else do I have to go?" Her voice broke, and the grief in her eyes was heartbreaking. "Bailey and Jack are my friends."

I reached across and took her hand. It was cold and lacking the strength I remembered from when I first met her.

"You're in love with her, Noah. Don't fight it," Sophie said softly, her eyes steady on mine. "She loves you too. Cherish the time you have or it'll become your biggest regret."

Her words hit me harder than anything I expected. Sophie wasn't just speaking from a place of hope, she was speaking from experience. She understood regret, and I realized she was right. Nothing could tear you apart more than guilt.

I slung my arm around her and held her close, not just for her, but for me too. I needed the comfort.

It felt like forever before I was allowed in to see them.

Bailey was sleeping. I stood by the glass, gazing at her. She looked so peaceful, like Snow White in a glass coffin, waiting for her prince to rescue her. But I wasn't a prince. I wasn't capable of the rescue, nor could I promise her a happily-ever-after, not when everything around us was in shambles. But I was in love with her, and I wanted to build that future with her. I just hoped I wasn't too late.

A nurse approached, interrupting my thoughts. "If you'd like to see your grandfather now, he's awake."

I nodded, though part of me didn't want to leave Bailey. I followed the nurse to a small cubicle, where Jack lay hooked to monitors, tubes snaking across his body.

The moment Jack saw me, his eyes welled with tears. "Where's Bailey?"

"She's going to be okay. Relax."

"Is the house completely gone?" His voice cracked, and tears slid down his cheeks.

"I don't know. We left before it was fully out. What happened?"

Jack sighed deeply, his chest rising and falling with the effort. "I don't remember. One minute I was cooking, and the next thing I knew, I was here. What about the dogs?"

"Bailey saved them. They're fine." I kept my voice calm, hoping it would help him relax. But it didn't. "I think you need to stop getting so worked up, Jack. You need to relax."

Jack's sigh was long and heavy. "Is this extreme enough for you to recognize what she means to you, Noah? You're a smart guy, but when it comes to Bailey, you've acted like a bloody fool."

The anxiety was killing me, and Jack wasn't helping. "I'm only allowed a few minutes, and I haven't seen Bailey yet—"

"Then why the hell are you in here?" Jack shot back, his frustration raw. "Honestly, are you trying to give me another heart attack?"

"Okay, okay. Settle down." I stood up, rubbing my temples in frustration. "She was sleeping, but I'll wake her up if it makes you feel better."

Jack closed his eyes and sighed again, as if he could hardly bear to be so worked up. "Good. Give her a kiss for me."

I patted his hand gently. "Don't give the nurses a hard time," I said with a small smile, and turned to leave the room.

When I entered Bailey's room, I moved quietly, sitting on the chair beside her bed. She looked so small, so pale. Her stillness was frightening, and the sterile scent of the hospital made her feel distant—like she wasn't even the woman I knew. It was a far cry from the vanilla scent that always lingered when she was near.

I reached out, taking her hand gently in mine. I kissed it, pressing my forehead to the edge of the mattress.

She stirred, and I looked up, watching as her eyelids fluttered open. Her eyes met mine, and there was a faint look of confusion in them, like she was trying to place who I was.

"You scared me," I whispered. "I didn't think I'd find you in time."

A smile touched the corners of her mouth, soft and fragile. "But you did." Her eyes widened as she remembered. "Jack."

"Shh." I stood, leaning over her, brushing stray strands of hair from her face. "He's alive because of you."

Her eyes closed, and I lowered my face to hers, kissing her forehead.

"He's going to be devastated. His house is gone," she said, and I could hear the pain in her voice, even as she fought back the tears.

"It's just a house." I touched my fingertips to her cheek, feeling the warmth of her skin. "You and Jack are safe. That's all that matters. I love you, Bailey."

Her eyes blinked slowly, and a tear escaped from the corner of her eye.

"I'm just sorry it took almost losing you to tell you that." I ran my thumb along her cheek, my voice thick with emotion. "But I love you, and I want to tell you every day for the rest of my life. We can rebuild a house, but I want us to make it a home—if you'll have me. I want to be with you, always."

Bailey smiled, her tears only making the moment more beautiful. "I wanted that from the moment I stepped out of my truck. I love you, Noah. Of course, I'll have you."

With that, I lowered my lips to hers, and in that kiss, I knew I had found my happiness.

MEET STEFI HART

By day, Stefi Hart is a dedicated Literary Curator, but by night, she immerses herself in the world of steamy small-town romance. With a gift for weaving heartfelt stories into country settings, Stefi creates swoon-worthy tales that are her perfect late-night escape.

When she's not writing, Stefi loves unwinding in the Margaret River wine region, savoring a glass of red and a good book. Family is her true anchor, and she cherishes every moment spent with her four children, three grandsons, and her very own real-life hero.

JOIN THE GRAPE VINE

As I spend most of my time writing or with my family, I won't be spamming you with emails. But, I will send updates about what's happening and what's coming next.

So join the grape vine to receive all the *goss*!

Thanks for reading!

Love Stef x

ALSO BY STEFI HART

Bennett Springs Series

Ravens Ridge Series

Angel Cove Series

www.ingramcontent.com/pod-product-compliance
Ingram Content Group UK Ltd.
Pitfield, Milton Keynes, MK11 3LW, UK
UKHW040929050225
454710UK00004B/191